"I dare yo[u]... through the door..."

Suzi had dared her...and Audra had failed. What kind of Wicked Chick was she? Now she had something to prove to *herself*.

"I need to do it," Audra said. "I'm going to do it."

Suzi shrugged. "So do the *next* guy to come through the door," she said.

Turning on the bar stool, Audra leaned her elbows back on the table and faced the door.

Holy cow. She eyed the sexy hunk standing in the doorway and exhaled a deep sigh of appreciation. Oh, yeah...he was hell on wheels. Audra took inventory, her gaze taking a slow, appreciative tour up well-worn denim, lingering on a few particularly rough places, then moving up to a well-defined chest and—mmm-mmm-good—perfect shoulders.

Very nice.

Audra flashed him a naughty smile, then turned back to Suzi. "Good thing I wore my sexiest lingerie...."

Blaze

Dear Reader,

Did you ever take a dare you just knew was going to get you in trouble?

Audra and Jesse are complete opposites. She's a bad girl who revels in the naughty side of life, while he's the epitome of a good boy (and boy, is he *good!*). But they have one thing in common... neither can walk away from a dare.

I was *never* as naughty as Audra, but she's definitely a heroine I can relate to. She's treading that fine line between indulging her wild side and trying to be a responsible adult. In her mind, the two don't mesh. Lucky for her, Jesse's there to teach her just how perfectly both sides combine. Talk about a lucky girl!

Who ever said being bad wouldn't pay off?

Thanks for picking up my first book, *Double Dare*. I had a great time writing this and I'm thrilled to see it in the Harlequin Blaze lineup.

I'd love to hear what you think of the story. Drop by my Web site, www.TawnyWeber.com, and check out my blog.

Happy reading,

Tawny Weber

DOUBLE DARE
Tawny Weber

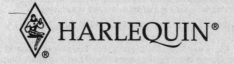

HARLEQUIN®

TORONTO • NEW YORK • LONDON
AMSTERDAM • PARIS • SYDNEY • HAMBURG
STOCKHOLM • ATHENS • TOKYO • MILAN • MADRID
PRAGUE • WARSAW • BUDAPEST • AUCKLAND

ISBN-13: 978-0-373-79328-0
ISBN-10:   0-373-79328-6

DOUBLE DARE

www.eHarlequin.com

Printed in U.S.A.

ABOUT THE AUTHOR

Tawny Weber has always loved romance—all the way back to when she was checking out couple stories in the grade school library. Despite her family's warnings, all that romance stuff didn't warp her (too much). What's more rewarding than reading about the crazy twists and turns to happy ever after, and even better...steamy-hot love scenes? Nothing—those are the good things in life. Add to that a lifelong wish to write and a nudge from her husband to pursue her dreams. She took the leap. The result? Three Golden Heart nominations and a Harlequin Blaze contest win on the way to her coveted first sale to Blaze. And she's just getting started.... Tawny's usually found dreaming up stories in her Northern California home, surrounded by dogs, cats and kids. Be sure to check out her Web site for upcoming books—www.TawnyWeber.com.

To my daughters, who gladly share me with the Muse and don't think it odd that Mom works in her jammies. Never give up on your dreams... they really do come true.

To James, for being the most incredible hero a woman could ask for. Thank you for the love, support and unfailing belief in me.

To my Critique Partners for the laughter, patience and gentle shoves when I was stuck. You ladies rock!

And to my editor, Brenda Chin, for not only helping me reach the point where she could buy my book...but for feeding my husband so I could write more.

1

MAYBE SHE should have seen it coming, but a girl just didn't expect to get knifed in the back by her best friends.

"Wanna repeat that?" Audra Walker requested in a smooth, calm voice. She was rather proud of that tone. It didn't show the anger or the gut-wrenching hurt she was feeling. She was sure her face, carefully made up for this evening of revelry and celebration, was equally calm. After all, hiding her true feelings was old hat to her.

She spared a glance at her surroundings. The Wild Thing was typical of most of the clubs Audra's friends frequented. The beat of the music and voices reverberated in time with teal lights flashing overhead. Places like this were always bright and loud and hadn't ever bothered Audra before. Then again, her friends hadn't been idiots before, either.

"You're just not into it anymore, Audra. Face it, you no longer qualify as a Wicked Chick," Suzi Willits said, her breathy voice as serious as it ever got. The buxom blonde shrugged one toned shoulder, making her ample breasts bounce under her leopard print tank top. "We might not mean much to you these days, but we do have standards to uphold, you know."

"The Standard of the Double D. Of course I know," she said with a roll of her eyes. Maybe this was a joke? They'd rib her for a while, then spring a congratulations-on-your-promotion present on her or something. To stifle the simmering panic in her belly, Audra shifted in her seat and breathed deeply. The scent of her friends' perfume was as familiar to her as her own.

"I'm the one who came up with it. Dudes and drinks, the Wicked Chick's tools of the trade."

"Right, so you know better than anyone how important it is to keep those tools sharp and fresh, don't you?" Suzi challenged. It wasn't her tone that forced Audra to accept they were serious. It was the fact that Suzi waved away the hot guy who'd just signaled her to come dance with him.

Audra's gaze flicked from Suzi to Bea Tanner. Rather than meeting her eyes, the redhead kept her gaze averted, making a show of swirling a piece of mango through the froth of her margarita.

Audra thought about laughing in their faces. It'd be easy enough to toss back her drink, slide from the barstool and tell them both to kiss her ass before sashaying out of the nightclub. The only thing stopping her was the fact that Suzi and Bea were two of her closest friends. And while they might not be the poster children for loving support, the three of them had been hanging together since they were Wicked Chicks in Training at fourteen, doing junior high detention together.

Ten years later, and still a hard-ass with a bad attitude, Audra didn't have many friends other than Bea, Suzi and Isabel. Most people, both back then and now, looked at her and saw imminent failure. She'd never cared, since those three were always there for her. With her dismal upbringing, she'd always considered these women her family, albeit a little dysfunctional at times. Without them, she was just a hard-ass with killer curves. They'd been the ones to show her how to *use* those curves.

She glanced over as the last member of their little party

rejoined them at the table. Slightly winded from her dance, the dark-haired woman gulped down her soda. Isabel Santos had been hanging out with Audra since they had both worn ruffled panties. Although not a member of the Wicked Chicks, Isabel had spent time with the other women off and on over the years. After school, though, Isabel had focused on her own career, while the Wicked Chicks had focused on enjoying life. At least, until Audra had the temerity to pursue an actual career.

"You're always hanging out with that Natasha chick now," Bea accused. She poked her silicone-filled bottom lip out in a practiced pout. Her newly colored titian hair framed a face that had graced a magazine cover, as Bea was always quick to point out. But the look on that face, half-sneer and half-dejection, assured Audra they were dead serious. They were kicking her out of the Wicked Chicks.

"That Natasha chick is a) my sister-in-law and b) my boss. And now she's about to launch a new lingerie line that is exclusively my designs." Which is what Audra had thought she was at the club to celebrate. Her promotion to head designer for Simply Sensual Lingerie. The achievement of her dreams.

"See, it's that kind of crap that's the problem," Suzi pointed out. "That's all we've heard this last year. You have to work. You have to study. You can't party with us because you have early classes. I thought it'd end when you graduated a few months ago, but now you're all about work instead."

"Oh, please," Audra scoffed, "like the two of you don't have jobs and responsibilities?"

Bea did tend to drift from job to job, but she always worked. Suzi cut hair in a high-end hair salon in San Francisco and Isabel's florist shop was flourishing.

"How come your jobs aren't the issue here?" Audra asked.

"*We* are able to maintain a balance between our jobs and our real lives," Suzi said in perfect imitation of an upper-class snob.

"And what am I doing?"

"You're building a career," Bea pointed out quietly. She said it as if Audra were building a weapon of mass destruction, her voice a combination of bemusement, aversion and fear.

"Why shouldn't Audra build a career? She's a great designer. This is her dream opportunity. Aren't you excited for her?" Isabel asked in a surprised tone. Her gray eyes flashed as indignation built. "Don't you guys think you're being a little unfair?"

"Fair, schmair," Suzi shot back. "Friends don't let friends blow their prime years chasing careers. That's the kind of crap you do later…after you've lost your sexual mojo."

Audra tuned out the inevitable debate between Isabel and Suzi over sexual status, aging, equal rights and staying true to friends. It was old news.

She bit back a scream. All she'd ever heard from her older brother was how her friends were trouble and would screw up her life. Isabel was always nagging her to set goals and prioritize her plans. And now she was hearing from her friends that she wasn't one of them anymore because she was trying to build a future. Not one damn person in her life was willing to simply accept her. All of her.

"I can have both a career and my friends," Audra insisted. Wasn't that the women's right of the new millennium? She could have it all? It wasn't as if Audra was looking to add a husband or anything stupid like that to the mix.

"Some career."

"I design lingerie," Audra pointed out, matching Suzi's sneer with one of her own. "That's hardly at odds with my Wicked Chick designation."

"You've always wanted to design sexy, wild lingerie," Suzi pointed out. And she'd know, since she and Bea spent years listening to Audra daydream about it, never once discouraging her.

"Instead," Suzi continued, "you settled for vanilla-sweet nighties for virginal brides."

"Everyone has to start somewhere," Isabel interjected in Audra's defense.

Before Suzi could retaliate, Bea pressed her hands to the table, bloodred nails spread like claws against the faux leather surface.

"Enough of this crap." The mellowest of them all, her distaste for the bickering and one-upmanship was clear on her face. "Audra, this is an intervention. You either prove you're still one of us, or you lose your Wicked Chick status."

Isabel gasped. "You've got to be kidding."

"Prove myself?" Oh jeez, it was junior high school all over again.

Suzi leaned forward with a challenging gleam shining in her midnight-blue eyes. "Prove yourself."

Audra rolled her eyes. "How? Outdrink you two? Dance topless on stage? Give up my job?"

Audra tossed the words out in an airy, unconcerned tone. But her insides twisted at the thought of either the first or the last. Given that she'd started her drinking in her early teens, she figured she'd done more than enough partying. That, and she'd watched what drinking had done to her mother, leaving her old and haggard-looking by forty. The booze wouldn't do Audra's skin, or her health, a bit of good. And she planned to keep both long into the future. Two drinks were her limit now, although she did a good job of hiding that from her friends.

And quit her job? Oh, God, no. She loved that job. Loved designing lingerie. She couldn't think of anything more satisfying than starting with a vision in her head, turning it into a reality and seeing a woman prance out of the boutique empowered by the result. They couldn't—wouldn't—be crazy enough to think she'd give that up.

"How about all thr—"

"No, much simpler," Bea interrupted with a dark look at the blonde. Suzi sat back with a huff and a roll of her eyes.

Audra waited. The music pounded a heavy beat around her, the cacophony of voices blending with the percussions.

"I dare you…" Bea began.

Oh, hell, she should have known.

"…to *do* the next guy to come through the door."

"This is silly," Isabel stated. Her gray eyes flashed with rare anger. She crossed her arms over her chest, her sweater pulling tight to curves she tended to hide, rather than display like the other three women. "Haven't you outgrown that silly game? I thought your club was all about empowerment, not pressure. Audra's your friend. She doesn't have to do anything to prove herself."

A voice in Audra's head agreed. She *didn't* have to. Like drinking, impersonal sex had long since lost its appeal. She could have just as good a time with her vibrator as with most guys. And at least her "D-celled" friend guaranteed she'd come. Swear to God, most guys didn't seem to know the difference between the G-spot and a parking spot.

But if she didn't, she'd be saying goodbye to something vital. Not just her friendships were on the line here, Audra realized with a start. So was her sense of self. The badass, wild part of her seemed to be fading away. And she didn't have a clue what, if anything, she'd find underneath.

"Hey, no problem. I never mind scratching that particular itch."

Ignoring Isabel's disappointed look, she gave the girls a wink, tossed back the last of her strawberry margarita and straightened her shoulders. Turning on the barstool, she leaned her elbows back on the table, faced the door and sent up a prayer that the next guy through knew how to park.

Holy cow. She eyed the sexy hunk standing in the doorway and exhaled a deep sigh of appreciation. Oh, yeah, he'd not only know how to park, but she'd bet he was hell on wheels. Audra took inventory, starting at what she estimated to be size twelve biker boots. Her gaze took a slow, appreciative tour up well-worn denim, lingering on a few particularly worn places.

Very nice.

She continued her tour over a well-defined chest and— m'm m'm good—perfect shoulders. The sleeves of the denim work shirt were rolled up to the elbows, and it was buttoned about halfway up to showcase that chest, wide and lightly dusted with a sprinkling of dark hair. How would that hair feel against her cheek? Soft and sensual? Wiry and erotic? Did it thicken as it meandered down his belly? Or did it taper to a very delicious point?

If he'd hurry up and walk through the door, she could find out. Anticipation made Audra antsy. She shifted in her seat and held her breath while her gaze rose to his face.

Oh, baby. Eyes half-mast, a wave of lust-induced appreciation crashed through her system. Now that was one hot man. Black hair tumbled around a face just this side of pretty. His full lower lip promised a sensual nature and, although she couldn't see his eyes in any detail, the man had cheekbones to die for. The only thing that saved him from being girly-pretty was a stubborn jaw and his nose, obviously broken a couple times.

"Good thing I wore my sexiest lingerie, hmm?"

Bea laughed and gave an appreciative hum. Even Isabel mouthed "wow," although the look in her eyes still screamed disapproval. Not surprising, since Isabel had never been comfortable with casual sex. At Suzi's silence, Audra glanced over. The blonde didn't look thrilled. If anything, she looked a little pouty. The rules of the dare were that neither of the others could come on to the dare guy. Which put hot, tall and sexy off limits for Suzi.

Audra couldn't resist taunting her. "One small step for him, one giant orgasm for me."

Suzi grinned and started to say something, then her eyes widened and she winced.

"Oops," Bea said under her breath.

Isabel cringed.

Stomach suddenly tight, Audra followed their gaze to the entrance where the hunk still stood in conversation with the bouncer just outside the arch that they deemed the official entrance for dares. Disappointment sunk like a chunk of lead in her stomach when she saw the source of her friends' horror. Shouldering the hunk aside was another guy. A nonhunky guy. A totally geeky, nonhunky guy. Audra's stomach turned, but did she see any way out of the dare? Not with her pride intact.

"Ya think he's got anything in that pocket protector you can get up?" Obviously trying to ease the tension, Suzi called the waitress over for a second round. "You'll need a drink before this one, Audra. My treat."

Was she supposed to be grateful?

"And as soon as you prove you've still got it in you to take a dare, maybe I'll go get myself a whole different kind of treat," Suzi mused. Audra followed her gaze to where hot, tall and sexy had taken a seat, two tables over from Audra's target. Rarely territorial over men, Audra was surprised to find that the thought of Suzi and the sexy hunk made her teeth clench.

She grimaced her thanks at the waitress and knocked back her margarita in one long gulp. Audra ran her index finger under her lower lip to make sure her lipstick wasn't smudged. Might as well get it over with. She slipped from the stool and sucked in a deep breath. A little shimmy of the shoulders to make sure everything was where it belonged, her fingertips brushed the hem of her leather mini and she let out her breath.

Isabel protested, "Audra, you don't have to go through with this. I'm sure Suzi and Bea are just riding you. You guys have been tight for years. You don't have to prove your friendship. Especially not by having random sex with some—" she grimaced at the geek "—creepy stranger."

She shot the other two women a dark look. Pink washed over Bea's cheeks and, with a half-hearted shrug, she averted her gaze.

Suzi, though, stuck out her chin.

"Hey, we never said jack about friendship. Audra knows we're all amigas. This is about being true to the Wicked Chicks code. Nobody's forcing her to re-up her membership. That's her call. *Hers*. Not yours."

With that statement, the underlying hurt and confusion in Suzi's tone, Audra realized her friends needed reassurance. This wasn't about where she stood with the Wicked Chicks. It was about where *they* stood with her.

Her friendship with Suzi and Bea was changing, sure. Did that matter?

Audra sucked in a breath. Yes, it mattered. These women were more than buddies to run around with. They were more than a part of her history. They'd accepted her, encouraged her. And, even if they were pains in the ass, they both gave her something nobody else, other than Isabel, ever had. Unconditional acceptance.

At least, they had until tonight.

The music pulsing around her, Audra knew she could shrug and—just like she'd grown out of acne, her spandex phase and the desperate anger that'd fueled her for so many years—let her ties with the other women go.

But being wicked wasn't just a designation. It defined her. She was a bad girl. From her prepubescent years under the bleachers to her wild cross-country rebellion when her father died, being bad was how she dealt with life.

Without it, what did she have left? Since she didn't know the answer, she obviously had no choice.

"I'm a lifetime member," she drawled. "Let's just hope the geek over there can handle me."

Isabel opened her mouth, probably to protest. Then, with a shrug and a sigh that summed up why she'd never quite fit in with the other women, she just rolled her eyes and sat back.

"Go get him, tiger," Bea said.

"Oh, yeah, have a great time," Suzi said with a wink.

Audra bit back a snarky response. Her gaze caught on the hunk again and she grinned. There was no rule against a nibble of an appetizer before hitting on the main course.

JESSE MARTINEZ looked around the nightclub and bit back a sigh. Purple walls were covered in teal neon lights. The dance floor was tri-level and the chrome bar wrapped around the room. The band was on break, but a deejay played Top Forty rock. Definitely not Jesse's kind of place. Crowded, loud and filled with psuedoperfect bodies, all on the make. How the hell had he ended up here?

Oh, he could blame it on work. Legitimately, he *was* on a job. But he could be back in his office with his computer. That was his job description, after all. A Cyber Crimes detective with the Sacramento PD, he wasn't required to follow dirtbags in person. He did it over the World Wide Web, instead. But, no, sucker that he was, he hadn't been able to back down from a coworker's dare that he get off his butt and get his hands dirty. Do real work. Show what he was made of. Damned if Jesse could back down from a dare, especially one couched in insults to his manhood.

He should probably work to reprogram that defective element of his personality. But since it was one of the few traits he actually appreciated having in common with his late father, he was loath to lose it.

Instead, he ended up in tacky nightclubs. Jesse sighed, but gave the waitress a smile and ordered a beer. He eyed the dorky dude a couple tables over. The guy was fidgety as hell, his fingers tapping on the table, his knee bouncing to a completely different rhythm. He looked like a virgin on a blind date with a porn queen. Or as if he were about to rob the place.

The guy's name was Dave Larson and he was a computer hacker with a taste for gambling. Jesse had it on good authority that Larson was butt deep in organized crime and determined to work his way up one of the dirtiest crime ladders in Northern California, the *Du Bing Li* Triad. Since there were any number of tasks a guy with Dave's computer skills could provide, Jesse wasn't sure just what the geek was up to. But one thing was sure, it was no good.

Which is why he'd followed him to the club.

The waitress returned with his beer. Jesse reached for his wallet when a slim hand pressed against his forearm.

"Let me get that for you."

Jesse's brain, at least the independent gentlemanly part, shut down. Apparently his vocal cords did too, because he couldn't say a word. All he could do was stare.

Temptation and pure sin, wrapped in black leather. The still functioning portion of Jesse's brain cataloged the woman's features. Huge doe eyes with a thick fringe of lashes dominated a narrow face. Shiny red lips looked as if she'd just eaten something juicy, tempting him to lean forward for a taste. Her short hair was jet-black, the spiky ends tipped with magenta.

Her body was a teenage boy's wet dream, all curves and sleek lines.

But it was her voice that had him in a trance. It was made for sex. The husky lisp brought to mind talking dirty in the dark. And he could tell in that one look, she definitely knew how to talk dirty.

The waitress snickered as she left and Jesse pulled himself together.

"Thanks for the offer, but I can handle paying for my own drink." He wished he didn't sound as if he had a stick up his ass, but that didn't appear to be happening.

A slow, wicked smile curved those sleek red lips and she leaned in close to whisper, "You look like a man who could handle just about anything."

She waited a beat, long enough for the image of just exactly how he'd like to handle her to fully form in his mind, then she leaned back and winked. "As for the drink, call it a welcome gesture. I haven't seen you in here before."

"You're here a lot, huh?" Jesse mentally groaned. Could he be any wittier? Of course she was here a lot; she obviously hadn't stumbled in on her way from a church social. For a computer geek like himself, she was the ultimate fantasy. Sexy as hell, and twice as aggressive. Not that Jesse didn't know how to please a woman in bed; he was damned good at it. But he was used to real women, flesh and blood. Not sexual goddesses such as the one standing in front of him. Close enough to touch, but totally out of reach.

"Actually I haven't been in here in, like, forever. But…" She looked left, then right, then whispered, "Shh, don't tell anyone or it'd ruin a great pickup line."

Jesse laughed with her, and just like that, she *was* within reach. He relaxed and lifted his beer to toast her.

"It'll be our little secret," he promised. "I'm Jesse."

"Audra," she said as she took his hand.

Damn. Jesse's body, all the vital parts, leaped to attention as sexual awareness surged through him at the touch of her hand in his. A hand that felt oddly delicate for a woman with such a powerful presence.

Which was closer to the real woman—the hot, sexy babe she appeared to be, or the soft, gentle woman both her fragile hand and her easy humor suggested? Unable to leave a puzzle unsolved, he knew his mind wouldn't rest until he'd figured her out. To say nothing of everything his *body* wanted to learn about her.

"The least I can do is buy you a drink in return," Jesse offered.

Her brown eyes lit up, then dimmed as her gaze slid away. "I'd love that, but I'm actually meeting someone else tonight. Blind date, of a sort, you know?"

Maybe it was ego, but he swore the regret in her voice was genuine.

"You don't sound excited."

"Hardly," she said with a laugh. She got a naughty look in her eye, shot a glance over her shoulder, then leaned close. "But you can help me."

"How?"

"A little fun, kind of like that spoonful of sugar that helps the medicine go down."

Before Jesse could laugh, she'd stepped close. So close only a bare inch separated her breasts from his forearm. Seated as he was on the stool, they were eye to eye. He automatically shifted so that his hand was on her hip, and she winked her approval.

Then she kissed him and blew his mind.

It started as a soft brush of her lips over his, just a whisper. Her breath mingled with his a moment as their eyes met, then something wild burned in hers before the thick fringe of lashes covered them. With a quick intake of breath, she slid her tongue along his lower lip. The act was so sensual in its simplicity, so seductive in its delicious temptation, Jesse almost whimpered.

Before he could respond, she stepped back and winked.

"Nice to meet you, Jesse. I'll see you later, maybe."

Fascinated, he murmured his goodbye and watched her walk away.

No maybe about it, he didn't plan to wait for later. Jesse started to slide off the barstool to follow her. Half out of his seat, he watched, baffled, as she stopped at Davey's table. She leaned across the narrow circular surface and said something that made the dork blush. Jesse watched the guy start stuttering and babbling.

With a frown, Jesse settled back on the barstool to watch. What did Audra have to do with a guy like Davey Larson? A simple blind date, like she'd said? A blind date, *of a sort?* What sort? Dave Larson was hip deep in crime, both organized and sloppy. Where did Audra come in?

Rumor had it Davey had caught the eye of the top echelon of a local crime ring. The head of that ring had a habit of using his women for deliveries. Was she the handoff? Delivery or receiving? Either way, it boded poorly for Jesse's shot at experiencing his ultimate fantasy.

A haze of jealousy blurred his vision when, instead of taking the seat opposite Davey, Audra slid around to sit next to him. Damn near in the dork's lap. When she tiptoed those delicate fingers of hers up the guy's butt-ugly tie, Jesse actually growled out loud.

Jesse watched Audra lean in close to Davey and whisper something. Whatever it was must have been a doozy, because Dave jumped as if she'd goosed him. A damp sheen coated his lanky face and his eyes bulged. Audra looped her finger through the knot on his tie and Davey skittered back. A group of partyers blocked Jesse's view. He craned his neck but could barely see the tops of their heads.

When the crowd shifted, Jesse saw Davey shaking his head like crazy. She said something, and Dave turned a little green around the gills, then jumped up from the table. Audra stared wide-eyed at him as he babbled. She was lucky not to get nailed in the face by the wild gestures the dork made. He finally ran out of steam. Mouth ajar, Audra looked stunned for a second, then said something. When Davey gave a frantic shake of his head, she held out her hand. Jesse couldn't see what she was holding, but Davey's eyes bulged in horror and he scampered away from the table, throwing one last comment over his skinny shoulder.

Jesse slid from his seat, prepared to follow Dave. He hesitated, glancing at Audra. Even with her mouth hanging open, she was the sexiest thing he'd ever seen. He debated between pursuing Dave or hooking up with Audra to find out what her connection was.

Before he could take a step toward her, though, she was surrounded by three women, their shocked expressions all matching Audra's. He eyed the blonde, redhead and brunette, but none popped up as criminals in his mental data bank. Then again, neither had Audra.

From the looks of them, the ladies would be around for a while. Davey, though, was scurrying off like a scared rat. Jesse hightailed it after the rat, but couldn't help shooting a final look of regret for the woman who'd briefly held the promise of fulfilling his every fantasy.

2

"WHAT THE HELL happened?" Suzi demanded, her voice filled with the same shock coursing through Audra's system. "I figured a geek like that would have lousy staying power, but you barely touched him."

"He didn't…" Bea gestured to her crotch area and scrunched up her face in disgust. "Just from you talking to him, did he?"

Audra squinted in question, then shuddered as Bea's meaning sank in. "Eww, no."

"Then why'd he run?"

Audra opened her mouth, then closed it with a baffled shake of her head. Her fingers clenched the strip of fabric in her hand. She had no clue. She'd made plenty of guys tremble over the years, but she'd never made one run before. When her friends had first started spouting off that she wasn't a Wicked Chick anymore, it had been easy to ignore them.

But now? Audra's breath hitched. Were they right? Was she losing it?

"I think he mistook me for someone else," Audra finally admitted. "He babbled a few things I didn't understand and when I suggested we get to know each other better, he ran like a sissy-lala."

Isabel took the tie from her, grimacing at the ugly green piece of patterned polyester.

Suzi flicked the flimsy fabric and wrinkled her nose. "Nice souvenir, Audra," she said. "What're you going to do with it?"

"I have no clue," she admitted. "I've rendered men dumb before, but none have ever hit the level of idiocy this guy did. I flirted, he babbled. I finally resorted to complimenting that ugly tie. He promptly ripped it off and tossed it at me just before he ran off like a scaredy-cat."

They all stared at the offense to fashion.

"Does this mean you failed the dare?" Suzi asked in a breathy tone of shock.

Audra's gaze shot to hers. Failed?

"She didn't fail," Bea snapped. "She isn't to blame if a guy can't keep it up. He obviously had issues and ran."

But Audra saw it in her friend's eyes. Even Isabel's held a faint glint of that dreaded emotion.

Pity.

Audra had failed. The first Wicked Chick to blow a dare.

"You're right, that wasn't failure," Suzi finally agreed. "Who knows, maybe he's not into chicks or something."

Bea gave a snort of laughter and shrugged. "So we, what? Chalk it up to a first? Wanna get another round of drinks and dance?"

Audra realized her friends would let it go then. They'd pushed the dare as a means to prove she hadn't moved on. That she was still one of the girls.

But now? Now she had something to prove to *herself.*

"Hey, I'm not done yet," she told them. "You dared me, I need to fulfill the dare."

"How?" Isabel wanted to know.

"New dare?" Bea suggested with a shrug.

"Like?" Audra asked.

"Simple," Suzi claimed. "You do the *next* guy to come through the door."

Audra sucked in a breath, ignored the voice in the back of her head claiming she was so over this dare crap, and nodded. Over it or not, she has something to prove. She eyed the tie as Isabel glanced at the ugly thing, then at Audra's tiny purse. With a grimace, her friend tucked it into her own hobo bag.

Audra glanced around for Jesse. Gone. At least he hadn't witnessed her failure. She didn't know why it mattered, but it did. Shoving the thought aside, she focused on the entryway and hoped to hell the next guy through the door wasn't a bigger geek than the one who'd just run away. It was probably asking too much for him to be as hot as the appetizer she'd enjoyed earlier.

JESSE SHOULDERED his way through the crowd waiting to enter the club and looked around for Davey. He didn't have to look far. The geek was huddled over his cell phone a few feet from the entrance, obviously waiting for a valet to bring his car around.

Jesse sidled closer, staying out of the guy's line of vision, until he could hear the one-sided conversation over the noise of the crowd.

"Look, I did my part. I passed the info to your bimbo. When do I get my money?"

Jesse leaned a shoulder against the building and let out a sigh. Not only could Audra undoubtedly talk dirty enough to have a man begging for release…she was dirty. As in, criminally dirty.

Damn.

He listened with half an ear as Davey negotiated fund transfers and time frames. He'd be able to track the payoff through Dave's computer, no problem.

Which meant he was that much closer to solving the case. At least, a part of the case. He'd come to realize in the last few days that Dave Larson was a small piece of a much larger puzzle.

And Jesse wanted the bigger picture. And the promotion that would come with it.

Hell, he was twenty-eight. His late father had already made lieutenant by this age. Of course, Jesse had spent four years earning his degree in computer science, but he should still be farther up the food chain.

This case, the undercover work and proving he could step outside his cozy computer world would seal that promotion for him.

And prove once and for all that he was just as good a cop as his father had been. He grimaced. Being the son of a legend was definitely a pain in the ass.

He watched Davey slide into his car. From the grin on the kid's face, he must've overtipped the valet. Jesse debated following him, but there wasn't much point. He could track the payoff money easily enough by computer.

Right now he needed to connect with the next level. Which meant Audra. He remembered the taste of those luscious red lips beneath his with pleasure. Some days he loved his job.

Anticipation spinning through his system, he reentered the club. His gaze sought out the table where she'd met the geek. She was still there, surrounded by friends.

When their eyes met, hers grew huge and she ran her tongue over her lower lip before flashing a delighted smile. She murmured something and three other sets of eyes glanced his way, varying degrees of naughty smiles on the women's faces.

With a look filled with sexual promise, combined with an unexplained gratitude that made his body go on full alert, Audra slid from the barstool in a slow, sexy move. Would she do everything with the same deliberate sensuality? Would he find out?

No. She was now a suspect. A criminal. His key to breaking this case.

But as she walked toward him, the last thing on his brain was the case. His gaze traced long, sleek legs encased in sheer black hose, and his fingers itched to glide up their silky length.

Jesse realized with a sinking heart that after years of wondering if he had any more in common with his late father than their coloring, he'd just found proof positive. Good ole dad had not only had a penchant for dares, he'd had a taste for women who spelled trouble. God knew, this was a rotten time for the grand discovery. Because this woman definitely spelled trouble, in glowing neon letters.

"Looks like it's later already," she said when she reached him. He smiled in response to the humor in her husky tone.

"What happened to your date?" he fished. "It didn't look like it went well."

"Oh." She glanced back at the table where her friends watched. She pressed her lips together, then shrugged. "You saw that, huh?"

"Bits and pieces. So that was your blind date?" He held his breath. If she admitted it was a business association, he could haul her in for questioning.

"Of a sort," she replied.

Damn it.

"A sort, huh?"

"Yeah, a sort." She hesitated, then gave a one-shouldered shrug. "You know, more like a dare. You ever get suckered into a dare? There is just no way out."

"Believe me, I know all about dares."

"Then you know how humiliating it is to back down from one, don't you?" As she spoke, Audra shifted so she stood between his legs. He wanted to pull her against him, to feel her body give way to the straining flesh pressing against his now too-tight jeans. She traced a finger over his mouth.

Jesse's lip tingled, and it was all he could do to keep from pulling that finger into his mouth and sucking on it. He was a passionate man—it was in his blood—but he'd never experienced this level of deep, dark excitement.

"Oh, yeah, a dare refused is a guarantee of humiliation," he agreed.

"Sometimes a dare accepted holds the same guarantee."

Was she talking about her deal with Davey? Larson could be involved in anything from credit card fraud to identity theft. What had he passed to Audra? Jesse was going to have to find out.

"It sounds like you're an expert on dares," he said.

Something dimmed the sparkle in her huge brown eyes. To Jesse, it looked like a combination of indecision and reluctance. Her gaze slid past him, a frown quirked her brow, and then she puffed out a little sigh.

"How about we blow this joint? Find a little privacy and get to know each other better?"

His mouth went so dry, Jesse couldn't reply. Instead, he nodded.

Desire ripping through him like a jagged knife, he followed Audra out of the nightclub, his gaze glued on the tantalizing sway of her leather-clad hips.

Jesse told himself he was just playing along for the case. He had to follow her to find out what she knew. That was all. He didn't intend to let it get out of hand.

But for the first time in his six-year career as a cop, he wondered if he could keep his pants on long enough to arrest a woman before having desperate, mind-blowing sex with her.

AUDRA WELCOMED the warm evening air after the stifling, sticky heat of the club. Her ears still ringing from the loud music, she took in a few deep breaths and wished for a breeze.

"Did you want to go somewhere? Get something to eat or some coffee?" Jesse offered. His hand warmed her hip as he shifted to protect her from being jostled by the partyers shoving past them to leave the club.

Did she want to go anywhere? Audra eyed the hunk at her side and puffed out a breath. He was hot, no question about it. But more, he had a layer of sweetness that had her alternating between wanting to hug him close and lick him all over. The latter boded well for her current predicament, the former was better avoided.

After all, thanks to that crazy man who'd freaked out over her offer to get friendly, Jesse had become her new dare. Not that she was proud to have the first failed dare chalked up under her name. But at least that failure came with a sweet reward. She eyed Jesse in delight. He'd make this dare a pleasure.

All she had to do was focus on the rush of sexual energy arcing between them like a rainbow, a bone-melting orgasm the promised reward. And ignore the spark of emotion, the weird desire to get to know him better. After a year of watching her brother and his bride grow closer, she'd probably just picked up on their couple vibe. Like a virus, that kind of thing could only be dangerous to her health, though. So she'd ignore it.

"How about we find someplace quiet," she suggested with a wink, "and see what comes up?"

From the widening of those delicious coffee-brown eyes, he got her message. The heat there told her he was all for it, but then his gaze shifted, became more reserved.

"There's a little coffee shop nearby," he countered. "We can order something to drink, maybe a piece of pie, and talk?"

He was kidding, right? Audra stopped and looked closer. There was a hint of color on his cheeks, but that could just be the neon lights. He was gorgeous, no question about that. And sexy as hell, but he didn't seem used to the club scene. Was he playing hard to get? Or was he one of those? A fabled good boy?

She squinted, taking in his shadowed jawline, his crooked nose, and the slight frown between his heavy brows. She couldn't tell for sure. After all, she'd never known a good boy.

"Wouldn't you rather go somewhere a little more private?" she asked.

He closed his eyes for a second, as if in prayer, then opened them and gave her a tight smile. "Let's talk a little first, huh?"

From the stiff set of his shoulders, he didn't mean dirty talk. Intrigued by the novelty, Audra smiled and nodded. "Okay, then. Your car or mine?"

"It's close. We can walk."

Audra laughed aloud. "Walk?" She lifted one foot to show off the four-inch heels of her spiked black pumps and pointed her toe. "These feet have been known to do many things," she paused suggestively, "but they don't walk any farther than necessary."

"Aren't you concerned about getting into a car with a strange man? A beautiful woman like yourself needs to be cautious."

From someone else, that might have sounded patronizing. Jesse, though, seemed genuinely concerned. His gaze locked on hers, warmth and sincerity clear in the brown depths. She noted the protective hand on her hip, not groping or sliding down her butt, but simply keeping her from being jostled.

Something warmed in Audra. Nobody had ever shown concern for her before. It felt…odd. A good kind of odd, though. Could he really be that sweet?

She gave him a warm smile and said, "I'm used to taking care of myself, promise. I'm a good judge of character and I fight nasty." The can of Mace in her purse didn't hurt, either. "Nobody tries anything with me I don't want without regretting it."

He gave a contemplative nod, but didn't try to pull any macho crap by arguing or trying to prove he was tough. Audra's respect rose a few notches. How wild. She was really liking this guy. She just might want to see if this dare could lead to something more.

Depending on his performance on her "O" scale, of course.

"Let's take my car," she suggested. "I prefer the driver's seat."

She slid her hand in his and shivered a little at the hard strength of his palm and long, narrow fingers.

"So," he said as they made their way to the parking lot, "that guy didn't look like your type."

Audra looked at the milling partiers in confusion. "Which guy?"

"The one in the club back there. You know, the dorky guy you had the 'sort of' date with."

"Oh, him. No, he's definitely not my type." Audra suppressed a shudder. What a geek.

"Do you have to deal with that a lot? I'd think a woman as gorgeous as you are wouldn't need blind dates."

"You know how that goes. You have to kiss a lot of toads before you nail a prince."

Thanks to the geek—or Dave, as he'd introduced himself—being a nervous wreck, she'd lucked out and wouldn't be locking lips with any toads tonight.

Would she be nailing this prince, though? Audra gave Jesse the once-over out of the corner of her eye. He sure looked like a prince. Hot, sexy and ready to be crowned.

They reached her car and she dropped Jesse's hand to fish through her purse for her keys.

"I'll bet you're going to have a few things to say to whatever *supposed* friend set you up, huh?"

"Why?"

"What kind of friend sets you up with a loser?"

"The kind who think they know best and are afraid I might break away from the gang."

"Gang?"

Audra frowned at the edge of cynicism in his tone. "Gang, club. You know, a group you hang with regularly? I take it you're not into clubs," she asked with a tilt of her head.

"I'm not into anything that pushes me to do things I'm uncomfortable doing."

She pursed her lips and gave him a long look. She'd bet she could push him to do quite a few things he hadn't been comfortable with before. And have him thanking her afterward. But she wasn't the kind to give away secrets, so she just smiled and gave a dismissive, one-shouldered shrug.

"Your date with that dork wasn't your idea, I take it?"

Audra grimaced. "Not hardly. More like I gave in to pressure and my need to keep my standing with my friends. And almost ended up with a very regrettable evening. Although—" she clicked the lock button on her key fob "—I have to say I came out the winner here. If not for them, I wouldn't be here with you, would I?"

Audra turned and in a smooth, easy move, pinned Jesse between her body and the car. She almost purred aloud. Even in heels, he still towered over her, the hard length of his body inviting her to lean into his warmth. Very nice. This dare was turning into pure pleasure, no longer a means to prove her Wicked Chick status to her friends. She wanted to get closer to Jesse. Just for herself.

With her slowest, most seductive smile, she watched him from under her fringe of lashes. His eyes had that slightly glazed look that assured her he liked the feel of her body against his. She shimmied a little, just to be sure she had his attention.

As she slid her free hand up his biceps, this time she did

purr aloud. "Yum. You're in fabulous shape. What do you do for a workout?"

"A little weights, some martial arts," he replied, his attention more on her caresses than her question. Both hands settled lightly on her hips, clenched, then gripped her curves fully. "So what made you pick this club tonight?"

"Hmm? Wild Thing? It's a fun place, one of the best in Sacramento. I'd planned a little celebration, although it didn't turn out quite the way I'd hoped. But I think you're the perfect celebratory present to myself."

Audra wrapped her arms around his neck and leaned further into his welcoming body. She brushed her lips over his, more a teasing temptation than a real kiss. Heated excitement swirled through her, making sensation spiral from her lips to the damp center between her legs. God, if he got her this turned on with barely a kiss, how would she feel when he put his hands on her? When he put his mouth on her body?

Desire was edged with impatience. She wanted to know. She had to know. She was sure Jesse would be a delicious lover. The kind that rated at least an eight on her "O" scale. She'd yet to find a perfect ten, but a solid eight could definitely be coached.

Backing off a little, she leaned her head back to see what he'd do. How he'd react.

"That's not much of a present," he commented.

Then he took her mouth. Took it in a way she'd only dreamt of before. His hands, gentle yet firm, cupped her head and held her where he wanted. Just for his pleasure. He nibbled at the corners of her mouth softly. Then, as she was smiling at the sweetness of it, he plunged his tongue between her lips in a swift, powerful move.

She was so used to being the aggressor that for the first couple of seconds she remained passive out of surprise. Then, pleasure shooting through her like an arrow, she met his tongue with hers in a dance of sexual delight.

Audra clenched her thighs to intensify the sensation. More. She definitely wanted more from this man.

"Wait," he breathed, breaking away from her mouth. "We should get to know each other better. You know, talk or something."

"I vote for 'or something.'"

"Did you say you got stuck on an almost sort-of date with that dork because your friend threatened you?" he asked, his words coming in a gasp as she pressed the beaded tips of her breasts against his chest. "Doesn't sound like much of a club to me."

"They're just worried about me."

Maybe they had reason to worry, too. Audra hadn't realized she wasn't much interested in meaningless sex and constant partying until tonight's fiasco. After all, at twenty-five, she was damned hot, exciting and interesting, even if she didn't get as wild as she used to. Maybe a part of her—deep inside— worried there wasn't any more to her than her bad girl persona. But as a rule, she tended to ignore that snarky worrying part. Even when snarky turned to screaming, as it had tonight.

"You know how it is when you get in tight with friends, people who've known you, like, most of your life? They want you to stay in their tidy box, keep with their perception of you. Sometimes you have to pacify them with proof you're still a part of the gang, you know?"

To distract them both, she pulled away a bit to run her hands up the delicious, hard expanse of his chest. "Why are we wasting time talking about this? Let's move on to more exciting subjects. Like, say, how you look naked?"

3

JESSE SWORE his heart stopped. All blood rushed from his head to his…well, other head. Damn, he'd never been as turned on or as unable to do anything about it as he was right this minute. Audra, with her promise of hot, sticky-sweet pleasure, was technically off-limits.

But her hands were doing incredible things to his body. Long, delicate fingers traced a path from his shoulders, over his nipples and down to his belt. Jesse wanted to say screw police procedure and guide those fingers lower. He breathed in the rich scent of her perfume and tried to remember she was still a suspect.

And after her comments, especially her confession of gang affiliation, Jesse knew she was Davey's crime ring connection. And it was his job to find out exactly how she fit into the organization and use it to break the case. He might prefer to do that job behind a computer, but there were definite benefits to this unfamiliar fieldwork. The temptation of Audra's body pressed against his was proving to be an almost irresistible benefit.

"So tonight was the first time you'd met that guy?" he asked. "He seemed a little overwhelmed when he saw you."

Not that Jesse was surprised there. Davey was a dork, sure. But Audra was the kind of woman that would overwhelm any guy, present company included.

"He was a bit freaked, I guess," Audra said distractedly. Her attention was focused on the soft, damp kisses she was scattering over his jaw and throat. Jesse's eyes fluttered shut as his body, already turned on by their kiss and the feel of her pressed against him, went into overdrive when she reached the open collar of his shirt and trailed her tongue across his collarbone.

"Why don't we take this inside," she suggested in that husky lisp.

"Back in the club?" Maybe that would be safer? She'd still be temptation in spiked heels, but at least he'd have a crowd to remind him why taking those heels off to nibble on her toes was a bad idea.

"In the car."

His eyes flew open. He looked at her. Huge doe eyes stared back at him. Her lips were damp, a sleek, succulent red and it was all he could do not to sink into their ripe promise. He tore his gaze from her mouth to glance at her compact silver car.

"That's a little cramped, don't you think?"

"Let's find out."

With that, she nudged him aside and tugged the passenger door of her toy-like convertible open.

"I think this probably isn't such a good idea."

Audra tilted her head to the side and arched one perfect brow. "No? I think it's a great idea. I think maybe you're just a little…reserved." She pressed against him again until he felt the edge of the door frame against his calves. "I think maybe you're not used to being seduced."

"Is that what you're doing? Seducing me?"

Had he ever been seduced? Jesse flipped through his mental database of his past encounters. He'd had his share of flings, a few deeper relationships and one lady he'd been serious enough about to bring home to meet the family. He wouldn't call any of the women repressed, by any means. But, he realized, he'd always been the aggressor. The go-to-it guy.

He couldn't remember ever being in the passive role of seducee. Most women he'd been with were happy to let him lead. Hell, he'd discovered getting a woman to even voice what turned her on was a major accomplishment. And Audra wanted to seduce him? Oh, yeah, baby.

"I'll bet I can seduce you with words alone," she suggested softly.

"Just words?"

"Just words. You, of course, are free to touch. I, though, won't use anything but my voice."

Jesse grinned. That sounded safe enough. Her touch, he was sure he couldn't resist. But words? Hell, words wouldn't be a problem for him.

"You're on," he said.

"Have a seat, then." She gestured to the open door.

Jesse sat, swinging his long legs into the small car. He was enveloped in her scent, seeped as it was into the smooth leather seats and gunmetal interior. Giving him an excellent view of her smooth cleavage under the neckline of her top, Audra leaned down. Her face almost in his crotch, she reached between his legs. Jesse's jeans grew tight and he caught his breath as anticipation hammered through him. "What happened to just voice?"

She turned her head, the parking lot lights making the magenta tips of her hair glow. She gave him a grin and he heard a click. Then the seat slid back. She rose with a wink and, leaning across him so her breasts were at eye level, she flicked off the interior light.

"Just making sure you're comfortable," she said. Then with a twist, a little shimmy in that tight black leather dress, she sat on his lap so that her back was to the driver's seat and her deliciously long legs were resting on the open door's armrest.

The nearest light was a half dozen or so cars away, and the parking lot deserted, so they had the illusion of privacy. But it wasn't private, and the door was wide open. Maybe if Jesse repeated that to himself a few dozen times, he could find the strength to care.

The temptation of those legs, encased in silky black stockings, was too much for him. Reveling in the feel of her toned limbs, he slid his hand down her thigh.

"Mmm, you have good hands. I'll bet you can work wonders with those fingers of yours." She laid her hand over his and guided it back up her thigh, just to the edge of the butter-soft leather hem. A hem that was inches, bare inches, from the promise of heaven between those glorious thighs. "I'd like to feel those hands on my body. You could start by unzipping my dress. All I'd have to do is stand up and it would slide to the ground, leaving me in silky little bits of nothing."

"Computers," he blurted.

"Beg your pardon?"

"I work with computers. That's how I keep my fingers limber." And how he'd dulled his social skills. Damn, could he sound any more stupid? Maybe he could sweet-talk her with some HTML code next? "Are you much into computers?"

Maybe that was her link with crime ring? Although with Davey on board, they probably didn't need any hacking help, as the dork was second only to Jesse himself in computer expertise. Nah, she had to be the handoff.

"Computers? I know about enough to turn one on."

"I'll bet you do," he murmured.

"I suppose that explains it," she mused.

He gave her a questioning look.

"Under that hunky exterior, you've got a brainy thing going on."

"Brainy?" Dammit, why brainy? Not that he sucked at attracting women, but there was always that layer of intellectual connection. His family was dead set on reducing him to a brain, albeit a handy brain when they needed heavy furniture moved. His coworkers and captain in Cyber Crimes valued his brains, counted on them to break the hardest cases. But the last thing he wanted to be noted for when he had the sexiest women he'd ever met in his lap was what was in his head. At least, not the one on his shoulders.

But, hunky? He knew it was immature, but his biceps clenched to support his hunk title. He could live with hunky.

"Yeah, you have a look in your eyes that tells me you think things through. Which is good. That means you'll think long and hard—" she paused for effect, then to punctuate her point, she wiggled her butt just a little "—about doing any job the best you can."

"Well, yeah. I do take pride in doing my best."

"I'll bet you do. Someone with that thoughtfulness, that attention to detail, you're sure to hit at least a seven, maybe even an eight, on the orgasm scale."

"Orgasm scale?" It was as if she'd posted a challenge sign. His testosterone demanded he grab that gauntlet and prove his manhood. "What's the scale? One to eight?"

Audra placed her fingers, just the tips, on the back of his hand and slid it under the edge of her skirt. Then she leaned close so he could feel her warm, sweet breath on his face. "Ten, baby. The top of the scale is a ten."

"What's the criteria for placement on this scale of yours?" He stifled a groan when he realized those luscious black hose covering her long legs stopped at the top of her thighs. He traced the rough, lacy band and told himself mewling pitifully would probably not rate high on her scale.

"Visual stimulation is the first step," she explained, her

husky lisp stimulating him more than most women could with a naked body and a can of whipped cream. "A look across the room, the sexual energy that sparks between two people when their eyes meet."

He slid his index finger under the band of her stockings, imagining how it'd feel to roll the silky fabric down her thighs, leaving her flesh bare for his lips.

"Do you know how it is when you meet someone's eyes, and your body responds sexually? For a man, you might get a little hard, might feel your muscles tighten. Me, I get damp. Damp is always a good sign in climbing the orgasm scale."

"I'll admit, I did get hard when our eyes met," he said.

She smiled her approval, obviously delighted he was willing to play along.

"Why don't you find out if I got damp?"

"We're a little past the meeting-of-the-eyes stage," he reminded her.

"Then why don't you see if I'm wet?"

Jesse couldn't resist. He slid his fingers higher on her thigh, brushing the tips over the lacy fabric of her panties. He groaned aloud. Wet. Deliciously wet.

"See, you're well on your way to an eight."

"I'm sure I can hit higher than an eight on that particular scale," he assured her fervently.

"Babe, nobody's gotten higher than an eight. That fabled ten on the orgasm scale is a myth."

"Then why not lower the scale?"

"Please," she insisted with a haughty look only a woman confident in her sexual worth could pull off. "Why would I lower my standards?"

Good point. Jesse grinned. It was a challenge he couldn't resist.

He leaned over and took her mouth with his.

And lost himself in the dark delight she offered. Pure sex, with that underlying sweet humor. She was his ultimate fantasy. When she sucked his tongue into her mouth, Jesse realized his fantasies were about to upgrade.

Audra's fingers brushed his skin like little electric shocks as she slipped the buttons of his shirt free. He nudged the elastic band of her panties aside to delight in her wet folds. When she scraped her fingernail over his nipple, an intense wave of desire washed over him and all thought fled.

With his fingers between her legs, his tongue working her mouth, Jesse gave himself over to a single goal. Bringing her that orgasm.

"Mmm," she moaned as he nibbled his way over the curves flowing out the top of her leather bodice. "I am so glad you came into the club tonight."

Club. Davey. The case. Dammit. Jesse lifted his head and blinked, shocked for some reason to realize they were still in the parking lot. A freaking parking lot, for God's sake. With a suspect of his case.

"I can't," Jesse said with a quick breath.

With not only his virtue, but his ethics on the line, he pulled back and shifted Audra so she was curled in his arms. And more importantly, so she was angled so he couldn't put his hand back up her skirt.

"Can't? Babe, you're hard enough to shoot for level nine if you tried. Believe me, I have faith you can."

Oh, God. Damned right he could. He was so hard, just the feel of her ass pressed against him was almost more pressure than he could stand. But he was pushing boundaries already. No way was he crossing that particular line.

"No condom," he claimed in desperation. "I don't have protection."

"Is that all?" Audra gave him a sultry smile that blurred

those ethical lines again. She reached behind her for the tiny purse she'd tossed on the driver's seat and did a quick finger rifle through it. Obviously not finding what she wanted, she upended the contents. Coming up empty, she frowned and gave a little shrug as she pulled open her wallet.

While she peered through the little pockets, Jesse eyed the disarray, looking for whatever Davey boy had given her. Lipstick, mints, a clear change purse holding a twenty and some coins. He spied her driver's license. Perfect.

"Wow, you look good," he said, slipping the small plastic card from the seat. He mentally patted himself on the back for such a sly move. "I thought crappy driver's license pictures were some kind of law."

"Laws aren't really rules, they're more like guidelines," Audra joked. Jesse cringed at her attitude but didn't figure he had room to take her to task, since he'd obviously broken a few ethical laws of his own. The underlying tightness in her voice distracted him from the pleasure of self-flagellation.

"And you aren't big on guidelines?" he asked with a frown. Frustrated with the lack of physical evidence of her connection to Davey, he told himself to get back in cop mode. Jesse memorized her full name, address and license number.

"Sure I am. It's a lot easier to break the rules if you know the guidelines first," she said with a wicked grin.

"Knowledge is the first step of preparation, huh?"

"Sure. And a Wicked Chick is always prepared." She leaned back toward the driver's seat and flipped open the glove box. She quickly shuffled through the messy pile of papers and frowned. "I have to have one in here."

She moved from shuffling papers to tossing them on the floor. "What the hell? How can I not have one? It's the Wicked Chicks number one rule. The only way to play safe is bring your own protection."

"I thought rules were more like guidelines." As soon as the words were out, Audra pinned him with a laser glare. Jesse winced. Maybe his sisters were right. Maybe he did always find the perfectly wrong thing to say.

Either way, he felt as if he'd been saved from a long fall off a very jagged cliff. He'd just ignore the part of him that was screaming in frustration at being denied that fall. Eight, his ass. He'd have shown her nine, easy. Ten, if he could use props and toys.

But that wasn't an option. At least, not right now. First he had to clear her or, if she was too involved with Dave Larson's current crimefest, bust her.

"To be honest, I'm not usually the kind of guy who gets that friendly on the first date."

Audra just continued to look at him, frustration and something deeper reflected in her eyes.

"I'd like to get together sometime, maybe a date?" Somewhere with a better setting for interrogation. First he'd do a little research, see if he could ferret out her connections. And practice the art of the cold shower.

"A date?"

"Yeah, you know, two people, out in public, getting to know each other."

"Sure. 'Cause guys are always interested in dating a woman they didn't get laid with, right?" she asked with a curl of her lip.

"Hey, what kind of guy do you think I am? I'm interested in you for more than sex."

"Sure," she repeated. With a wiggle that made him want to beg, she used her foot to push wide the partially open car door and slid off his lap to stand outside the car. As Jesse painfully unfolded himself from the vehicle, she reached into her purse and pulled out a piece of paper.

"Tell you what, here's my business card. You go ahead and give me a call, we'll do that date."

Jesse read it. Audra Walker, Simply Sensual Lingerie. Designer. "Lingerie, huh?"

"Oh, yeah, lingerie. And I'm damned good. Give me that call, I'll model some for you."

Maybe it wasn't too late to climb back in the car? He'd make do without intercourse. They could skip the whole condom issue.

She swung the car door shut and leaned against the fender. Smoothing her hands over her hips, she winked. "Don't forget the condom, huh?"

EVEN AS A BAD GIRL, lies didn't come easy to Audra. She hadn't been able to admit another failure, so when she'd sashayed back into the club, she'd smiled and let her friends assume she'd done the deed.

Five blood-pumping dances and an order of nachos hadn't blunted her sexual frustration. Finally tired of the unearned congratulations from Suzi and Bea, and the unspoken judgment of Isabel, she'd told the girls she was heading out. It would've been a clean break if not for the fact that she was Isabel's ride home.

Now, with her oldest friend in the passenger seat next to her, Audra flew down the freeway toward Auburn and the small neighborhood they'd grown up in.

Unlike Suzi and Bea, Isabel was into the whole focus-on-building-a-career thing. She'd taken over her parents' florist shop and was looking for ways to turn it from a small-town posey-pusher into one of the area's prominent florists.

Audra and Isabel had grown up next door to each other, both living over their parents' business. That Isabel had lived over the florist and Audra over a bar probably played into their personalities a bit. As a child, Isabel had been quiet, sweet and a little pudgy. Audra? She'd always been trouble.

Somehow, the two balanced each other out, though.

"Congratulations again on netting that deal with the mall," Audra said, remembering Isabel's earlier news. "You've been trying to snag that account for almost a year now. That's great that it finally came together."

They shared a smile. It was obviously a night to celebrate career achievements. Then Audra remembered the by-product of her latest achievement, her failure to live up to the code of the Wicked Chicks, and her mouth drooped.

"There's nothing wrong with being ambitious, Audra," Isabel said, obviously misreading her expression and figuring her frustration was career-focused. After all, for Isabel, most things were. "You worked your butt off going to school full-time and working in the boutique, too. You deserved to celebrate your success."

"Designing vanilla fluff."

"Oh, c'mon. Don't let that kind of defeatist thinking take hold. You have to start somewhere. How many people can claim the title of head designer right out of school? So you're not creating quite the kind of thing you want. Put in your time, pay your dues, and you'll be there soon enough."

Audra lifted her chin and pulled back her shoulders. Right. She'd get there. Damned if she wouldn't.

"Did you want to read that book I was telling you about yesterday?" Isabel asked, referring to the latest motivational tome she'd discovered. Audra had to hand it to her friend: Isabel was just as confident and determined to make her business a success as the Wicked Chicks were to live life to the fullest.

"Nah, I'll let you read it and give me the rundown, as always," Audra said with a wink.

Instead of her usual nod of agreement, Isabel frowned.

"You know," she said hesitantly, "you might want to read it yourself. Maybe it'd help you figure out why you agreed to debase yourself with meaningless sex, just for the sake of a girls' club you've outgrown."

"Debase?" Audra asked, ignoring the club reference, "What's so debasing about doing a hot, sexy guy?" Now, if she'd had to do that geek, well, that would've been beyond debasing. But Jesse? Her mouth still watered at the memory of his fingers, his lips. Oh, God. His tongue. She squirmed in her seat and shook her head at Isabel. "Look, I like sex. Just because you're trying out this chastity thing doesn't mean my choices are wrong."

"But this wasn't your choice, Audra. Why do you let them push you into those dares? I thought you said you were glad you'd grown out of that type of thing."

Audra's jaw worked. So what if she'd backslid a little? It wasn't just that Suzi and Bea were two of her closest friends. Her image, the sexy persona she'd developed in her teens, defined her. It made her special. Made her more than the pitiful little castoff of dismal parents who fought over her custody. Not over who got to keep her, but over who *had* to keep her.

It gave her control. Over herself, her life, the people around her. Isabel just didn't get that. She had two parents who adored her, who thought she'd hung the moon. Sure, she'd dealt with her share of crap growing up. But not like Audra.

Unlike the Wicked Chicks, Isabel preferred to stay in the background, to live the quiet life. In a lot of ways, it was amazing she and Audra had been able to maintain their friendship all these years.

Especially in the face of snotty-ass attitudes like she was currently copping.

"Look, Audra, I'm not judging you."

At Audra's sneer, she shrugged and admitted, "Okay, maybe a little. But that's just, you know…me. I don't get the whole sex-without-emotions thing."

"Emotions can't be trusted. Not when it comes to men," Audra stated adamantly as she pulled off the freeway. She'd learned that the hard way. The only guy she even considered semireliable was her brother. And that was more because she trusted his wife than out of any deep faith in him sticking around.

"Think of guys like dessert. Some you want to spend a lot of time on, savor. Get to know, maybe try a few more times to see if they're as good as you remember. Others are like M&M's. Quick, easy and clean. An easy between-meal treat that satisfies, but isn't really worth remembering afterward."

Isabel's laughter gurgled out, as Audra had intended. She glanced over and gave her friend a wink. Isabel rolled her eyes and shrugged. They'd been through over this same ground too many times before. They knew the drill.

Audra focused on negotiating streets she knew like the back of her hand. Finally, she pulled up in front of the small building that housed Isabel's flower shop and her apartment above. Audra's gaze landed on the neon lights flashing beer logos in the windows of the Good Times Sports Bar.

The difference in the two was as glaring-bright. Audra's brother, Drew, had taken over the bar after their father died. He'd put some effort into cleaning it up, but it was still a bar. Its edgy brick facade was in sharp contrast to the pale green florist shop with its apricot trim and flower-filled window boxes.

It was above that bar Audra had learned to set her goals, bust her ass and stand up for herself.

"So…what was this guy?" Isabel asked. "Tiramisu or M&M's?"

After barely a taste, she'd bet he was tiramisu all the way.

Since Wicked Chicks didn't admit failure, Audra gave her friend a wink and her naughtiest grin.

"Let's just say it would be my pleasure to try another taste of him," she drawled.

"It's probably just as well you won't," Isabel advised as she gathered her bag and opened the car door. "You need to focus on your career. This is no time to let some three-course dessert pull you off track."

"Hey, when have I ever let a guy matter enough to distract me from anything?"

As soon as the words were out of her mouth, Audra winced. While that would have worked with Suzi or Bea, Isabel knew Audra's history as well as her own. Once upon a time, Audra had thought love might exist. She'd believed a guy was more important than she was and had gladly handed him her dreams on a silver platter. Too bad he hadn't been interested enough to even lift the lid.

Luckily, her friend didn't press her advantage. She just patted Audra's hand where it rested on the gearshift knob and slid out of the car.

"Oh, hey, I almost forgot your souvenir." Isabel grinned and pulled a long strip of tacky green fabric from her bag. The tie. Audra took it with a wince. Ugly.

Isabel's grin faded as she shut the car door with a little wave. "You're there, Audra. Staring success in the face. Don't blow it."

Audra rolled her eyes and, without a word, slammed the car in gear and shot away from the curb.

Tension flamed its way over her shoulders and down her neck. And no wonder. She'd been fighting to prove herself all freaking night. Sure, she'd convinced her friends to chill out.

The cost? Instead of celebrating the first step of achieving her dreams, she was now wrestling with a pack of doubts. To say nothing of feeling overwhelmed by what could only be described as an identity crisis.

At this rate, she'd soon be one of those boring goody-goodys who worked all week for someone else's glory. Then spent Saturday night home alone. Maybe a pint of Chunky Monkey for company. Her friends would drop her a line now and then, a pity call for old times sake.

She was worried. Hell, she should be worried.

And yet all she could think about was whether or not she'd ever hear from Jesse again to finish what they'd started.

Maybe Isabel had a point?

4

AT HER DRAWING TABLE Monday morning, Audra stared at the design she was supposed to be finishing. Instead, she'd been sitting here, staring, for over an hour. Blocked. She'd never been blocked before. But now, she looked at the sketch of a white silk chemise and all she saw was blah, boring, vanilla.

Had she sold out? Had she put the idea of building a career, of making a name for herself in the lingerie design business, ahead of her individuality? Hell, did she even have individuality anymore? The things she'd counted on most of her life seemed to be slipping away. Her friends, her wicked persona. Her sexy attitude and ability to wow a guy speechless.

She eyed the tie she'd tossed on her table and rolled her eyes. Well, maybe she hadn't lost the speechless thing. That geek hadn't been able to weave three words together.

Audra looked at the wall over her table, sketches for the fall line in various stages of completion tacked across it. Some were, yes…vanilla. But only a couple. Most were hot. Empowering. An invitation for a woman to embrace her sensuality, to dress herself up in a way that would guarantee she felt strong and sexy.

Dammit, she was proud of those designs.

For a girl with few standout traits—at least, ones she wanted to market—the acclaim and attention she'd received designing lingerie were amazing. Audra had never stood out for anything but her looks and her badass attitude. So to take the sexy little designs she dreamed up from sketch to finished product gave her a sense of accomplishment she'd never imagined growing up as a number on a social worker's case file.

To have others actually pay money for that lingerie? It rocked, plain and simple.

So maybe she was focusing on the vanilla aspect, for now. It was a place to start. Soon, she'd layer in some rich, bittersweet chocolate syrup, maybe a little whipped cream. If she followed Isabel's advice and all that career planning stuff her friend spouted, Audra figured she'd have her cherry-topped dreams before she was thirty.

Nothing to worry about. She wasn't losing herself in the dream. Just working toward making her starring role a little better.

Semireassured, she forced herself to shake off the irritating introspection and took a swig of her energy drink.

She fingered her memento from Saturday night, the geek's hideous tie. It was a poorly-sewn-together monstrosity of blue geometric shapes strewn over an eye-watering green polyester background. She ought to toss it in the trash, but for some reason she couldn't. Probably because it reminded her of the delight she'd almost had, and how she'd let it get away.

"What's that? A new design?" Natasha, Audra's sister-in-law and boss, asked as she entered the small office-slash-design room. She reached out to touch the tie and grimaced. "No offense, Audra, but that's butt-ugly. Is that the kind of thing you're going to do now that you've graduated textile design school with all those honors?"

Audra fought back a blush. Honors. Who'd have thunk it? She was so *not* an honors kind of chick. For a woman who'd gotten her high school diploma through the G.E.D. program, school was not the gig of choice. But the Textile and Fashion

Design Academy? She'd found heaven. People who admired her for more than her bust, who were more interested in the designs she envisioned and brought to life than how much she could drink.

"No," she said in answer to the question, "this isn't a design for Simply Sensual. It's more like a reminder."

"Of what not to wear, I hope."

More like of the hottest guy she'd ever almost had, to say nothing of her fall from Wicked Chick status. Two dares failed in one night. How humiliating. A wave of despair washed over her. Were her friends right? Was she changing? Losing her edge in her drive to build a career? The missing condom definitely supported that theory.

She looked around the work space, its soft blues and deep burgundies edged with gilt and curlicues. Pure femininity. The colors and lines definitely weren't what she'd call her style, yet she was perfectly comfortable here. Productive, even more so than in the vivid purple and red decor of her apartment.

It was a Monday morning, and she'd shown up at work before Natasha to open the shop. Again, a sign of responsibility at odds with her bad girl reputation of swinging in whenever the whim took her.

It was enough to make a girl panic. But Audra ignored the sick tension in her stomach and the freaked-out thoughts swirling through her brain. She was made of sterner stuff than that. Dammit, she could have it all. She'd prove her badness, *and* make her mark on the lingerie world.

Since that wasn't the kind of thing she could share, though, she just smiled. In looks, Natasha was her complete opposite. Blond, ladylike and subdued. It was only after Audra had gotten to know her that she'd recognized the wild woman under Natasha's tidy exterior.

"I like to think of it as a design with an identity crisis," Audra said of the tie. Like a game show hostess, she held it high in one hand and trailed the back of her fingers over it with the other. It was so poorly constructed, it felt as if they'd left a needle or something between the layers.

"Identity crisis?" Natasha repeated with a laugh. "That tie is just ugly."

Damned good thing she hadn't ended up with its owner. Who knew what else of his was poorly constructed? Audra suppressed a shudder and shrugged. "Some ideas might come of it."

Hopefully ideas on how to find balance between her ambitions and her friends instead of the sexual fantasies she'd entertained about Jesse and all the alternate endings to their encounter. Alternate endings she had no way to engineer since she'd not only become wuss girl without the condom, but hadn't even got the man's phone number.

God, what was happening to her?

"If anyone can find inspiration from it to use in a lingerie design, you can," said Natasha. "After all, your latest nightie is selling like gangbusters. Didn't you say it was inspired by one of those plastic six-pack carriers?"

Audra grinned. She loved the nightie Natasha mentioned. Its random circles of opaque fabric stamped over sheer organza offered tantalizing peeks of bare flesh, all in a baby doll style that screamed sassy fun.

"This just goes to prove the brilliance of my decision to make you head designer," Natasha claimed with a satisfied smile.

To hide her infinitesimal wince, Audra shrugged. Head designer. It sounded so…uptight, official. So not her. She wasn't sure if it was the designation or the implied responsibility that gave her the willies. Then again…if it kept her on the road to that cherry-topped dream, she'd deal with it. Willies and all.

She pinned the tie to the wall next to her sketches. She was just about to pitch the changes she'd been dying to make for the new fall line when Natasha jumped up and clapped her hands.

"Oh, that reminds me." Excitement rang clear in her sister-in-law's voice. "I had a call. A very special call, as a matter of fact. From Hantai Lingerie. They definitely want to talk business."

Audra's mouth went dry. Business? International business? Visions of her latest design ideas flashed through her mind. Now that she was head designer, she'd be able to get a little wild, instead of the more demure, subtle designs Natasha favored. Where better to launch them than in a new country? Excitement whipped through her.

This was why she was teetering on the edge of losing her Wicked Chick status and even the respect of her friends. For a shot at making these visions a reality. To make her mark on the design world with lingerie and finally prove she was a success. Go beyond bridal fluff and get into truly sexy creativity.

"This is it, Audra. We're heading for the big time. That makes the third China-based lingerie distributor wanting to carry our fall line."

Natasha grinned and grabbed Audra, pulling her out of her chair for a hug. Still unused to the ready affection, Audra was stiff at first, but Natasha didn't let up. A few seconds was all it took Audra to loosen up and join her sister-in-law in the celebration. They did a wild butt-swinging boogie and slapped hands before dropping to their chairs.

"Rock on. I've been thinking of some designs to spice up the line. You know, add a few options to grab the more adventurous customers." It was all Audra could do to keep her cool and not bounce in her seat like a little schoolgirl.

Natasha's smile dimmed and her face got that let's-let-her-down-gently look.

Audra didn't even need to hear the words to know she was being denied.

"I'd love to see your ideas. I'm sure there's a solid market for more adventurous designs. I'll bet you have some exciting things in mind."

Nice words, but a shutdown, none the less.

"But…"

Here it was.

"Simply Sensual has built its reputation in a more demure and subtle direction. I think, at least for the fall line, we should keep our focus there. That's what these distributors have recognized us for, what they are interested in. After all, we can't afford to experiment at this point. We just don't have the time or the financial resources."

In other words, more fluffy sweet designs. Audra bit back a sigh. Not that she didn't enjoy the challenge of making something demure scream "Do me." But she'd thought she'd be able to spread her wings a little now. Wasn't that what head designer meant? That she was in charge of the designs?

Before she could find an unchallenging way to ask, Natasha leaned forward to tap the papers spread over the drafting table.

"Let's focus on signing these Chinese distributors. We'll keep the fall line in sync with our current image. But draw me up these designs you have in mind, and we'll see what we can do about incorporating some aspect of them into the spring additions, okay?"

After a brief struggle with impatience, Audra grimaced and shrugged. Heck, she was getting her way, right? Maybe not as fast as she'd prefer, but Natasha's explanation made sense.

"I've been thinking about it," Natasha said, her fair face

flushed from dancing. "I know I said I didn't want to borrow any money from a bank because I need all the capital and collateral available for this next big order. But I talked to my aunt last week. She's willing to loan me enough money to guarantee we nail this deal."

Natasha's aunt was rolling in snooty, upscale money.

"I think it'd be smart if one of us went over to Beijing and met with these companies," Natasha continued. "You know, talk us up and personally present the designs. Be there to get them to sign the contracts."

From the serious look on the blonde's aristocratic face, she'd put a lot of thought into this. The lure of China stifled Audra's still simmering impatience to branch out with her designs.

"Okay. That's smart," Audra agreed with a nod. She didn't even ask which one of them would go. She might be the newly appointed head designer, but the businesswoman thing was obviously not her specialty. "It'll cost a bit of capital, but if the loan will cover it, it's worth it. I think the connection we'll make by face-to-face meetings will pay off in the long run."

But didn't this mean there was more money available? Like, money that could go toward some hot, sexy designs? Audra pressed her lips together, but didn't say anything. Bottom line, it was Natasha's business. As much as Audra might want to push for her rights as head designer, she'd wait. She'd watch for the opportune moment. Any bad girl worth her garter belt knew how to turn a no into a yes. It was all in the timing.

Simply Sensual would be a success. Thanks, in part, to her. This would be the first major step they'd taken since Natasha had bought the company from her aunt almost two years before, one they couldn't have made without Audra's talent.

She sucked in a breath and held it, her cheeks puffed out.

Focus on the trip. China, so much to see and do. She'd never traveled outside the country. Not that she'd be going this time, but wouldn't it be cool if she could? Make big deals, wow the distributors with her charm and moxie.

"Which one of us is going to go?" she asked, just in case a miracle happened and Natasha thought knowledge of the designs would be a bigger asset on this trip than knowing the business.

"I'm not sure," Natasha admitted with a grimace. "You did the designs. But I know the business end. You know, what we need to make this deal work."

Not sure, her ass. When it was put that way, Audra could hardly argue. She really wasn't disappointed. And maybe if she repeated it enough, she'd believe it.

Besides, she had enough at stake already, trying to wade through her personal identity crisis. The exhilaration fading, Audra wanted to sink into her chair and bury her head in her hands, but couldn't. Not while Natasha was here. To admit such a problem—hell, to admit any weakness—wasn't her way.

"You'd make a stronger impression on the suits" was all Audra could come up with. And it was true. While Audra might wow them, the impression Natasha would make would likely net more business.

"Are you sure?"

"I'm sure. You go. Hell, you should take Drew," Audra suggested, certain her brother would love the idea of a second honeymoon. He'd been so focused on saving their deceased father's bar, then on building enough business to keep Aaron Walker's legacy in the black, that he hardly ever took time off. Besides, not only had he been the one to nag Audra into going to design school, he'd even paid her way.

The least she could do was make sure big brother got a little international nooky with his wife. "He'd get a charge out of it. I'll bet it'd make a better impression on those business-men, too, you being solidly married and all that."

"Oh, good point." Natasha scooted around the desk and grabbed a pad and pen. Audra grinned when she started scratching out a list of things to do. Then Natasha paused and tucked a long strand of hair behind her ear and peered at Audra.

"Um, you'd have to handle the boutique on your own. I think I could get Aunt Sharon to help behind the counter once in a while, but mostly it'd fall on you. I'd have to be gone about two weeks, I think."

Unspoken was the fact that the longest Audra had been re-sponsible for Simply Sensual was a three-day weekend. That was the weekend she'd ended up hosting an impromptu bridal shower in the boutique, complete with male strippers. It probably wouldn't have been too big a deal if Natasha's aunt hadn't chosen to stop in just as the bride-to-be and the stripper had been acting out an explicit sexual act on the checkout counter. They'd sold a hell of a lot of lingerie that evening, she remembered, suppressing a naughty grin.

Natasha's doubts, so politely unsaid, were clear on her face. Audra knew her sister-in-law would be enlisting her aunt as a babysitter, as well as temporary clerk. Audra's amusement fell away. No matter how she sugarcoated it, her sister-in-law expected her to drop the ball.

Jeez, how hard could it be to take charge of the boutique for a couple weeks? Audra ran through a checklist of what she knew about running the business. It was a dismally short list.

Damn.

Maybe Natasha was right to worry about the wisdom of leaving it all in her hands. But if there was one thing Audra refused to do, it was to appear needy. Nope, she'd suck up the insecurity and do a kick-ass job.

"When do you think you'll go?"

Natasha tapped the pencil on the pad of paper, the dull thump keeping rhythm with Aerosmith belting out "Just Push Play" on the radio.

"I can call Aunt Sharon and get the money transferred today. The sooner we get the contracts and an idea of what kind of numbers we'll be producing, the faster we can deliver product. What do you think about me leaving tomorrow? It's like an all-day flight, but I can set up meetings starting on Wednesday."

"Sounds like a plan. Let's get this party rockin'."

Natasha settled behind her desk with a cup of peppermint tea while Audra knocked back a Red Bull. For the next half hour they sketched out a plan of action, then went over the boutique responsibilities for the next week or so.

"I think that's everything," Natasha said as she tidied her notes into a stack. "And just in time to open the doors."

She came around her desk and gave Audra an excited hug.

"We're making it, Audra. Big-time. Drew is so proud of you." She pulled back, obviously realizing all this sentimental stuff made Audra uncomfortable. "So we're set. Are you sure you can handle everything alone?"

Audra considered her performance over the last week since graduating the textile and design academy.

She'd lost an order, told a customer the fishnets made her cellulite look like a bag full of marbles and almost got the delivery guy fired for flirting on company time.

Hardly management material.

But if she wanted to be trusted with something as major as bringing her vision to the spring line, she'd have to prove she could handle running the boutique.

Rarely felt nerves made their way through her stomach with a nasty flutter.

"I can handle it," she vowed. She'd make sure of it. "As long as I don't have to remember to bring a condom," she muttered under her breath.

"Um, no, I doubt you'll need to worry about that. At least, not for the boutique—unless you're planning another party," Natasha said with a wink and laugh.

Maybe she'd overreacted and Natasha wasn't worried about leaving her in charge. Audra frowned.

Dammit, she should worry. Two years ago, heck, two months ago, she'd have worried. Now, though, Audra was, what? Such a goody-goody she could be trusted to be well-behaved? She sank into her chair with a morose sigh. All these yo-yoing emotions were exhausting. Just because she wasn't a loser didn't mean she was a goody-goody. There was an in-between there. Somewhere.

"But, you know it's better to be safe than sorry. I'd strongly suggest keeping a few condoms on hand, since you never know what will come up." Laughing at her own joke, Natasha headed out to the showroom to open the boutique for the day.

Audra made a face at her sister-in-law's retreating back and mocked, "Ha ha."

But inside, she groaned. How freaking pitiful was she? Even Natasha knew to be prepared.

After Natasha left, Audra contemplated the ugly tie pinned to the wall. The green was an insult to the eyes, and the crappy construction mocked her devotion to design details.

She should throw it away. It was stupid to hold on to some geek's tie. A geek who'd run out on her, making her a loser in her friends' eyes. Sure, they'd tossed her a second dare. But look how that had turned out.

But no, here she was, a sappy sentimental wuss who should have her Wicked Chick membership revoked. Courting silly thoughts about what a guy was like out of bed and wondering if he'd really call her for a date. Holding on to some butt-ugly memento as a reminder of the night she'd met the hottest guy to ever keep her awake without even being there.

Talk about an identity crisis.

A JUMBO COFFEE at his elbow, heavily laced with cream to disguise the bitter taste, Jesse's fingers cruised with loving familiarity over the computer keyboard. He ignored the usual Tuesday morning noise in the cop shop as he patiently hacked through Dave Larson's personal life.

Two steps forward, five steps back.

A dance Jesse loved. Larson was dirtier than a meth fiend on a street corner. The last two years he'd been up to his ass in debt, conning Peter to rob Paul. Now, suddenly, he was rolling in the green. Enough cash flying through his secondary account to rent a BMW, pay for a Nordstrom shopping spree and buy one hell of a lot of porn on the Internet. Davey Larson was definitely being paid well.

Jesse hit Print to add the financials to his file and continued digging. An hour later, the phone on the corner of his desk jangled. He ignored it until someone yelled his name.

"Hey, Martinez. Phone. Dude wants to talk to you."

Jesse waved his thanks and grabbed the phone, still working the keyboard with one hand.

"Martinez here."

Five minutes later, he stared at his scribbled notes. It wasn't the chicken-scratch mess that had the coffee churning in his stomach. His informant had confirmed the rumors. Dave Larson wasn't just dabbling in organized crime. He was playing with the big boys. Chinatown-based mafia *Du Bing Li* big. It seemed Dave had finally scored the underworld connections he'd sought through the most unlikely source. His porn addiction.

And the woman who'd lured him in was said to be one hot babe who favored The Wild Thing as her club of choice.

Audra's image flashed through his brain. Jesse tried to wash out the dirty taste in his mouth with a swig of tepid coffee. Pulling a face, he shoved the cup away. He couldn't stand the flavor of the stuff, but it was the best caffeine bang for the buck, and his energy level was nil in the morning.

Dammit. Jesse slapped the notepad aside. He hated that she was dirty. Sure, she came across as a man-eater who knew the score, but there was an underlying sweetness that had tugged at his heart.

"What's up?"

Jesse glanced over at Rob Dutton, the cop whose desk faced his. A tall, lanky redhead with a penchant for practical jokes, he was the reason Jesse found himself in this moral mess. After all, it'd been Rob who'd dared him to get out of his comfort zone and try a little undercover for a change.

The bastard.

"The evidence against Larson is building," Jesse told him.

"Good thing you tailed him, huh? Did you get the goods Saturday night?"

Not for lack of willingness on his body's part. With a shiver, Jesse remembered the cold shower he'd taken Saturday night after leaving Audra.

"I trailed him, identified his connection and made contact." The memory of that contact sent a wave of heat over Jesse, making him shift in his chair.

"Dude, you crack this case, you might snag a promotion. Your work here in Cyber Crimes is noteworthy, sure. But the extra steps you're taking, going undercover? The brass will love that. Hero stuff must run in the family," Rob teased.

Jesse responded with a shrug as Rob took a phone call, but his mind raced.

The brass. Always close to the surface, the memory of his late father rose in Jesse's head. Even though he'd been gone five years now, Jesse still imagined his father was watching over his shoulder—always judging his job performance, his life choices—and shaking his head with a frown of disapproval.

A man's man, Diego Martinez had been one hell of a cop. The brass said he'd died a hero's death. Jesse knew the reality was Diego had trusted the wrong woman. While Jesse might feel compelled to constantly prove he was as good a cop as his father, he wasn't about to repeat the man's mistakes.

So he would run an in-depth check on Audra Walker. As soon as he'd built enough evidence against her, he'd lose this fascination. Maybe then he could lay off the cold showers. His body would thank him. Hell, just the thought of Audra got him horny as hell. For another chance to see her, touch her, his body would weep in gratitude.

Ten minutes later, Jesse was wishing he'd started his day with something stronger than coffee.

"Damn," he breathed. He hadn't even had to dig. It was all right there. Cocky and in-your-face, just like Audra herself. It hadn't taken Jesse more than a couple of keystrokes to find the proof he needed.

He stared at the monitor with a sinking feeling in his gut. A part of him had secretly hoped he'd discover her innocence. The evidence pointed to the contrary.

"Martinez? Report."

This day was going downhill fast. Jesse grimaced. Then, clearing his face, he spun in his chair to face his captain.

"There's a break in the Larson case. I've solidly tied him to the *Du Bing Li* triad."

Captain Shale's bushy blond brows rose, and he tugged at his chin, signaling he was cautiously impressed.

"We've been trying to infiltrate *Du Bing Li* for months now. We've got a guy from San Francisco PD working Chinatown, but nobody's been able to tie them to the Cantonese *Wo Shing Wo* triad. Do you have anything solid?"

"I know he's passing information, sir. It could be fraud, ID theft or, given Larson's history, credit card theft. I haven't narrowed down the specifics yet. But I'm close. Give me a few more days." Jesse pulled out a file on the triad and handed it, along with the Larson file, to the captain.

Shale flipped through the report, humming a couple times, but otherwise silent. When he got to the most recent pages Jesse had added, the captain's brows rose again and his hum turned into an *aha*. He'd obviously reached the part pertaining to Audra Walker.

Jesse felt like hurling those large quantities of coffee he'd used to pry his eyes open that morning.

"Walker? You run her sheet?"

"Yes, sir. Her adult record is clean, but she's got a sealed juvie."

"You verified this deposit?"

"Yeah, the money was deposited in the account last night. It's not her account, but the business she works for." As if that minute detail mattered. "I haven't been able to track the source yet." The sick feeling spread from his stomach to his head. It just felt wrong planning to arrest a woman after he'd had his hands in her panties. Unlike his father, he didn't prescribe to the any-method-to-crack-the-case code. Jesse stretched his neck from side to side with a loud crack of tension.

"Two plane tickets to Beijing?"

"Yes, sir. They're booked in her boss's name, though."

As if that were any big defense. It only meant both women were involved. Jesse hadn't had time yet to check further into

Natasha Walker, other than to discover she was related to Audra by marriage. A family that plays together stays together.

"Your cover is solid? You've made contact with her?"

With all parts of her. Jesse's fingers tingled at the memory of the sweet heat of her juices.

"Yeah, it's solid" was all he said. He knew there were officers who had no problem going into deep cover, could justify any action in the name of getting the job done. His father had been one of them.

Jesse, though, didn't. Couldn't.

"I don't have a case against her, yet," he reminded his boss. "So far, what I have is all circumstantial. It's possible it's all a coincidence."

"I don't believe in simple coincidence, Martinez, you know that. Keep digging on Larson, see if you can follow him, strike up a friendship. Maybe use your computer connection or check into infiltrating one of his online porn chats. But focus on Audra Walker. She's tied in somehow. I want you to find out how. Stay undercover, use whatever means necessary to get close to the woman. Break this case," he ordered.

His head pounding like a sledgehammer, Jesse thought of the condom he'd taken to carrying in his pocket. That probably wasn't the kind of means the captain had in mind. Then again, given the potential of this case, maybe it was. Knowing he had his captain's blessings didn't help Jesse's resolve to keep his dick in his pants and his hands off the luscious suspect.

"I JUST DON'T THINK naughty undies are in good taste," tittered a thirtysomething woman who looked as if she could use a good dose of naughty. Her mousy hair was pulled back so tight it made Audra's own face hurt, and her high-necked blouse did a damned good job of disguising her femininity.

"That's the great thing about lingerie. It can suit any mood from naughty to sweet," Audra assured her. "First and foremost, lingerie is about feeling good with yourself. It's like an affirmation of a woman's sexuality, her sensual self-worth."

"I just don't think I could wear some of this stuff," the woman murmured as she fingered a pink satin merry widow with rosebud detailing. She wrinkled her nose at the cord that comprised the G-string. "Wouldn't this chafe?"

"It's an acquired preference." Audra managed to keep a straight face and resisted adjusting the strap of the red leather bustier she wore with jeans and her cropped denim jacket. If the lady thought satin chafed, she'd definitely not be into leather. "If you're just beginning to explore lingerie, you might start by examining your own sexual fantasies. The merry widow is a popular choice. Sometimes you want to work up to that, though."

"Maybe I should start with something less intimidating?"

"Great idea." Audra gestured to a different display, this reminiscent of vintage Victorian. She held up a semisheer cotton sheath, and the woman's eyes lit up. "Something like this looks innocent and offers body coverage. Feel the fabric."

Hesitantly at first, the woman rubbed the cotton between her fingers.

"Oooh, so soft."

Audra quelled her triumphant grin at the look of delight on the woman's face.

"If you like that, wait until you see this corset set. It's the most comfortable thing you'll ever wear." Audra let her voice drop to a whisper as she leaned closer. "And the things it does for the cleavage. Very impressive."

The woman grinned and nodded enthusiastically.

Oh, yeah, baby, haul out the plastic.

Audra kept her smile in place as she rang up the sale, but

as soon as the door closed behind yet another lingerie convert, she let it fall away. God, what a week. Natasha had only been gone three days and Audra was ready to scream.

Only a half hour until closing. Then she'd be able to relax a little, shake off this stressed-out feeling. Maybe she should call the girls, see if they wanted to get together? She could loosen up and relax. And best of all, there was a good chance she'd meet a guy, get lucky and take the edge off.

Didn't it freaking suck that the only guy she wanted was Jesse? At least half her distraction this week could be firmly placed at his feet. After all, sexual frustration was not something Audra was used to feeling. Until now.

The soft chime of bells indicated a new customer. She wiped the pissy expression off her face and looked at the entrance.

Like a dream conjured from her naughtiest wishes, Jesse walked through the door. She gave an unconscious sigh of appreciation. He really was as hot as she remembered. Well-worn jeans cupped a promising package, while a plain black workshirt covered his drool-inspiring chest. Lust rushed through her at the delicious sight.

"Hey, gorgeous," she said leaning forward on the counter in a way she knew gave a generous view of her cleavage. "What a *very* nice surprise."

With a sexy grin, he held up a condom. The sunlight coming through the large plate glass windows glinted off the foil wrapper. "Didn't you say something about modeling lingerie for me?"

5

DAVE LARSON stood in the entrance to The Wild Thing and swiped the back of his hand over his forehead to keep the sweat from trickling into his eyes. He'd gone through two sticks of antiperspirant in the last week. Ever since he'd found out he'd handed off the computer chip to the wrong woman, he'd been sweating like a pig. For a fastidious man, it was pure hell.

That triad pinhead had woken him Sunday morning from a dead sleep, beating down his door and spouting a whole litany of threats. It had taken Dave a few minutes to figure out what the problem was. After all, not that he'd admit it to the pinhead, but it wasn't like women came on to him all that often. How the hell was he to know the hot chickie wasn't their connection? Hell, she'd fit the look, she'd complimented his tie, not quite the code word, but close enough. What more was he supposed to have waited for? Her friggin' ID?

That'd been when the pinhead had got pissed. The guy had started talking conspiracy, rival gangs and infiltration. Dave had just rolled his eyes. It was all too much paranoid drama for his blood.

It hadn't been until the pinhead had sicced his goon on one of Dave's computers, beating it into a pile of plastic and metal, that Dave had gotten scared.

It seemed that even though Dave had been a loyal employee for the past six months, although he'd followed their instructions, he'd worked his fingers sore hacking enough numbers to meet their dirty needs, the mix-up was all *his* fault. And while Dave was willing to take the blame—especially since the goon had still been hefting the baseball bat he'd whacked the computer with—the pinhead wasn't willing to let him off the hook.

Probably because Dave had gambled away a good portion of the first installment *Du Bing Li* had fronted. Not that he'd told them that, or apparently that it would have mattered. They wanted the chip. The original, not a copy, not a new batch of names. It had to be that one.

As proof of Dave's desire to live.

Here he was, Mr. Nice Guy, doing them a favor by offering up the goods. Dave knew the value of the info he'd hacked. Full identities. Names, addresses, social security numbers, mothers' maiden names. The works. All those tidy little tidbits of information a savvy group such as *Du Bing Li* could use.

Dave was a smart man. He knew *Du Bing Li* was tied to *Wo Shing Wo,* and the word on the street was they were looking to start transporting their human cargo into the good ole U.S. of A. For that, a computer chip of cleanly hacked IDs was a goldmine.

Now he had to get it back from some club tramp, or lose his ass.

"Move, dude."

Dave waited until the refrigerator-sized bouncer was past him before he sneered and gave him the finger.

He swiped his forehead again and stepped into the club. Damned flashing lights made it hard to see, so he squinted, looking for the woman.

He could barely remember what she looked like. Hot, sure. But the details? Jeez, all women looked alike from the neck up; he never paid much attention.

Finally, he spotted a blonde who seemed familiar. She had

been here that night. He was sure, because he remembered thinking that in the animal-print thing she'd been wearing, she'd looked exactly like one of the porn queens he idolized. She wasn't the woman he was looking for, but maybe she could help him find her.

He timed it right, waiting until she and the woman she was with waved to the waitress for drink refills. Then he sauntered over, hand on his wallet ready to make an impression.

"Ladies, how ya doin'?"

"We're out of your league, dude. Get lost," the blonde said, with barely a glance his way.

The other one, a redhead with a nice rack, gave him a sympathetic look and little shrug. It was that shrug, the dainty apology of it, that made Dave look again.

She was gorgeous. It wasn't just the sweet curve of her breasts pressing against her dress or the way her hair curled down her back, inspiring one of his favorite fantasies. It was the polished, moneyed look of her. Dave was an expert at recognizing money and what it could do for a person. Which was why he'd dedicated his life to amassing as much of it as he could.

A man such as himself could definitely appreciate the silky richness of a woman like this one.

"Don't underestimate me," he told the blonde. "There's a lot more to me than meets the eye."

The blonde snorted.

Normally, that kind of crap would send him back to the safety of his computer and his agreeable online ladies. But damned if he'd be brushed off when he'd found his dream woman. Especially when his ass was on the line, too.

"You might be overestimating yourself if you think you could handle either of us, dude." This time, the blonde actually turned to face him. Davey recognized the look in her eyes, the combination of pity and disinterest.

Davey fought off his natural instinct to run away. He needed the chip. To get the chip, he needed to find out who that woman was, and once he did, find a way to get to her. He was sure she'd been with these women that night. Which meant they might know her name and address. And hopefully, they meant enough to her to be bait if necessary.

"Let me buy you ladies drinks and I'll show you how wrong you are." Dave pulled out his wallet and, hiding a grimace, handed the waitress enough to cover the drinks she'd just delivered. "I'll bet women as hot as the two of you are used to all the studs hitting on you. Bunch of egocentric, selfish guys, all out for whatever they can get off you."

"Obviously any guy can hit. Who we let connect is what counts."

"Sure, sure. You're hot, you're in the driver's seat. But what I'm saying is, you ladies, hot as you are, have to get sick of the users around here. Me, I'm all about what I can do for you."

"Nice try, and points for creativity." The blonde rolled her eyes at him in obvious dismissal. "But, no thanks."

Davey ignored the blonde's disinterest. It was the redhead's reaction that sent the surge of triumph through him. Her slight nod and the droop of her mouth screamed "Score."

The gorgeous rich girl was the key. Anticipation swirled through him at the idea of working on her to get the information he needed.

Like a hawk focused on its prey, he shifted his weight just a bit. Enough to face her, but not enough to scare her off.

Her soft blue gaze met his, sending Cupid's arrow straight through his heart. He skimmed his gaze over her, taking in the designer clothes, flash of sparkles at her ears and pricey cosmetics. The only thing that turned him on more than a gorgeous woman with a C cup was one who came wrapped in wealth.

Unfortunately, as he did whenever he was faced with a fantasy woman, his tongue tied itself in knots and he lost the ability to think coherently.

Dave quelled the panicky feeling in his belly and tried to get his brain to work. He needed that chip. To get it, he needed the name of their friend. That wasn't gonna happen unless one of them trusted him. Since his body screamed out for the hot redhead, he'd focus on her. After all, the blonde scared him.

Dave put on his most trustworthy face and hid his fists in his pockets. Sucking in a deep breath, he almost choked on the mix of perfumes, BO and booze in the air. He ignored it and pasted a big smile on his face.

"Your friend's loss is your gain," he said to the redhead. Davey looked at her glass, almost empty, and hid a wince. She sure drank fast. Dammit, he might have to fork out more dough than he'd wanted. "Let me buy you a couple more drinks and tell you how well I'd treat you if you were my lady."

Three drinks, two painful dances and countless barbs from the blonde later, Davey was pretty happy with his progress. He had his hand on the redhead's—Bea's—ass. He'd got a buzz going and lost some of the edgy nerves that had dogged him since the pinhead had slammed down his door. Now to get that name.

"You ladies look familiar. Have you been in any commercials or print work I'd recognize?" he asked.

Bea's eyes lit up and she did a sweet little wiggle that sent her chest swaying. Before she could reply, though, the blonde gave a mean little laugh.

"Oh, please," sneered Suzi. "You're already feeling her up. Can't you do any better than that cheesy pickup line?"

"No, no. I've been on the cover of *California Girl*," Bea said with a glare at her friend. "He probably recognized me."

Davey didn't even recognize the magazine. But he grinned anyway and nodded.

"Of course, of course. I knew it. I've seen you recently, though. Maybe in person? Do you come in here a lot?"

"Actually," Bea said, giving him a long, slightly wasted look, "you look familiar, too."

"Gag me," Suzi murmured.

Davey had to force himself not to take her up on the offer. Instead, he offered her a sneer and his shoulder. She just laughed.

"I was in last Saturday scoping out talent. I'm a photographer," he told Bea, who's eyes sparked with excitement. "Maybe you were here then?"

"Saturday?" the blonde said with a shrug. "Maybe. We hit a lot of clubs."

Bea narrowed her eyes, then nodded. "We *were* here Saturday. That was Audra's party. Remember, Suzi?"

"Oh, yeah, I remember." Suzi giggled, the softest sound he'd heard from her. A self-professed expert at reading people, Dave wondered at the affection and regret in the blonde's eyes. "She hit on that geeky loser and he ran like a scared little girl, remember Bea?"

Bingo. Davey cracked his neck, pasted on a fake smile and hoped they didn't recognize him as the scared little girl. The Audra chick must have his computer chip. Dave wasn't too concerned, though. It wasn't as if she was the competition, out to sell it to the highest bidder. Nah, this was all gonna be fine. Just fine.

Davey leaned his elbows on the high table and turned on the charm. He'd find out if he had anything to worry about, get a name to retrieve his chip from and romance his dream woman in the bargain. Nobody was better at getting his way than Dave Larson.

AUDRA'S SMILE drew Jesse's attention away from the mouth-watering view of smooth flesh showcased in red leather. He knew the flesh was smooth because his fingers had memorized the feel of her.

"You'll have to tell me a little bit about your preferences," Audra told him. Straightening slowly, the view shifted and he saw her top only reached her midriff, leaving her stomach bare above low-slung jeans.

A bare stomach adorned with not only an ultrafine gold chain, but also a belly-button piercing—a glittery red jewel with dangling stars.

Jesse did his damnedest not to swallow his tongue.

"Preferences?" he asked. The possibilities ran through his mind at the speed of light, each one featuring a deliciously naked Audra.

"Yeah. You know, what look you like. What gets you excited?"

"You."

And she did. Instead of the magenta-tipped spikes he'd seen before, today her hair was fluffed around her head. Still edgy black, it was just a little softer. Her face seemed softer, too. Maybe it was the girly atmosphere of the boutique instead of the harsh lights of the club or the parking overheads. This easy, approachable look made it damned hard to think of her as a criminal.

Especially in this confection-style shop, with its gilded edges, swirly decorations and mass of frilly sex-inspired nighties.

She laughed a little and shook her head. "I mean what lingerie looks are you into? Any fashion preferences?"

"I like the look you have going on," he reiterated. "What style is that?"

Audra looked down at herself, then shrugged and grinned. "You won't find this in here. For the most part, Simply

Sensual's stock is more subtle. You know, satin and lace. Someday, I hope to bring in a little leather, maybe some metal detailing. But for now, the stock here is pretty sweet. I call this my last rebellion style."

"Do tell."

"When I started working here, I was the ultimate rebel. It was all about the design, not the boutique. Shop, retail, that was boring. I'd show up for work whenever I felt like it, take off when I wanted."

"Didn't your employer object?"

"Believe me, I didn't come with references," Audra said with a rueful laugh. "I remember my first job. I worked at this trendy little boutique. One day I saw a list of 'employee rules' posted in the office and realized I'd broken them all."

"Don't you worry about breaking rules?"

"Nah. I'm not big on rules. Usually the worst I get is a lecture and I'm used to that. I had a social worker once who was the queen of lectures."

"Social worker, huh?"

"No biggie," she said with a shrug, "I had a high school counselor who doubled as Dottie Do-Gooder. She was so sure I was gonna end up in jail or on the streets, ole Dottie called in Child Protective Services. They'd already tagged me as a lost cause, but this social worker figured she'd hang out and make me her project child."

Even though her tone was light, it was clearly a closed door. Jesse noted the tight, pained look around her eyes as she talked about the past. From the info he'd dug up, she'd never actually been in the foster system. It didn't sound as if she'd gotten off unscathed, though.

"So you're not big on rules, huh? What about losing your job?"

Her wide smile was obviously in thanks for changing the

subject. Jesse ignored what it did to his body and told himself to focus on the case. His body, of course, ignored him.

"Natasha knew what she was getting into when she signed me on. Actually, I started in the back doing design work while I went to school. Simpl Sensual has two functions. The boutique and the lingerie company. My focus is design, first and foremost. But somehow I got conned into creating displays, eventually got suckered into working the cash register."

"Sounds like your—" Jesse stopped himself before he let slip *sister-in-law* "—boss is pretty wily. She obviously knew what it would take to entice you into becoming the model employee." He eyed her bare belly and winked. "Especially if you get many men in here shopping."

"We get a few. And yeah, Natasha's okay. She just promoted me last week. Now I run the design department of the lingerie side of the business."

"And you still rebel?"

Audra laughed, a husky sound of delight.

"I'll always be a rebel. I'm just a little…less, now." Her tone drooped, kind of like the wispy bit of silk that dangled, one strap hanging forlornly, from the padded hanger. She reached over to adjust it, securing the loose strap over the fabric-covered button.

"Over the last few months, I suppose I have become the model employee. Hell, I even put the money in the cash register now so it all faces the same way." She gave a rueful laugh and walked toward him. The effortless swing of her hips tempted him to forget his resolve to stay on track. Jesse caught her distinctive scent and felt his body reacting with remembered yearning. "But a girl loses her edge if she doesn't keep that naughty side alive and kicking. So now I find other areas to be…bad."

His mouth watered as he envisioned her being bad on him. Over him. Under him. *Oh, hell. Focus, Martinez.* He needed to get a grip. She'd given him the perfect opening, he needed to think with his cop head.

"So what kind of bad are you into now?" he asked.

"Just about anything you have in mind, I'll bet I'd be into," she said, taking a few steps closer. So close, he could feel the heat radiating from her lush body. So close, his fingers tingled with the need to touch her. She was like a drug. She'd wormed her way into his system and he couldn't get enough of her. Then he frowned. Anything?

"Like what? I mean, how far do you go to be bad? Drugs?"

When her eyes popped wide, Jesse winced. Dammit, he belonged behind a computer keyboard, not here trying to sneak information out of a woman whose scent fogged his brain.

She gave him a long look, the most serious he'd ever seen from her. Then she offered a one-shouldered shrug. "I guess, given what some people call bad, I don't mind clarifying for you. I'm anti-drugs, and to be honest, I'm a very light drinker. I'm not big on artificial stimulation."

She paused, inspecting his face. She must have been satisfied with whatever she saw there, because she ran her tongue over her lower lip and moved close to him again.

"I am, however, very into physical stimulation. If memory serves, you're pretty good in that area."

"I can work magic with my hands," Jesse assured her. Sure, it was usually on a keyboard, but all that finger work limbered him up for much more intricate maneuvers.

"Really? Does that mean your wand is magic, too?" Her comment, combined with her wide-eyed innocent look, made him laugh with pleasure.

"You're so damned cute, you know that?" He was surprised at how much fun she was. How at odds her playful side was to the hot packaging.

"Cute? I don't think I've ever been called cute," she said with a snicker.

He winced. That probably wasn't the kind of thing a woman over twelve took as a compliment. But she didn't seem offended, just amused.

"Is that a bad thing? I know my sisters have this need to be taken seriously, and cute isn't synonymous with serious. Other women I've known seem to need compliments and—" he almost said "to be fawned over," but stopped himself in time "—you know, to be treated so carefully. You're probably the most comfortable person I've ever met."

"Comfortable? You're kidding, right?" She furrowed her brow and gave a little curl of her lip. But, again, she didn't seem offended.

"Comfortable with yourself, I mean. Not comfortable to be around. After all, I get a hard-on the minute I see you. That's not exactly what I'd call relaxing."

Her face cleared, and a wide smile flashed. With an impish look, she raised a brow and dropped her gaze to the zipper of his jeans. Already semierect, his dick reacted as if she'd run her hands, instead of just her eyes, over it.

"You know how to play, if that makes sense. To laugh and not take every little thing seriously."

"Why bother? Life is too short to be all uptight. I'd much rather play, as you put it. Have a good time, enjoy myself. As long as I don't hurt anyone else, why shouldn't I do whatever makes me happy?"

Damned if he didn't want to see what he could do to make her happy. Desire, never far from the surface when he was with her, engulfed Jesse. He reached out to grip her hips, his hands smoothing over the silky skin along the edge of the waistband of her jeans.

Intrigued by her body decorations, he traced his index

finger over the gold chain settled in the curve of her waist. He glanced up to meet her eyes. They had a soft, bidding look in them that invited him to enjoy himself.

And she was involved with one of the nastiest crime rings in the state?

It didn't compute. This woman, with her freewheeling-but-hurt-nobody-else philosophy, just didn't seem like a criminal. For all her bad girl image, Audra really wasn't hard enough. Which meant she was just entering the criminal life.

He bit back a sigh and ignored the bad taste in his mouth. If he could get her to turn evidence on Davey and the triad, he could get her out of the picture fast, solve the case. Then maybe ask her out for real.

With that promise to himself, he forced himself to stop playing with her belly chain and let go of her hip.

"So, you know, in the name of physical stimulation, are you into porn?" he blurted out.

Audra's mouth dropped, her eyes growing huge. Like he'd asked her to have a threesome with a goat.

Lucky for him, she recovered with a shake of her head, and rolled her eyes. "I know some people really get into it, but it's not my thing. Who needs to watch someone else get off? I'm selfish. If there's any moaning going on, I want it to either be me, or because of me."

Jesse frowned. His informant was sure Larson had been lured in by the triad through his porn obsession. The guy had even hinted that the hot babe Larson made the handoff to dabbled a bit in movies herself. That had purportedly been the clincher—the opportunity to be face-to-face with one of the women he fantasized about.

"Then you probably haven't done any films like that, huh?" he asked. As soon as the words were out, Jesse wanted to slap himself in the forehead. So much for subtle investigation.

"Films? You mean porn? As in starred in a skin flick? Me?"

"Yeah. I mean, I hear that's a hot turn-on for some people, doing it on film."

"I know a few who are into taping their personal encounters for their own viewing pleasure, if you know what I mean. But even that's a little much for me. I'm not shy, I've just never felt the need for a souvenir."

She squinted at him, a bemused smile on her face.

"What?"

"Nothing, really. I just wouldn't have taken you for one of those guys."

"What guys?" Jesse asked blankly.

"A guy with a porn fetish. You seem more into making your own moves than watching someone else's."

"You think I meant I…? No, I mean, sure I have, but I don't. I have, of course. That is, you know, bachelor parties and stuff. But not like date replacement or anything. I don't, um, you know, watch it for sexual aids or whatever."

Jesse wondered if he babbled long enough, whether he could distract her with bullshit so that she wouldn't notice the color heating his cheeks. He hadn't blushed this much since puberty. And that had probably been because of porn, too.

Audra gave a husky laugh. She curved the back of her hand over one of his still warm cheeks, then stepped closer. She leaned into his body, just the barest brush of her breasts against his chest. Before Jesse could moan, she'd pressed a soft, friendly kiss to his other cheek and stepped back.

"And you said *I* was cute?"

She turned away to lean over the counter, giving him a sweet view of her denim-clad butt. Turning back around, a set of keys dangling from her fingers, she winked.

"I have to lock up. Then I'll be happy to give you that show you asked for."

Shit. Now what was he supposed to do? The plan had been to get her to tell him what porn link she'd used to hook up with Davey. He'd figured he could use that to make his own connection with the guy, then lure him in. But it seemed she was somehow unconnected. Or one hell of an actress. But why would she bother to hide something like that? It would be pointless.

Since the porn thread had gone nowhere, he should tug on the gang affiliation. He needed a few names, maybe an idea of what other pies the triad had their sticky criminal fingers in.

He could hardly ask her if she was in a gang. Not after his rookie porn questions. So he'd go along with the fashion show and wait for the opportune moment.

And maybe if he told himself often enough that she was a suspect, seeing Audra in a few dozen slinky, sexy outfits wouldn't make him explode with desire.

6

AUDRA USED the time it took her to lock the boutique door and shut the blinds to catch her breath. She'd met a lot of different guys in her Wicked Chick days. Maybe, sometimes late at night, she might admit to herself that some of those men she regretted. But with all her experience, she'd never before met a guy like Jesse.

There was something special about him. She wasn't sure what it was, exactly, but she'd have to watch out for it. After all, he'd actually had her opening up about her past. And that was something Audra never did. Especially not crap about CPS and the endless stress dodging them had brought to her teen years. Other than her endless truancy reports, her only real run-in with the law trying to spring a dog from death row. Of course, the cops had always harassed her anyway, just because they thought she looked like the type to be trouble.

It was all a part of her life she was more than happy to lock the door on. The only information she shared with guys was the turn-them-on, keep-them-guessing kind.

Then again, Jesse wasn't her average kind of guy.

He was an intriguing mixture of sweet and sexy, shy and sensual. The way he flirted was a major turn-on for her. In her considered opinion, he could definitely deliver on the promise of that flirtation. After all, she hadn't been able to get the memory of his talented fingers and delicious mouth out of her head all week.

How many guys talked porn in such a cute, unobnoxious way? Audra had a strict personal policy to only do what brought her pleasure, what felt good to her. If a guy was into a form of kink she didn't like, she'd say so, straight up. Like she'd told him, she wasn't into watching sex. She was more a kinesthetic, hands-on kind of girl.

Having closed the boutique for the night, she turned to face Jesse. He stood there, all sexy male confusion, fingering a purple silk chemise.

Yum.

"So you never answered my question. What's your pleasure?" she asked him.

His gaze shot to hers and he grinned, a boyish flash of white teeth.

"Such a leading question," he returned.

"Isn't it, though? The real question is, do you want to do the leading or be led?"

"I think I'd like both, depending."

Audra sauntered over to where he stood, the purple silk between his fingers. His obvious sensual appreciation for the tactile fabric was a good sign. One she wanted to explore. Enough of this chitchat prelim crap; it was time to rock and roll.

"Why don't we take turns? I'll start." With that, she looped her arms around his neck and gently pulled his head down to meet her hungry mouth.

Mmm. Delicious.

She traced his lips with her tongue, reveling in their soft texture and the hint of something hot and dangerous just beneath the surface. Impatience, with its rough, edgy bite, ripped through her. She wanted more. Wanted to taste him, see how fast and far he could take her.

So she did. With teeth, tongue and lips, she gave herself over to desire. At her assault, Jesse groaned. He gripped her hips in his hands and pulled her tight against him. Pleased to feel evidence that he was as into the kiss as she was, Audra rubbed herself against the hardening flesh behind his zipper. Need, already coiled tight, sprang loose to spiral through her. From her avid mouth to the wetness between her legs, she was ready for him.

"Now," she gasped. She pulled back from his mouth just long enough to make the demand before trailing kisses over his rugged jaw and down the smooth flesh of his throat.

"Lingerie," he mumbled, one hand roaming her back while the other gripped her hip as if it were a lifeline.

"Huh?"

"Show. You said you'd show me your designs."

Audra pulled back to look into Jesse's eyes. He wanted a show? Now? Instead of sex? A woman with less faith in her sexuality might worry that he wasn't interested. Given her track record this week, Audra's own faith in her sexuality was teetering on a fine line. But she knew the signs. Not just the woody pressing into her belly, but his dilated pupils, slightly labored breathing and the way his fingers smoothed over the small of her back as if it were a precious jewel.

She narrowed her eyes. Was he playing a game? He stared back. There was nothing in his eyes except desire. So why was her bullshit meter sending her caution signals?

Audra's breath caught as she tried tamp down the panic at the idea that she wasn't the sexy, hot chick she defined herself as. If she'd lost her identity—her sexual mojo, to quote Suzi— to ambition, what the hell did that leave? Her self-image was so wrapped up in her sexuality that without it, she was lost.

"You'd rather see my designs than get hot 'n' heavy with me?" she asked.

"Hell, no," he exclaimed. "But I want to see those designs. You intrigue me. I want to get to know you better. You know, things besides what will make you scream in ecstasy."

Letting herself be soothed out of the panic-inducing identity crisis, Audra considered him. When had she become so cynical and jaded that a guy looking for an actual relationship would have her so suspicious? Was she stupid enough to walk away from someone who might want more than just sex from her? Because he wanted to get to know her?

To quote Jesse, *Hell, no.*

"As long as I don't lose out on those screams of ecstasy, I'd be happy to show you my stuff."

Audra looked around the boutique, hoping something would spark inspiration. The guy wanted to get to know her? Maybe she could get to know him, too. She'd never spent as much time wondering about a man as she had Jesse. Why not get a few of the answers to her musings? As the idea took hold, the odd feeling of rejection she'd barely admitted fell away and she started to get excited.

If nothing else, finding out what lingerie he preferred would be an interesting peek into his sexual fantasies. What would prime his pump? Stir his juices? It'd be fun to find out.

"As the guest of honor at this evening's private showing of Simply Sensual Lingerie, I'd like to invite you to peruse our wares. Choose as many outfits as appeal to you."

"Anything?"

"Sure. It's all pretty tame, to be honest. Simply Sensual caters to the upscale, ladylike sexual fantasies. I'm hoping to change that soon, though."

"Really?" Jesse's intrigued glance, and the clear interest in his voice, encouraged her to open up.

"I'd like to bring in some naughtier stuff," Audra said with a laugh. "Something more adventurous. You know, the exotic and erotic, the leather, the merry widow, the role-playing-styled lingerie. Fun stuff aimed at sexual fantasies of the wilder kind. I've got a few things in the works that I figure will make all my dreams come true."

He shot her a weird look, a deep frown creasing his forehead, but all he said was, "Sounds like that promotion is going to bring some interesting changes here, huh?"

She sure hoped so.

Audra watched Jesse take his time, carefully inspect each outfit on each rack. Every time he seemed interested, he stopped to rub the fabric between his fingers, then looked at her as if gauging how it would feel with her in it. Since her shopping MO was based on the thrill of impulse buys, this was killing her. Or maybe it was the ever-tightening thread of desire that curled through her. After all, she was going to be getting next-to-naked with this guy soon. If he'd just hurry up.

Finally, he'd chosen a half-dozen outfits. Audra cast a quick eye over them and grabbed a few accessories as well as boots from the shelves, tossed them in a wicker shopping basket then winked.

"It's showtime." She gestured to the hall. "Shall we?"

Jesse shot a confused look at the flowing letters over another hall marked Dressing Room. "Where are we going?"

"A few months after I started working here, I realized we were missing out by having those tiny dressing rooms up front. They're fine for women shopping alone, but it can be a major turn-on lingerie shopping with your man along. You know, letting him be a part of the fun."

He followed her down the short hallway. There were two doors, the second being her and Natasha's office. They stopped at the first one. The interior had been fitted as a comfortable waiting area.

A manly leather couch offset the overt femininity of the rest of the boutique. A low table in front of it to hold a drink or for a guy to put his feet up while he waited, with an array of magazines, including *Car Craft* and *GQ,* spread over the smooth wood surface. The corner had been fitted as a dressing area, with deep burgundy curtains for privacy. And in front of the small, mirrored wall was a pedestal, perfect for modeling purposes.

"It's not just about couples. We get brides in here wanting to try on their trousseau for their entourage. Sometimes girlfriends have fun putting on a group show. But the couples seem to appreciate it the most."

"Nice," Jesse said, taking it all in. He gestured to the couch. "That'd probably put a guy at ease, huh?"

"It does, yes. And guys at ease tend to hang out longer, buy more."

"Smart business." He sauntered over as if he was going to sit down, then hesitated. "Maybe this is a tacky question, but don't you worry the privacy, combined with the sensual atmosphere, might…you know?"

Faint color washed his cheeks. Damn, he was cute. Audra couldn't help but tease him.

"You know? What? Try on more lingerie?"

"No. You know, this place, the clothes, you. It's all so sexy. A guy comes in here, he's gonna be thinking sex. He gets back in this room, he's gonna be tempted to have sex. Some guys even get off on the semipublic aspect of it. Just knowing customers are a few feet away, it adds to the excitement."

"Do you?"

"Huh?"

"Do you get off on the semipublic aspect of it? You were asking about porn earlier. Is this another form of voyeurism?"

Jesse swallowed audibly.

"Yeah. In a way, I guess it is. I mean, I'm not into porn. Like you, watching isn't my thing. But I can see where there might be an added edge, an extra element of spice, to doing it in a semipublic place. Kinda like the other night in your car? Public parking lot, dark night. It was… Well, it was sexy as hell."

His voice gruff with emotion, combined with the look in his eyes, made Audra catch her breath. The memory of that night, of his fingers on her—in her—made her shiver with desire.

Had she ever wanted a man like this? What was it about him that had her at war with herself, wanting equally to get to know him better and to rip his clothes off and get him naked?

"It *was* sexy, wasn't it?"

Spying the brass rack, Jesse hung the lingerie on the bar and turned toward her. He took the basket from her hands, set it on the low table and faced her again. Excited by the anticipation, the wonder, she tensed. Her entire focus centered on him. On what he'd do next.

He stepped close, so close she could feel the heat off his body, smell the subtle spice of his shaving cream. Without actually touching her, he flicked the tiny stars dangling from her belly button, watching their movement with heated eyes.

"That night was about the sexiest experience I've ever had without an actual orgasm," he told her. "Everything with you seems to have that extra edge. A special something that takes it past anything I've ever felt before."

Audra didn't know what to say. She felt the same. Her feelings about Jesse, her reactions to him, were all new to her.

But she'd learned when she was young to guard her emotions, to keep those vulnerabilities to herself. After all, she'd tried that relationship thing once. But then she'd realized that she just didn't have it in her to change enough to make another person happy. Even though Jesse's honesty inspired her to share the same, she couldn't. Maybe that made her defective, or just overly cautious. But she couldn't open her heart. Couldn't let him peek into her soul.

Not out of any sense of privacy. No, Audra could admit to herself it was fear, pure and simple. Fear that if anyone ever saw into her heart, into her soul, they'd find out there was nothing really there.

Instead, she fell back on the tried and true, gave him her sexiest smile and leaned in close. With the softest brush of her lips against his, she whispered, "If you thought that was good, you ain't seen nothing yet."

Jesse laughed, and the air cleared of all that heavy emotional expectation. Relieved, Audra winked and gestured to the couch. With a flip of a couple switches, she dimmed the lights and cued the music. A low, bluesy tune wailed softly through the tiny speakers in the corners of the room.

"Get comfy," she suggested again. She waited until he settled on the couch before she made her way to the dressing area. "Do me a favor. Think of those outfits you picked out. Try and imagine me in each one. Picture what it will cover, what it will show. How the light will shimmer as it touches my skin. Imagine how the lingerie will look on my body. How it'll feel as you run your hands over it. Over me."

She watched his eyes dilate, grinned and slipped behind the curtain.

"Be right back."

JESSE SHIFTED on the couch, guilt making him wince. Damn, could he get any lower? A snake would look down on him in contempt, with good reason.

This kind of thing—a sexy suspect, questionable circumstances—had been tools of the trade for his father. Diego Martinez'd had a reputation for breaking his cases by using any method at his disposal, especially romancing the ladies.

Because of that, Jesse'd long ago promised himself never be in the position to borrow any pages from his father's book.

So much for promises.

Granted, he wasn't overly experienced with fieldwork or working face-to-face with suspects. But Audra simply didn't seem crooked. She was hot, sexy, sweet as hell. She might be aggressive and a little wild, but those things didn't make her a criminal.

Jesse shoved a hand through his hair and sighed. Since he'd already landed in a typical Diego Martinez situation, his father's philosophy was screaming in his head. *The more innocent they looked, the guiltier they were.*

Disgust with himself churned through Jesse's stomach. He didn't want to break the case this way. Audra wasn't a means to an end. Even knowing she was guilty, he was dangerously close to falling into serious lust with the woman. Bad business.

On top of that, she knew nothing about the porn connection. He'd do better to focus his investigation on Dave Larson. If he left now, he could get home in plenty of time to cruise the online porn sites Larson frequented, try and connect with the guy. He had a few other lines he could tug, too. Such as hacking into Larson's computer and finding a trail to his backup system. Jesse knew there had to be a backup system. The trick was to find it.

Either way, there was plenty Jesse could be doing. None of which included the torture of sitting here while Audra got naked behind that curtain. He couldn't even see her bare feet, but just knowing she was on the other side of that flimsy barrier— slipping those jeans down her long, sleek legs, unsnapping that leather bodice to free her lush breasts—was killing him.

He should skip out now, before she came out and gave life to one of the many fantasies he'd envisioned as he picked out lingerie. He could claim to be sick, to get a call, a forgotten emergency. Anything.

He'd tell her he'd call in a couple weeks. Go solve this case, arrest Larson, break up the *Du Bing Li* triad. Maybe by doing so, he could find a way to help Audra out of the criminal organization.

Jesse stood up. Just as he started to yell to let her know he'd had an emergency and had to run, she flipped aside the curtain.

His breath caught in his throat and his body went from semierect to rock-hard in three seconds flat. God help him. He couldn't walk away. Hell, he'd be lucky if he could *even* walk, as hard as he was. Standing before him, Audra made him want to weep. Hands down, she was his ultimate fantasy.

From her red velvet choker to the black satin corset with red lacing up the front, her look screamed wild sex. Golden flesh peeked through the crisscrossed laces, and the red satin ends hung loose, untied. A promise of easy access to the heaven beyond.

The skirt, some sheer material that gave him tempting glimpses of the outline of her legs, flowed to her calves. And beneath it? The one thing guaranteed to send Jesse into a drooling mess of testosterone. Boots. Knee-high, black suede, lace-up-the-front boots.

She'd fluffed her hair, done something to make her skin sparkle in the soft lighting. His gaze followed the glittering trail down her throat, over her collarbone and watched where it sank between her cleavage. He wanted to take that same path with his tongue.

Jesse groaned.

Audra gave him a saucy grin. Pure female confidence, she

stepped up onto the platform and pressed a button on the wall. The music changed from soft blues to the quicker, heavy beat of rock and roll.

Her gaze locked on his, Audra danced the length of the platform.

"You like?"

"I like very much."

Audra nodded as if she'd expected nothing less. She danced, totally unself-conscious, her moves both sexy and graceful.

"You have good taste. This is one of my favorite outfits. I call it Dominate Me. It's about the edgiest design we carry. It's turned out to be one of our best sellers."

"I can see why," he said, his vision glazed with desire. "You look good enough to make me hand over a whip and ask you to punish me, mistress."

Audra's brows winged up, a wicked grin curving her full lips.

"I like the way you think. Very sexy. I've never met such a sexy computer geek before." She sauntered off the platform, her hips swaying in hypnotic time to the rock beat. "Maybe you can take a look at my PC sometime? It's been acting funky lately."

"Sure," Jesse said with quick enthusiasm. It was all he could do to not jump up, grab her by the hand and run from the room. "We could do that now. Let's go."

Audra stopped, inches in front of him, and gave him a puzzled look.

"Now? You're kidding, right?"

Jesse's gaze swept the delicious feast of flesh encased in smooth black satin and tried not to groan. Hell, no, he wasn't kidding. He didn't know how he could stay here and resist touching her. Tasting her. He needed to get out of here, fast.

"Why not? Your computer is here?" Since the tickets to China had been purchased through Simply Sensual it was feasible any connections she had with Davey or *Du Bing Li* would be on the company computer. Give him a half hour with that PC and he'd have all the evidence he needed to nail her. He just hoped it was enough to push her into turning evidence on Davey and the gang.

"Nah, I don't have a personal computer here. Natasha handles all the books and business stuff on one. But I rarely use it. It's better that way. If I started thinking of computers as workhorses, I'd never play with one again."

She took a step closer, and Jesse almost swallowed his tongue. Just centimeters away, he could feel the heat from her body. He could see the outline of her nipples beneath the midnight satin. Her perfume, something musky and evocative, enveloped him. His mind fogged, and thought dribbled away like water between his fingers.

"My computer is at my place. Maybe we can go look at it later."

"Later?"

"Mmm-hmm. Later. We're busy right now. After all, you don't want to miss any of the show, now do you?"

AUDRA HELD her breath, waiting for Jesse's response. Her sex appeal on the line, she wasn't sure what she'd do if he said he'd rather check out her computer than her body.

Any other guy, she'd have flicked him off, sent him on his way at the slightest hint he wasn't totally into her. But Jesse? She couldn't help it, but she was mortally afraid she'd do whatever it took to get him—keep him—interested.

Lucky for her, those gorgeous brown eyes of his glowed with heated interest, and he gave her a slow, sweet smile.

"Show, huh? I did like that dance. You have a way of moving that makes a man want to give thanks."

"I have a few other moves you might like to see."

Jesse's eyes darkened to a deep, rich chocolate and muttered what sounded like a prayer before he reached out to pull her toward him. One hand flat against the small of her back, he combed the other through her hair to tug gently, holding her head.

"I've got a few of my own. Why don't we share?"

"Why don't we," she murmured just before his mouth took hers.

It was like a wildfire. The heat had been there already, swirling between them. But the touch of their lips set off the spark, sending those smoldering embers of desire into flames. Engulfing, life-changing flames that Audra welcomed like nothing she'd ever felt before.

She gave herself over to the kiss. Every slide of their tongues, nip of their teeth, fanned the flames hotter. She ran her hands down his arms and gave a shiver of delight at the clenched muscles beneath his shirtsleeves. Nothing turned her on more than a dude with a hot bod. She wanted to see just how hot Jesse's was.

She slipped her hands between their bodies and worked the buttons of his shirt loose. He released his hold on her head and, oh baby, cupped her breast instead. Audra paused on the buttons to fully give herself over to the pleasure of his fingers working her nipple beneath the slippery satin.

He pulled his mouth away and with two quick steps, swung her around so that she lay beneath him on the couch. She shifted so one leg wrapped around his and cupped him between her thighs. The feel of his hard flesh pressed against her swollen, aching center made her moan. Audra moved against his leg in a subtle, easy rhythm to enjoy the slow climb to ecstasy.

Jesse buried his mouth in the curve of her neck and slid his fingers up her thigh. She could feel the heat of his hand through the silky smooth stockings and waited, a half smile on her face. She let her head fall back, eyes closed to heighten the sensations, as he discovered her thighs were bare above the elastic thigh-high stockings. Her thighs and everything else.

He slid his body down just a bit, and she moaned as the movement put more pressure on her wet, throbbing nub.

"More," she demanded breathlessly.

Jesse used that oh-so-talented mouth to tug at the laces between her breasts. Loosened, the bodice fell open and she heard his hiss of pleasure at the sight. With her free hand, she reached up to cup one of her own breasts, offering it up for his pleasure. Then she felt his mouth on her flesh. He used his tongue to lightly circle her nipple, teasing, taunting. Audra wanted to scream. She needed more. Needed pressure.

He must have read her desperation. In a deliciously quick move, Jesse took her nipple in his mouth. He suckled it deep as he ran the tip of his finger over the wet, straining folds of flesh between her thighs.

Audra felt the climax building, a tight coil of sensation. She tried to pull back. It was too fast, and while she was all for selfish pleasure, she wanted more with Jesse.

But he wouldn't let her. With a gentle scrape of his teeth over her nipple, he worked her clitoris and sent her flying over the edge.

Audra gave a keening moan of pleasure and shuddered as the orgasm took her breath away. Lights flashed behind her closed eyes and she felt as if she were surfing on a wave of delight. Her body clenched, shuddering as the climax rippled through her.

While she floated somewhere in a cloud of bliss, Jesse gathered her close and shifted so that they lay side by side on the couch.

Her hand still clenched on his bicep, Audra slowly opened her eyes to see him staring down at her.

He winked and raised both brows. "I know it was just an opener, but I'd say that had to rate at least a six on your scale."

She stared blankly for a second, then burst out laughing. "At least a six. Probably even a six and a half. I can't wait to see what you do when we're naked."

Before she could make a move to find out, a tinny chime rang out. Jesse started, then looked around in confusion. A few notes into the tune, and Audra grimaced.

"Isn't that the song from *Pinocchio?* What's it called?"

"'When You Wish Upon a Star,'" she muttered, not meeting his eyes.

Five solid seconds of stunned silence was more than she could handle, though. She glanced up from his chest to see the look of bafflement in his eyes.

"Disney? Your cell phone rings Disney?"

"Well, not really."

He squinted at her.

"I have ring tones programmed in for some of my friends. That would be Isabel, and it's a joke. Sort of."

"Sort of?"

Audra sighed. Why did she have the feeling she wasn't going to get his clothes off without an explanation?

"When we were kids, Isabel had a habit of acting like that annoying little cricket."

His frown faded, and he laughed. "Your conscience?"

Give the man points for being quick. At least on the uptake. She'd bet he took his slow, sweet time with other things. Impatience rippled through her, since she wanted to get back to finding out.

"Right. And since she has a freakish record for interrupting me when I least want her to, I haven't changed it." Audra shifted and her still-sensitive nipples brushed against the hard planes of his chest. She sucked in a breath, then let it out as she pressed herself closer.

"She's gone now, so let's get back to more important matters. Like if you can top six and a half."

Impatient to find out, she shifted so she could undo the remainder of his shirt buttons.

Jesse's hands folded over hers. Audra looked up with a frown and tilted her head in question.

"We need to stop," he murmured. Regret shone in his brown eyes, still hot with desire.

"What? You're kidding, right? You just gave me one sweet little orgasm, but that's just an appetizer. I won't be satisfied unless I get the whole meal." Brows furrowed, she brushed a soft kiss over his mouth. "I want you to get the whole meal."

He gave a strained laugh and rested his forehead against hers. Sweet pleasure, something on another level than the physical release she'd just experienced, rushed through Audra.

"I'm sure it'd be one hell of a meal, at that. And I want to. You have no idea how bad I want to. But…I can't. I just can't."

"Why? What is it? You have a condom. I saw it. I even have a box of them here. Is there another reason? The phone call? Did you lose the mood?"

She shifted against his still straining hard-on and grinned. "You definitely didn't lose it where it counts."

"No, it's not that."

"What, then? Something physical?" A million thoughts ran through her brain, all of them a little gross.

He looked blank at first, then screwed up his face in denial. Relief surged through Audra.

"No! I mean, it's nothing physical. It's just…well, as insane as this sounds, I'm not that kind of guy."

All she could do was stare, her mind blank with shock.

"Oh. My. God," she breathed. She reached up to pull her bodice over her bare breasts. "I knew it. The signs were all there, but I kept sidestepping them. That voice in the back of my head kept pointing out the obvious, but I kept telling myself I was wrong."

He winced.

"You are a *good* boy, aren't you?"

"A good boy?" He squinted at her in silence for a few seconds. Then he frowned and nodded slowly. "Yeah, that's one way to put it. I'm a good boy. And, well, I can't do this yet. I want to. I want *you* insanely. Past the edge of reason. But…I can't."

"What? Is there some good boy code or something?"

"You could say that."

She waited.

He shrugged and gave her a sheepish smile.

"I'd really like to get to know you better before we make love."

Audra just stared. It sounded like a brush-off to her. She wasn't really sure, having never been brushed off before. But she'd brushed plenty herself, and it was definitely following the same pattern. She bit her lip and told herself she wasn't hurt.

The pain in her chest said differently. She was a big girl, though. She could ignore it.

Something must have shown on her face, because Jesse's expression clouded with concern. He slipped both hands, so warm and strong, over her jaw to cup her cheeks.

"What? You don't believe me?"

"It's not that, really. I mean, I don't think you're lying to me or anything." Maybe lying to himself? He seemed too sweet to try and deliberately deceive her. She'd known plenty of guys who were pros at the scam. Jesse radiated pure honesty. Such a good boy trait.

"I swear, I want to spend time with you. I can't think of anything I want more than to make love with you. To drive us both crazy, to see how many ways we can bring each other pleasure. You know, strive for that ultimate ten."

Audra, still damp, felt herself heat up again at his words. If she closed her eyes, she knew she'd be able to visualize them together. To imagine all the things they'd do with each other. To each other.

"I just… Well, I want to get to know you better first. So when we do get together, it means something."

Her eyes grew huge. He wasn't thinking all that mushy emotional stuff, was he? Obviously reading her, he grinned and shook his head.

"Not like that. As much as I want to see where this goes between us, it's not like I'm not looking for something permanent or, you know, all serious. I just, well, I believe that when two people get together, it should be more than the moment."

His wince was infinitesimal, but Audra saw it anyway. Maybe he figured she was such a hard-ass, she'd blast him for being a sentimental goofball. Once, she might have. But now?

Now the sentiment was appealing to her, for some reason. Maybe it was the source?

"So, dating, huh?"

"You game? Call it prolonged foreplay."

When Audra laughed, Jesse hugged her close. She closed her eyes and let herself absorb the warm comfort of his arms.

"It'll be cool. You'll see. Besides, I'm just not the kind of guy who goes all the way on the first date."

She laughed again and pulled away from him. Both arms outspread, she jutted one hip and tilted her head.

"You sure you want to wait?"

Jesse closed his eyes and groaned. But he still nodded.

"It'll be cool," he repeated. "We'll talk, get to know each other. Just the two of us, hit some hot spots, do things."

"What kind of things do you want to do?" Audra strained to think of nonsexual things to do with a man, but she came up blank. She tried to tell herself it was the remnants of heat, the faint tremors of that orgasm still coursing through her.

"What about a trip to Napa? Check out the wine country. Or we can go to San Francisco and hang out on Fisherman's Wharf. See a movie, catch a concert. Dinner and dancing? You know, dating things."

Audra frowned. They all sounded great. They'd all be better capped off with a night of sex, but who was she to quibble. Had she ever dated? For a woman whose longest relationship could be counted in weeks, it was a foreign concept.

To date and not have sex? It was more than foreign, it was totally alien.

But…for Jesse? She was drawn to him, and as much as she wanted to screw his brains out, she was intrigued by the man as much as by the body.

Just one more out-of-character thing to worry about.

Dating? It was worth a shot.

"For a while," she agreed. "But you have to promise, after the third date we get to have sex."

7

CLOSING TIME had never been so welcome, Audra thought. Or, she glanced at Bea, so distracting.

"C'mon, you have to help me out," Bea wheedled. She leaned against the boutique's sales counter and batted her lashes. "You're always there for me, right? Best buds?"

As if Audra was going to be influenced by a pair of big baby blues and carefully displayed cleavage? She knew it wasn't deliberate, though. That was just what Bea did. They'd met when Bea had rebelled against her rich daddy by talking her stepmom du jour into enrolling her in public school. The helpless sex-kitten persona was as much a part of Bea as her porcelain complexion and the way she cried at Hallmark commercials.

"Look, normally I would, you know that." That was the great thing about the Wicked Chicks, they *were* always there for each other. "But I don't have time right now. I've got too much to do here in the boutique. Between that and my deadline for the fall designs, I'm buried."

She'd be a lot further along with the designs if she hadn't spent so much time daydreaming about her time with Jesse on the couch the night before. And reliving the sweet rush of pleasure he'd given her.

"I'd pay extra," Bea offered. As soon as the words were out of her mouth, she winced and held up one hand in protest. "Don't say it. I'm sorry. Reflex brought on by retail mania."

Audra quirked a brow, but didn't respond. After all, Bea's generosity was as big as her heart. Unfortunately, the woman was getting used to daddy's money buying anything she wanted—again. It was a habit the Wicked Chicks had broken her of in their teen years. The girls had come from drastically different places—Bea, the poor little rich girl, Audra, a social worker's obligation, and Suzi, an orphan with a chip on her shoulder. But they'd all had the same badass attitude and faith in each other. Audra firmly believed it'd been that faith that had kept the three of them from becoming sad statistics.

Lately, though, Bea had given in to her father's nagging and emotional blackmail, and after his last divorce, had agreed to act as his hostess and social assistant.

The man was obviously a bad influence on her.

"It doesn't have to be a special design, then," Bea continued in her relentless way. "I mean, I love your stuff, you know that. I'd rather wear it than anything else. I just need some hot lingerie for this shoot."

Audra glanced over to see the redhead's lower lip hanging, her eyes puppy-dog sad.

Oh, jeez. As if she cared about a guilt trip? Audra ignored the subtle pressure of both Bea's pout and her own conscience. She continued counting Saturday's till. The boutique had just closed. All she needed to do was finish the deposit and grab her sketches, and she could hightail it home to a pair of cozy slippers, a cup of hot chocolate with extra whipped cream and her waiting pile of work.

That thought, the mundane boring reality of it, scared the hell out of her. Her fingers clenched the bills she was counting. It was Saturday night. She should be planning to go clubbing. Considering what hot outfit to wear, which of her three new pairs of heels would be best for dancing.

Contemplating what flavor of sex she was in the mood for.

Panic whispered in her ear, assuring her she really was washed up. She'd lost it.

Audra sucked in a swift breath to quell the freaked-out thoughts and tilted her chin at Bea.

"Tell me the deal again. Why has this photo shoot got you so excited?"

"I met this up-and-coming photographer and he's going to shoot a few rolls of film for my portfolio," Bea explained in a giddy tone. Bea dropped a name but, since she was unfamiliar with the fashion scene outside lingerie, Audra just shrugged. "This is it, Audra. With his edgy, high-fashion shots, I can have it all. Modeling, magazines, maybe even TV commercials."

"This guy told you all that?" Audra had to work to keep the sneer out of her voice. When would Bea learn that guys lied like rugs?

"Yeah. Suzi said he was full of shit and was just trying to get laid."

Suzi was smart that way.

"But he gave me his business card this morning, told me to check him out if I had any worries."

This morning. As in Bea had already done the guy. Audra sighed and wondered when she'd turned into Isabel. Who knew meaningless sex could bother her so much?

"Did you check him out?" she asked.

"Well, no. I mean, I don't know how to check a guy out, other than the obvious package assessment." From the look on her face, the guy's package hadn't been too impressive. "He did say he's not really computer savvy, so he just recently hired someone to set up a Web site for his company. He even mentioned using my picture for the launch page of his site after this photo shoot."

Maybe she was just jaded, but it still sounded like a line

of bullshit to her. Then again, he'd already got into Bea's panties, so why would he lie after the fact?

"Take a look around. You're welcome to anything here."

Obviously not thrilled to be shopping off the rack, Bea wrinkled her nose. But she started flipping through the lingerie racks anyway.

Five minutes later, Audra's jaw hurt from clenching it. Not that Bea had been bitchy or rude about the designs, but her expression was crystal clear. She was very unimpressed.

"What's the problem?" Audra finally challenged.

"Nothing. Really, these are sweet." Bea hesitated, obviously not wanting to be ungrateful. Then she shrugged, her hands lifting in defeat. "It's just… Well, they *are* sweet."

"Sweet?"

"Yeah. You know, the kind of thing you'd get your little sister for her wedding night or something. They hint at naughty, but don't scream *hot sex*."

Audra opened her mouth to protest. Then with a snap, she shut it again. After all, Bea was right.

"I just wanted something more, you know, spicy. Hot. Dirty, ya know?"

She knew. Stuff like she'd been seeing in her head. Leather, zippers, chrome. Designs that got a woman excited about herself. Dared her to push her own envelope a little. The kind that promised a guy he'd have to work damned hard to keep up.

The kind of design she'd been itching to create.

But couldn't, because she was already behind the eight ball with her current commitments. Maybe after Natasha returned from China?

Then again, she mused, this *would* be a great opportunity to sketch out a few of her visions, use Bea's request as an excuse to pitch them to Natasha.

"Tell you what," she proposed, "I don't have time to work

up anything new right now. But I can modify a couple to suit you. When did you say the shoot is?"

"Hopefully next week. He's going to book the studio and let me know the date."

"Okay, I'll work on it tonight." She shouldn't have too much trouble fitting a little altering and modification in between designs.

"You won't regret it," Bea promised. She giggled and gave Audra a tight hug. "I'll be a huge star and everyone will be clamoring for your lingerie."

A warm feeling, friendship mingled with comfort, settled over Audra. She might not be as bad as she once was, but at least she still had her friends.

That, combined with a chance to run with these design ideas, and her upcoming date with the sexiest man she'd ever come for… Well, her life was rockin' along nicely.

WITH A HUGE YAWN, Audra stretched her arms overhead and tried to work the kinks out of her shoulders. She glanced over at the stack of designs, in various stages of completion, scattered over her home drafting table. She'd spent the previous evening working on three outfits for Bea. She'd tailored each to showcase the redhead's curvy figure and rich coloring.

Sexual images, always at the forefront of her mind because of her nature and the nature of her work, had bombarded her all night. All she'd been able to think of was her not-even-close-to-enough sexual encounter with Jesse. She'd spent hours staring off in space, reliving the whole evening. Here she was, all hot and bothered, and the guy wanted to date.

Dating. Who'd figure she'd be excited about the idea? Maybe it was the novelty. Possibly the distraction from all the responsibility of Simply Sensual, or the worries over the unclear direction her life was going—or, rather, not going. Whatever the reason, she was fascinated with the concept.

Too bad their first date wasn't until Thursday night. She wouldn't mind a repeat of that level-six orgasm. If he could do that fully clothed, she just might have found a level-eight guy. With extensive coaching, possibly the fabled nine and a half.

She glanced at the clock on the wall, a Betty Boop figurine complete with finger on chin and her butt hitched in a seductive stance. Audra needed to get these designs done.

One of the keys to Simply Sensual's sales pitch was, in addition to key pieces from their current line of lingerie, a first look at their fall line and three exclusive designs to any distributor committing to a certain quantity.

While the current line was already available to show, the fall line wasn't complete yet. Which was what Audra was supposed to finish this weekend.

She'd lost a lot of time already, and Natasha was going to want the sketches faxed to her on Monday. Since that was tomorrow, Audra didn't have the luxury of daydreaming. Not if she wanted make good on Natasha's faith in her. And given that Natasha had given her a job, a career and a chance to prove herself, Audra was set on proving that faith justified.

She looked around her apartment, its funky style making her smile. Rich, jewel-toned paisley fabric covered the walls in lieu of paint. Peacock feathers, Mardi Gras masks and a black boa provided wall art, and the furniture was overstuffed and sensual. Tall pillar candles filled the air with musk, their flickering flame dancing with warmth. All in all, an invitation to play. Just the way she liked it.

She'd been on her own forever, it seemed. But this apartment, even months after she'd moved in, still made her proud. It was the most expensive place she'd lived. Very different from growing up with her father over the bar, or her mother in whatever dive she happened to be flopping at the time.

When she'd reunited with her brother, she hadn't had much faith in him. Or, to be honest, in herself. But he'd come through for her. He'd been determined to do whatever it took to fulfill their father's last request that they reconnect and that Drew help her get a job, get her life on track.

At first, Audra had screwed with Drew's head a lot. She'd told him she wanted work in a circus, a lemonade stand and her own phone sex business. Despite her crappy attitude, he hadn't given up. He'd pushed until she finally admitted her interest in design and lingerie.

Lucky for her, Drew's wife had just bought out her aunt's share of Simply Sensual and she'd taken Audra under her wing. Natasha had mentored her, given her a job both in the boutique and designing lingerie. While Drew had footed the bill, Natasha had helped Audra get into school to get her degree in fashion and design. The more Audra learned, the more Natasha had let her do, until Audra was doing all of the designs in-house.

Natasha has promised if Audra stuck with it and graduated, she'd make it worth her while. There weren't many people Audra trusted to keep their word. After all, other than Isabel, Bea and Suzi, nobody else in her life ever had. But Natasha and Drew had come through for her.

It still amazed her.

Finally, about six months ago, Audra had been comfortable enough to trust the income would last and had settled into her dream apartment. Two bedrooms, a sunken tub and, her secret passion, a gourmet kitchen. Not that she could cook more than microwave dinners. But there was something so sensual about food, and places where food was prepared. Like sex, she figured when she learned to cook, she'd be damned good at it.

She forced herself to concentrate on her current design. An oriental-inspired teddy, it was a combination of silk, embroidery and a modified mandarin collar. But she couldn't focus. Her mind was fogged with exhaustion and she could barely keep her eyes open. With a shrug, she decided she had the rest of the day. She could get it done later.

Audra gave into the decadent lure of her bedroom and cuddled under the downy warmth of her purple velour comforter. After a little nap, she'd be recharged to work on the designs.

THE JANGLING PHONE shrilled in Audra's ear. She moaned and pulled her pillow over her head, trying to ignore the summons.

Her answering machine, idiotically placed on the bedside table, whirred as it delivered the outgoing message.

"Audra? You have to be around. Where are you?" Natasha's voice crackled over the line. Not even the thousands of miles between them were enough to dull the sharp, frantic tone of her voice. "I have to talk to you right away. Can you—"

Audra grabbed the phone. "Yeah," she said.

She leaned on one elbow and squinted through the dusk-darkened room at the luminescent numbers of her clock radio. She'd slept two hours. At least she'd had a nice, hot erotic dream to show for it. Images of Jesse, leather wrist straps and decadent delights still flashed through her head as Audra stretched, one hand holding the phone and the other trailing down her body, over her still peaked nipples. Even awake, she could feel the heat, the wet pleasure between her legs.

"I'm here. What's up, Tash? You sound a little freaked."

"Freaked? Oh, man, that's putting it lightly. These people are crazy. They want the designs immediately."

Audra winced and sent a squint-eyed look past her

bedroom door to the drafting table backlit by the kitchen lights. Okay, no problem. She'd work all night, get the fall designs done and faxed first thing in the morning.

"The fall designs? Um, okay. I'll get them to you this week. I have the hotel's fax number, right?"

"Wrong. Hotel address."

"What? You need them expressed or something?"

"No." Panic came through the phone line loud and clear. "They aren't satisfied with the *promise* of three exclusive designs in addition to the fall line. They want to see what the designs will be."

"What?" Audra yelped, sitting up so fast her head spun.

"They want to see actual design boards on the custom designs. The real deal. No rough sketches, no samples of past designs to prove our quality. They want, in their demanding little fingers, the actual prototype designs. Fabric swatches, bead samples. The works."

"Shit." This sucked. Audra threw off the comforter and bounded out of bed. Maybe they could substitute a few from the fall line she'd been working on? She hurried into the living room and started flipping through her completed designs. Five. Dammit.

She had to do it, though. Natasha had gone all the way to China to court these distributors in person. To take Simply Sensual out of the domestic market and go international. This was their big break.

"How soon do you actually have to have them?"

"The sooner the better. I can send you their preferences, the looks they're hoping for. You have my appointment schedule. If you can get me the individualized design boards at least a day before each meeting, that'd still work."

"I doubt I can get them ready that fast, Natasha. I thought we had time. I thought you were just presenting ideas, remember. I was waiting to hear what they wanted for their custom look before I even tried to come up with designs."

Audra frowned and set aside the almost-complete design for a lace bridal teddy. Before she could think of another alternative, her sister-in-law was wailing again.

"This was crazy. We jumped before we were ready. I'm going to come home, we'll regroup, think this through. We might lose these distributors, sure, but we can pick up others."

"No!" Audra exclaimed. "No damned way. We spent a lot of time researching *these* distributors. We busted our asses finding companies that met all our requirements, including your demanding work ethic. That wasn't easy, Natasha. This is our shot. You're already there, you've had the initial meetings with them. If you leave, we've blown it."

"I don't want to leave, either, but I just don't see how we can do this. There is so much work involved. Work you are going to be stuck doing."

"We'll make it happen," she vowed. Somehow.

"Are you sure? Because if you can do it, I'm sure we'll snag at least two of these accounts. And on top of that, I was approached by a different distributor yesterday who's interested. We're meeting this week, as well. I need to research them, but it could mean an even bigger order. More success." Natasha sounded giddy and terrified, all at the same time.

Audra pressed a hand to her stomach. She knew how her sister-in-law felt.

"The thing is," Natasha continued, "this puts it all on your shoulders, Audra. That's four accounts to design for now. Can you handle it?"

Her anxiety came through loud and clear. It had been one thing to leave the boutique in Audra's hands while she was away for a short trip. But now? Now Audra was responsible for the boutique *and* the success of Simply Sensual.

The only thing Audra couldn't tell was whether Natasha felt bad about Audra carrying the extra load or if she simply didn't have the faith that Audra could pull it off.

Did it matter? Either way, it would take a miracle. But she wasn't going to tell Natasha that. The last thing she needed to do was confirm she couldn't handle the responsibility of the shop. Instead, she offered bogus assurances, hurried her sister-in-law through goodbyes and hung up.

"Shit," she said to the empty room. "Now what?"

Now she proved she was a responsible designer worthy of her new title, and not a pity case. Or she confirmed to the world at large, or at least her family, that she would never amount to more than an unreliable bad girl with a flair for design.

JESSE RUBBED his eyes and glared at the computer screen. He was finally getting a solid hook on Dave Larson. The guy had more screen names than Microsoft had patents. So far, though, he'd connected him with the enforcer of *Du Bing Li* triad, at least through e-mails, as well as three of the lower-ranking gang lieutenants. A couple were stupidly chatty in their online exchanges, probably thinking Dave's computer skills would shield them from detection.

Who knew the computer was the communication of choice for up-and-coming gangs?

"Martinez?"

Jesse turned to face his captain.

"Sir?"

"Any breaks on the triad case? Word on the street is they're moving on something big, but nobody can pinpoint what it is. Vice wants in, so give me something to keep this in our department."

Jesse bristled. "This isn't their arena, it's ours. From what

I've tracked so far, we'll be able to link them to high-level identity theft. Possibly credit card fraud and some money laundering, as well."

Shale grunted and took the file Jesse held out. The furrow between his brow deepened as he read through the case notes.

"If you're right, they'll be moving on this fast."

"I'd estimate they'll want to move before the month's out. I'm surprised they haven't already. All I can think of is maybe they had some trouble with the information? From what I can tell, Larson is scrambling. It looks like he screwed up somewhere."

"His loss, our gain."

"His loss might be more than he bargained for. He's always been small potatoes. This screwup, whatever it is, might cost him more than he'd imagined."

"Has a hit been ordered?"

"Not yet, but my narc seems to think it's in the works."

"Can you use that?"

Jesse considered. "Maybe. I've made contact with Larson online in a few different venues using different personas. He must have something else going on, though, since his online activity level is a lot lower than his M.O."

"Like you said, he's scrambling. Maybe he's busy trying to rebuild his info?"

"Or trying to recover it," Jesse mused. He had to nail down what had been handed off to Audra. Once he did, he'd have the evidence he needed to pull the guy in. Audra too, unfortunately. As far as he could tell, though, she hadn't had any further contact with Larson.

At Shale's look, Jesse shook his head and indicated the file. "Either way, he's on shaky ground."

"The shakier the better. See if you can set something up with him. Get his trust, see if he'll turn."

"Turning on anyone connected with *Du Bing Li* is dicey. I'd have to have some damned good incentive."

"If he did screw up, his ass is on the fast track to dead. That might be all the incentive you need."

Jesse nodded. It might. He'd see if he could come up with a little more, though.

"You nail the Walker chick yet?"

Didn't he wish? Jesse mentally groaned at the memory of Audra's body beneath his on the couch. The slide of her flesh against the slick leather. The feel of her exploding around his fingers. Damn.

"Not yet, but the evidence is building. Her business partner is over in China. So far, she's met with a few different lingerie distributors, which is in keeping with the lady's business. Nothing hokey until yesterday, when she had a meeting with a new company. A little digging and I found out they're a money laundering front for the *Wo Shing Wo* triad."

Shale nodded, obviously unsurprised. Unlike Jesse, who had been a little shocked to have the evidence drop into his lap that easily. He wanted to think it was too easy, but he was pretty sure that was the lusting side of his brain talking, not the cop side.

"Did you track the money?" Shale asked, tapping the printout of Simply Sensual's bank account and the large sum deposited the previous week.

"Not yet, except that it came from an offshore account."

"Both women have clean records, though. They're probably new," Shale mused.

While his boss focused on the file, Jesse didn't inform the captain that he'd broken into Audra's sealed juvie record. His superior would have no interest in the fact that Audra had been arrested for breaking into a dog pound.

Jesse, though, was fascinated. The woman was a mass of

contradictions. Sweet as hell, and equally hard. Funny and sexy, and now this humanitarian side? All he could think about was their date on Thursday night. If only he could break the case before then. Because it was going to be pure hell resisting her otherwise.

Jesse had never found a woman who appealed to him on so many levels. It was as if she was the answer to all of his most tempting dreams.

It was going to suck when he had to arrest her.

8

"HEY, AUDRA. You look whipped."

Audra glanced up from the counter, where she'd spread her designs, trim and the ugly tie the geek had tossed at her that night in the club, to see Isabel let the boutique door swing shut behind her.

"Hang on," she muttered. "I've almost got this design just right."

Sure, Natasha wanted to stick with the tried and true. But if Audra had to make up design boards to present the exclusive designs these distributors wanted to see, why not offer an interesting option?

She'd woke that morning from a hot dream where Jesse had tied her to the bedposts. All morning, she'd been trying to get the wild dominatrix idea out of her head. She hadn't been able to pull it from dream to reality until she'd spied the butt-ugly tie draped behind her desk. As soon as she'd seen the strip of tacky material, something had clicked. It was the color, the vivid garish rainbow, that she'd used for the wrist straps. The way the straps contrasted with the sexy black leather really made the design pop. It looked even better on paper than it had in her imagination.

She smothered a naughty grin. It wasn't that she was trying to get her own way by ignoring Natasha's wish to stick with the sweeter stuff. It was just that she felt sure she knew what was best for *her* designs. Wasn't that what a head designer was for?

"Party hard this weekend?" her friend asked. "You look like you haven't slept in days.

Dropping her pencil on the counter, Audra rubbed her burning eyes and glanced at the clock. It was only Monday morning and she was ready for the weekend. She'd been in this seat since six and her brain felt as if it were going to explode. She flexed her stiff shoulders and wished for just a thirty-minute nap. She swiveled to face Isabel and pasted a cheeky smile on her face. It was all she could do to keep it there when she got a good look at her friend's face.

"What's wrong?"

Isabel's lip jutted a little, and she tucked a black curl behind her ear as she shrugged. She flicked a finger down the peach lace of a chemise, then met Audra's eyes.

"I lost the account."

Her mind went blank for a moment. Audra started to ask what account, and then it hit her.

"The mall?" At Isabel's morose nod, she forced her stiff body off the stool and came around the counter. "What happened? You were meeting with the manager, right?"

"Right. This morning." Shoulders slumped, Isabel made her way toward Audra.

Her eyes still on her friend's face, Audra moved to grab a Red Bull from the minifridge behind the counter and handed it to her.

"Here, a shot of energy should help you shake it off. Then you can tell me the details."

Still droopy, Isabel popped open the can as she glanced over the sketches spread across the counter.

"See," she said with a sniff. "These designs are like us. The sweet florals are me. The leather and studs are you. Even if it does have those freaky-looking wrist bands."

Her brow wrinkled. What the hell was Isabel babbling about?

Audra looked at her little bit of rebellion. The leather teddy, complete with ugly-tie-inspired wrist restraints. Who knew such a blight against design as that piece of neckwear could inspire such a hot idea?

"Which one of these two can handle heavy flirting?" Isabel continued. "Which one screams, 'Do me with a dollop of whipped cream'? Which one would a guy go for?"

She took a swig of her drink. Then she faced Audra, her sweet face hard with determination.

"For the first time in my life, I want to be leather and studs," she declared.

Audra's eyes widened. *Come on over to the dark side,* she wanted to say. Afraid to jinx this breakthrough, though, she swallowed the invitation.

"What actually happened?" she asked instead.

Isabel took another look at the designs, then rolled her eyes. "Did you ever meet a guy who made you want to give him a bath with your tongue?"

Jesse's face flashed through her mind. She hadn't considered a tongue bath before. But now that she did, it had definite possibilities.

"I showed up this morning for my appointment. I was supposed to finalize everything and sign the contracts, right?" Before Audra could comment, Isabel continued, "I'm waiting in this guy's office and he's like twenty minutes late. I'd rather walk out, you know? Because the last thing I want to deal with is a rude client. If he's late for meetings, who knows what other bad business habits he has?"

Audra had barely finished nodding when Isabel barreled on. Now, though, she was pacing. Her wide-flying gestures didn't bother Audra so much as the open can in her hand.

"Finally, just as I decided no account, no matter how pretty a feather in my cap, was worth that rudeness, in walks this guy."

"The manager?"

"I wish. I've met the manager. He's balding, short and has an overbite. This guy is tall, hot and sexy. I guess he's the general manager or something."

"General manager? That's good, though, right? I mean, he's got the power to hire you for a lot of malls, not just one."

Isabel winced.

"Did he turn you down? He reneged on the verbal agreement?" Audra growled deep in her throat. Anger, rarely expressed, surged through her. With swift strides, she started pacing the length of the boutique, too. "I'll go to that mall myself and kick his sorry ass. Where does this guy get off?"

"He didn't renege, Audra. I ran."

Stopping so fast that her spiked heels should have been smoking, Audra squinted at her friend. "Huh?"

"I ran. He came in, all hot and sexy and I got tongue-tied. All I could think of was stripping his suit from his body and having him for breakfast. Then he…"

"He what?" Images flashed through her mind, none of them pretty. Her stomach cramped again.

Her voice so low that Audra had to strain to hear her, Isabel said, "He flirted with me."

Huh?

"Did he take his clothes off while he flirted?" Audra asked, perplexed.

"Of course not."

"Did he make kinky suggestions? Make you feel pressured to put out? Invite you to a threesome with the balding missing manager?"

"Don't be ridiculous. He didn't do any of that. He was just…you know, flirty. Like he was interested."

"So you ran away? Not only from a hot dude who'd likely give you a nice lube job, but from a huge business deal?"

And Isabel had worried Audra would blow *her* career?

"It sounds stupid when you say it. But I was overwhelmed. I'm not like you. I'm not used to such intense interest from a guy. I guess I ran from it. From him."

Isabel tossed her empty can into the trash and threw up her hands. "It's not like it really matters, right? I mean, I don't have to move on to the next stage of my business plan yet. I've improved the flower shop a lot already, right? Money is okay. So I've hit a career plateau."

Audra thought of her own struggles lately. That plateau seemed to be going around. Sure, she'd got a fancy promotion to head designer, but she was starting to feel that it was an empty promotion. Pretty words, no substance. Since she'd been fighting that particular perception most of her life, she should recognize it when it stared her in the face.

"No law says I have to move up *now*," Isabel continued. "I'm fine waiting a few months. Maybe years."

"Years? Oh, my God, no way." The glaring comparison to her own situation was too obvious to ignore. Audra smothered the thought with a determined jut of her chin. She wasn't waiting years to have her cake. And neither was Isabel.

"Years, my ass. You get your butt back to that mall, sex that guy up and get that account."

"Sex him up? You're insane."

"You don't really have to sleep with him. Just flirt. Give him back the same as he's giving you. You know, go for the gusto."

"Isn't that a beer slogan?"

Audra rolled her eyes. "You know what I mean. You want to be leather and studs, go for it. Who's to say you have to take it slow? Don't you owe it to yourself to give every shot one hundred percent? Even if it might not be the perfect time?"

"I can't mix business with pleasure like that," Isabel objected. "It'd be like using my body to get the account."

"Jeez, Isabel. You were already promised the account. So go get it. If you use your body at this point, it's to celebrate the success. Quit making it a crime to have sex."

"Meaningless sex."

"There's no such thing," Audra reminder her. "Even M&M's satisfy."

Considering her words, Isabel flicked a finger over the leather design board. "I haven't seen any designs like this in the boutique. Are you branching out? To be honest, this is the kind of thing I'd always imagined you designing. You know, something that screamed naughty sex."

Audra contemplated the leather-studded design she'd been doodling. Isabel was right, this *was* one of the things that had attracted her to lingerie in the first place. And exactly what she intended to market. Some day.

"We don't carry this kind of thing yet, it's just something I'm working on. You know, kind of like cleansing my palate. I'm on overload right now and was hitting the point that if I had to draw one more pink rosebud, I'd scream."

"Well, this definitely isn't pink." Isabel wrinkled her nose and looked around the boutique. "Of course, I'm sure carrying something like this here is way down the road. After all, this store caters to the sweet, wedding trousseau styles. I doubt this will fit your target market or Natasha's marketing plan."

Audra sniffed, but didn't answer. Instead, she tidied up the counter and focused on building Isabel's confidence back up so she could take that manager by storm.

Five minutes, a few pats on the back and a satin chemise later, she waved Isabel out the door. Audra eyed the stack of custom designs she was sending to Natasha. The courier was due any second. Lips pursed, she eyed Leather Submission, as she'd titled the teddy she'd just finished, and the tie that had been its inspiration.

It wasn't a big deal to include it. She was just showing Natasha a few options. With a sly grin, she cut a chunk off the tie and stapled it to the design board. Natasha would recognize it from their conversation and realize the butt-ugly tie had inspired a design, just like she'd predicted. Audra slid the tie-decorated board and the other designs into the mail pouch going to China and sealed it all with a kiss.

Sure, she got the whole careful planning thing. She did appreciate the progress. Slow and steady. But dammit, she wanted the whole dream. Designing things that inspired her. For women like her.

She wanted the gusto for herself.

And she was gonna get it.

DAVE LARSON was living on easy street. Life didn't get much better than this. He lay back on the foofy pillows of Bea's overstuffed couch and toed off his shoes. He had it all. A hot chick and a growing reputation with the right people looking for his particular skills.

And thanks to his handy-dandy off-site backup system the triad had no idea about, it'd taken him a couple of keystrokes and he'd made a spanking brand-new copy of the chip they wanted. No point in wasting time chasing his tie and the other chip when it wasn't any kind of real threat. He'd asked Bea enough questions to know her friend wasn't a problem. If there was one thing Dave prided himself in, it was his judgment of people.

"Hey, snookums, did you want a beer?" Bea asked as she curled up on the couch next to him. "I'll get you one and you can tell me what you've heard about my photo shoots. I'm ready, you know. I've got the perfect lingerie coming and everything."

Dave grimaced. He might actually have to find a way to make that happen for her. But at this point, he didn't have a clue. Time to change the subject.

Even though he'd intended to wait until after sex, Dave pulled a box out of his jacket and handed it to Bea. Before, after, either way, he'd be getting sex. This little gift would just ensure it'd keep coming.

"A present?" Bea said in that cute little girly voice that got him all excited. "For me? How sweet of you."

She leaned over, her lush breasts pressed against his shoulder giving him shivers, and brushed a lip-gloss-infused kiss against his cheek. Even knowing he'd have a breakout as a result, Dave couldn't bring himself to wipe the stain away.

He forced himself to sit still as nerves scratched their way down his spine. This was the first present he'd given a woman, if you didn't count his mother. And he didn't. Had anything ever mattered as much as this moment? He felt he was putting everything on the line.

In the blink of an eye, Bea ripped through the wrapping he'd made the clerk redo three times until he'd been satisfied. When she lifted the lid of the velvet jeweler's case, her grin sparkled as bright as the diamonds nestled on the white satin.

"Oh, Davey," she squealed, leaping across the couch to wrap those long, tan arms around his neck. Dave groaned as he slid his hands over her curves. She was a dream come true. Sweet, a little dumb, with a body better than any of his favorite porn queens. He couldn't get enough of her.

She rained kisses over his face and neck, all the while hooking the five-carat diamond bracelet around her wrist. Dave sighed in pleasure.

"You like?" he asked as she held her arm out to admire the dangling ice. This was definitely worth tapping into his un-

traceable overseas account for the funds. "That's just the beginning. You stick with me, you'll be wearing jewels from
head to toe."

Bea leaned back on her heels, her short dress hiked up to
the thighs that he'd beg to taste again. The look she gave him
was at odds with the airy persona he'd come to count on. "I
appreciate the gift, Dave. But I'm not with you for presents.
Or even for that magazine shoot you've promised me. I'm
with you because I like you. I really admire what you've
made of your life."

Dave ducked his head to hide his wince. Sure, she liked
the picture he'd painted. Who wouldn't? He was custom-
made for her, thanks to his ingenuity and brilliance. Not that
he believed for a second that she'd stick around without jewels
and incentives. But that was fine with Dave. It wasn't as if
he'd stick around if she didn't have such well-stacked incentives herself.

"I mean, how many guys orphaned so young make a huge
success like you did? You're a photographer to the stars.
You're a self-made man. I admire all of that, especially what
you told me about investing in the arts." Bea gave him a sexy
look through her lashes. "I'd really love to learn more about
art. It's so sexy."

Dave chewed the inside of his cheek while he tried to
remember what he'd told her. He really needed to start writing
these things down.

Before he had to come up with anything, though, his cell
chimed.

"Hang on," he told her as he pulled it from the leather case
on his belt. The tension in his body went into overdrive when
he saw the three X's on the readout.

"Can I take this in your room? It's business and, you
know, private."

She didn't even take her eyes from the sparkles as she waved him on his way. Dave hurried to the lush delights of Bea's bedroom, and, with a wince, answered.

"Larson here."

"Larson, my man. You've done us proud." The voice was as smooth as glass, but Dave knew it could cut deep enough to slice his jugular. A man didn't make top lieutenant in a group as powerful as the triad without a deadly reputation. "I wanted to personally thank you for the information on that chip. It's exactly what we were hoping for."

Dave wiped the bead of sweat from his upper lip. "You, uh, you got it all to open, right? No questions on anything?"

"You're information was both concise and user-friendly. Well done."

Dave tried to swallow, but he didn't have any spit in his mouth. If it was fine, why was the enforcer calling him?

As if he'd plucked the question straight from Dave's brain, the man continued in his whiskey-smooth tone, "I like to make it a point to let my people know when I'm pleased with them."

Dave's heart skipped a beat. *His* people. *Yes!* He'd made it. Time for the cushy jobs, the prime benefits.

"Of course, I was a little disturbed when I'd heard of your earlier…mistake." His pause was just long enough to let Dave become very aware of the sweat raining down his spine to soak the waistband of his slacks. "But you retrieved the temporarily misplaced information in a timely manner and didn't cause undue hardship for my people. I hate it when they have to take time away from their day-to-day jobs to…deal with issues."

Retrieved. Dave's vision blurred just a bit around the edges. Remade, retrieved. They were so close to the same thing. It didn't matter. Bea's friend was harmless. Just some bubbleheaded bimbo, hardly anyone to worry about. Hell, she'd likely tossed the tie by now.

"Hey, no problem," Dave finally said. "I mean, it was a simple mistake. Easy enough to rectify, ya know?"

"But it was rectified, which is what matters. I'm sure I don't have to tell you how damaging it would be to our operation should any of that information ever be used by any party other than us. An identity is a precious thing, and, of course, an exclusive thing. Should anyone else have the same identity, the same information, well…the picture isn't pretty, is it?"

Since the picture flashing through Dave's mind was of his body, dead in any horrifying variety of ways, he had to agree the image was ugly.

What if the chip slipped into the wrong hands? What if Bea's bubblehead friend somehow found it, even though it was expertly hidden in Dave's favorite tie? What would she do? Dave swiped the sweat off his chin with a shaky hand. Maybe he should check things out, try to get it back.

"As you know, I appreciate thoroughness in my people. After all, finding new ones is such a trial."

Since the triad had a reputation for never letting anyone leave employment alive after they'd "found" them, the threat was clear. The line went dead. Bile rose in his throat. Needing to wipe away the sweat dripping down his forehead and soaking his shirt, Dave headed for the bathroom to wash up.

He had to get that chip back. Not that the lieutenant had any idea the chip the triad had was anything other than the original. But just to be on the safe side, Davey'd better hook up with Bea's friend, Audra. He'd get his tie back, secure his deal. After all, he'd finally achieved his dreams. No way some loose thread was gonna screw that up for him.

By Wednesday, Audra was worn out and ready to scream. She'd just finished the final modifications to one of Simply Sensual's hottest designs for Bea. Now, the lilac lace screamed down-and-dirty sex instead of sweet, demure seduction.

It wasn't leather, but it'd suit Bea to a tee. She just hoped Bea wasn't disappointed. Her friend seemed to be putting a lot of hope into this guy's promises. Promises that sounded too good to be true.

Not that she hadn't cared about her friend's welfare and happiness in the past. She just didn't know how to interfere without sounding like an uptight idiot. As a rule, the three Wicked Chicks tended to live by a sink-or-swim policy, never interfering with or advising the others.

She thought of the final adjustments needed for Bea's last outfits.

Discontent weighed at her shoulders.

She didn't want to work.

No, what she wanted was Jesse. It'd been a long time since Friday night. Much too long since that delicious orgasm on the back couch. Even the barrage of erotic dreams she'd been enjoying all week weren't enough to satisfy her anymore.

She wanted Jesse.

She pulled a slip of paper out of the back pocket of her denim skirt. The creases were worn fuzzy, and looked about ready to rip apart from her unfolding and folding it. She stared down at the angular scrawl. *Jesse Martinez—cell.* Seven digits to delight.

She never called guys. Not out of any ladylike reserve, but because she never had to. But now? If she couldn't have Jesse's body, she'd settle for his voice.

Battling down nerves, she grabbed the boutique phone. Then, doubts racing through her head, she put it down and hurried back to the office for her phone. If she got lucky and it was a long call, she didn't want to have to hang up if she had to leave the boutique for any reason.

Cell phone in hand, she looked at the numbers again.

Two rings later and his deep voice was on the line. Anticipation made a heated journey through her erogenous zones. Audra settled in the plush chair toward the back of the shop and relaxed for the first time in days.

"Have you ever played Truth or Dare by telephone?" she asked in her sexiest voice.

Silence.

Then, "Audra?"

"How many other women are you playing phone sex games with?" she teased.

He laughed and she could almost hear his shrug. "I guess only you. Although, I have to admit, I've never seen Truth or Dare as a sex game."

"Then let me teach you the right way to play." Audra scanned the empty shop. She wanted to go back to the dressing room, take off her clothes and lay down on the leather couch. She could almost feel the cool grip of the leather against her hot, naked skin.

But it was still a half hour till closing. Damn this streak of responsibility.

"Is it a lot different than regular Truth or Dare?" Jesse asked.

"Just a smidge. Are you alone? Somewhere you can get comfortable?"

"Yeah," he said slowly. "I'm home alone. How comfortable?"

"Comfortable enough to touch yourself," she said in a husky voice.

His groan was as clear as if he'd been standing next to her. Audra grinned, biting back a giggle.

"How about I stick with truths?" he suggested. But Audra

was skilled at reading people, and she could tell from his voice that the truths held just as much worry as the dares.

Interesting.

She glanced around and spied a package of Naughty Games dice. With a grin, she grabbed it and ripped it open.

"We'll roll," Audra explained, making up her game as she looked at the hot pink dice. "Even number is truth, odd is dare."

"You carry dice with you?"

"You never know when you'll have the urge to do a little gambling," Audra teased. "After all, what's life without a risk?"

"Risk? Right."

Audra frowned at his tone. Was he too much a good boy to play with her? Maybe she was crazy to be drawn to someone so much her opposite.

"Okay, roll," he instructed.

"You're comfy?"

"Hell, no. But I'm ready to play with you."

With a grin of appreciation, she tossed the dice on the low display table.

"Odd."

"So you have to take a dare?"

She'd thought she was rolling for him. With a mental shrug, Audra stretched one arm overhead to release the tension in her lower spine. She wished she had one of those headsets in case this got to be a two-handed game.

"I have to take the dare," she agreed. "What's your pleasure?"

"My pleasure? I'm thinking more along the lines of what's your pleasure."

"Now that'd be a truth."

"Good point. Are you in a private place?"

Audra glanced toward the boutique door and raised blinds

on the bank of windows. She was partially obscured by a couple of clothes racks, but she'd hardly call it hidden.

"Private enough. Go for it."

His pause was filled with sparks of sexual awareness. Audra imagined him sitting somewhere, maybe a semidark room, fantasizing about her. Or more specifically, what he wanted her to do to herself.

She shifted a bit, adjusting her denim miniskirt in anticipation.

"Close your eyes," he instructed.

With a smile, anticipation coursing through her, she did.

"Now with your free hand, I want you to touch yourself."

She lightly scraped her nails up her thigh, heading toward the hem of her skirt.

"Start at your forehead," he instructed.

Audra's eyes flew open. Huh? What happened to phone sex? Was this some dumb idea of romance? What a waste of orgasm potential.

Before she could redirect his dare, he continued.

"C'mon, it's a dare. You have to do what I say, right?"

She pulled the phone away from her ear with a frown. How'd he know she wasn't? After rolling her eyes, she closed them and put the phone back to her ear. Then she followed the dare instructions and reached up to smooth her forehead.

"Imagine it's me, lightly tracing your face. Imagine that I'm sitting with you, staring at your beautiful features. Those sharp cheekbones, the little point of your chin. Imagine I'm rubbing my thumb across the full softness of your lower lip."

Audra's breath shuddered. Had any man ever looked at her like this? Ever memorized her features or taken such pleasure in imagining *himself* touching them?

"Slide your tongue out and wet your bottom lip," he said,

The Harlequin Reader Service® — Here's how it works:

Accepting your 2 free books and 2 free mystery gifts places you under no obligation to buy anything. You may keep the books and gifts and return the shipping statement marked "cancel". If you do not cancel, about a month later we'll send you 6 additional books and bill you just $3.99 each in the U.S. or $4.47 each in Canada, plus 25¢ shipping & handling per book and applicable taxes if any.* That's the complete price and — compared to cover prices of $4.75 each in the U.S. and $5.75 each in Canada — it's quite a bargain! You may cancel at any time, but if you choose to continue, every month we'll send you 6 more books, which you may either purchase at the discount price or return to us and cancel your subscription.

*Terms and prices subject to change without notice. Sales tax applicable in N.Y. Canadian residents will be charged applicable provincial taxes and GST. All orders subject to approval. Credit or debit balances in a customer's account(s) may be offset by any other outstanding balance owed by or to the customer. Please allow 4 to 6 weeks for delivery.

NO POSTAGE
NECESSARY
IF MAILED
IN THE
UNITED STATES

BUSINESS REPLY MAIL

FIRST-CLASS MAIL   PERMIT NO. 717   BUFFALO, NY

POSTAGE WILL BE PAID BY ADDRESSEE

HARLEQUIN READER SERVICE
3010 WALDEN AVE
PO BOX 1867
BUFFALO NY 14240-9952

If offer card is missing write to: Harlequin Reader Service, 3010 Walden Ave., P.O. Box 1867, Buffalo NY 14240-1867

GET FREE BOOKS and FREE GIFTS WHEN YOU PLAY THE...

SLOT MACHINE GAME!

Just scratch off the silver box with a coin. Then check below to see the gifts you get!

YES! I have scratched off the silver box. Please send me the 2 free Harlequin® Blaze® books and 2 free gifts for which I qualify. I understand I am under no obligation to purchase any books, as explained on the back of this card.

351 HDL ELXA   **151 HDL EL4X**

FIRST NAME   LAST NAME

ADDRESS

APT.#   CITY

STATE/PROV.   ZIP/POSTAL CODE

7	**7**	**7**
🍒	🍒	🍒
♣	♣	♣
🔔	🔔	🍒

Worth TWO FREE BOOKS plus 2 BONUS Mystery Gifts!

Worth TWO FREE BOOKS!

Worth ONE FREE BOOK!

TRY AGAIN!

www.eHarlequin.com

(H-B-05/07)

DETACH AND MAIL CARD TODAY!

© 2007 HARLEQUIN ENTERPRISES LTD.
® and ™ are trademarks owned and used by the trademark owner and/or its licensee.

his voice a lyrical seduction. "Then suck your finger into your mouth. Imagine it's me."

She gasped, then squirmed in the chair. She wanted to touch herself, to ease the building pressure. But she couldn't. Not with one hand on the phone and the other in her mouth. Did he know that?

"Your turn," he said after a few seconds. From his indrawn breath and labored tone, she could tell he was imagining himself in her mouth, too.

Audra hesitated, not sure what to say. Usually phone sex was down-and-dirty instructions. Touch this, do that. Imagine me this way.

But with Jesse? She felt she had to dig deeper. To reach inside and really ask herself how to make this a special experience. To make it about more than simple physical release.

And damn if that didn't scare her.

"Audra?"

"Yeah. Um, hang on, I'm rolling the dice." She sucked in a breath and told herself to get a grip. Sex was sex. And she'd never run from sex.

"Even," she told him, looking at the snake eyes. "So you have to tell me the truth."

"Okay," he drew out. He sounded a little unsure.

Ha, served him right. He'd pushed her emotional buttons, she was gonna push his.

"Tell me, truthfully…what's your ultimate sexual fantasy?"

His laugh was low and slightly wicked. More wicked than she'd have thought a good boy would sound.

"Ooh, this sounds like a good one."

"I don't know if I can say it over the phone," Jesse admitted.

"Sure you can. Just pretend you're with me. We're lying together in a dark room, and you're whispering in my ear."

Would he share? How truthful would he be? He'd agreed, and Audra had the impression that Jesse's word was gold. So if he bared his soul and shared his real fantasy, how sexy was this gonna get? She was willing to bet it was either one of two fantasies. The tie-'em-up-in-the-bedroom naughtiness, or the two-women-pleasuring-him scenario.

Audra glanced at the clock. Twelve minutes until closing. Screw it.

"Hang on," she ordered.

She flew from the chair to the front of the store. A quick glance outside assured her nobody was heading toward the boutique. With a flick of her wrist, the door was locked. A quick tug had the blinds drawn.

"Okay, start talking," she demanded as she headed down the hall toward the dressing room.

"Well," he started, sounding uncomfortable, "I guess it starts with dinner."

"Dinner?" Audra pulled the phone away from her ear to give it a baffled look, then shrugged. Without bothering to turn on the lights, she dropped to the couch and lay her head on the arm, with one leg thrown over the back. "Like, what? A family dinner? Dinner out at a restaurant? What?"

"No, dinner in. Candlelight, roses, wine. Just me and, well, in this case, you."

She grinned. "Me, huh? So you've had this fantasy recently?"

"Oh, yeah. It's been getting a lot of mileage this last week. Although the memory of you on that couch in your dressing room has been replayed a number of times, too."

"I'm on that couch now," Audra said in a husky tone.

Jesse groaned.

"Nope, no sidetracking," she demanded. "So we're having a candlelit dinner?"

"No. I'm sitting at the table. The room is dark except the

candle flames. Soft rock, something with a solid beat but not a lot of lyrics, plays in the background."

Audra heard a creak, as if he was settling back in his chair or something. He sounded more relaxed, like he was getting into the story.

"Sounds pretty," she said softly. It did. Very romantic and nice. Not really a turn-on, though. Oh, well, so the guy didn't have a wild imagination. He was definitely talented with his hands and had one wild mouth. Phone sex might have added more to her fascination with him, so this was probably just as well.

"You walk in," he continued, "completely nude. Except for thigh-high leather boots, of course."

"Of course," she agreed, swallowing a surprised chuckle. So maybe he wasn't so tame, if he wanted her, naked, for dinner. "Am I carrying food or something? Maybe serving you dinner?"

"Nope, there's a sideboard filled with everything I need."

"Need? Like…?"

"You come to me and lean over for a kiss. It's hot, a lot of tongue. Like we're battling it out for who gets to be boss. The winner will eat dessert off the other's body."

Oh. Audra hummed her appreciation of the image, her eyes dropping to slits as she imagined eating off Jesse's hard body. Yeah, that was working for her.

"I win, of course."

"Why?"

"Because it's my fantasy," he said with a laugh.

Audra frowned. Wouldn't a guy's fantasy lean toward being pleasured?

"I grab you, kind of quick and rough, and you give this breathy little moan and curl up on my lap. You run your hands over my body, using your nails a little to scrape at my skin. Nothing hard or painful, just a little wild."

Her breath short, she ran her tongue over her bottom lip to wet it.

"I grab a jar of chocolate-butterscotch fudge off the table," he told her.

Audra sighed in pleasure. Her favorite flavor. How perfect.

"I scoop it up with my fingers. I rub some on your lips, and you lick it off. Then you lie back in my arm so I have full access to your breasts and stomach."

Audra curved her hand over one of her already aching breasts and squeezed.

"My hands sticky with the chocolate, I hold your breasts, squeezing at the same time I flick your nipples. I lick the chocolate off your mouth, careful to get that little drip from your chin. You taste delicious." His voice trailed off and she heard the snick of a zipper through the phone. Eyes closed, Audra smiled her pleasure and with one last tweak of her nipple, slid her hand down to the hem of her skirt.

She pulled it up, then pressed her fingers to her damp panties.

"You pull away from me," he said, his voice rougher now. "You slide up onto the table and take the chocolate from me. Then you scoop some out and swirl it over your nipples. As soon as I lick it off, you wipe more on yourself, this time a little lower. I keep licking, you keep going lower."

Audra's panties were off now. She carefully traced her swollen lips, letting the pleasure build as she let his words, his obvious delight in this fantasy, take her higher.

"With just my tongue and fingers, I get you moaning. You beg me for more, beg me to drive you crazy. I make you come. You scream out my name over and over."

"Mmm," she moaned. The pleasure was building, tightening. She'd be screaming his name, all right. Any minute now.

"Your screams die down, and you slide from the table. You take that syrup and do the same thing to me, nibbling your way down my body. Eating the sweet dessert off my flesh. I get harder, bigger. I feel like I'm about to explode as your mouth gets closer and closer to my dick."

Imagining it, Audra used one, then two fingers to take her pleasure to the next level. Desire tightened deep in her belly, and she pressed the phone between her ear and the couch so she could use both hands on her body.

"Jesse?" she gasped.

"Yeah, babe?"

"I'm about to come."

She was. The tension had her back arching as she dug her heels into the leather couch, her pelvis thrust high in the air. She wished he were there to watch her. She imagined him standing at the end of the couch, his eyes hot on her body as she showed him how wet she was.

"Me, too," he admitted in a low voice. "But first I want to know how you like the taste of me. Imagine me in your mouth, Audra. Imagine me as you come."

The image of Jesse's face as she pleasured him exploded in her mind at the same time the orgasm ripped through her body.

From a distance, she heard his groan, and knew he'd found his own pleasure. A ghost of a smile flitted over her lips.

So much for him not having a wild imagination.

Audra felt too good to even care about her emotional warning alarm's scream of caution.

Because if the guy could make her feel this good over the telephone, there was no way she was running away until she had his body inside hers. Until she'd had the whole package.

Even if she was in mortal danger of falling in love.

9

AUDRA SMILED her goodbye to the last customer of the day and flipped the sign to Closed. She didn't lock the door, since Jesse was supposed to pick her up here instead of at her apartment, but she did pull the blinds.

Stress rippled across her weary shoulders as she turned off the display lights. What a hellish week. She'd had less than twenty hours of sleep in the last four days. For a woman who deemed anything less than nine hours a night roughing it, this had been pure torture.

The only thing that was going right was Jesse. Oh. My. God. The man was incredible. He'd sent her flying with his chocolate fantasy, then proceeded to make her come three more times as he'd shared his shower fantasy, then listened to a few of her hot thoughts.

She couldn't wait to try them all out with him for real.

Of course, who knew when she'd find the time? Even though she'd refused to give up her date tonight, she'd be busting her ass as soon as Jesse dropped her off.

She'd managed to ship the completed design boards to China. They should have arrived by now. She was dying to know what Natasha thought about the slick little leather number she'd slipped in.

Audra wasn't sure what was hurting more. Her fingers from the fine detail of the designs. Her eyes from strain. Or the crick in her neck from having to work while Natasha yammered in her ear to the tune of a hefty long-distance phone bill.

Like the call of the devil, the phone rang. She didn't even have to look at the caller ID screen to know it was her evening China call.

"Hey, Tasha," she said in lieu of hello.

"Audra, I received the couriered designs today. I have to say, you really outdid yourself this time."

Audra wanted to grin at the words, but the tone made her hesitate.

"You don't sound too thrilled," she said.

"I'm pleased with most of them," Natasha said, speaking slowly, as if she were choosing her words with extra care. "I'm a little confused why you'd send me this one, though. Leather? I thought we'd discussed this already and agreed to keep the designs in the tone Simply Sensual is known for."

Audra made a face at the phone. "It was just a fun idea I'd come up with. Remember we'd discussed that butt-ugly tie and how it might inspire a design? Well that's what I came up with, something a little kinky and a little crazy. You know, like the kind of person would have to be to wear that tie?"

She waited for Natasha to laugh.

She was met with dead silence.

Her own amusement faded, replaced by irritation. Damned if she wasn't tired of justifying her tastes, her choices and her hopes. It was a great design. Natasha should be excited her head designer had such insight. Not pissy because it wasn't covered in pink roses and foofy lace.

"What's the problem?" she asked. "It was just an idea. I didn't send it to get your knickers in a twist. It was something I thought you'd enjoy seeing. It's not like I mass-produced it and set up a display here in the boutique."

"No. But the designs arrived as I was on my way into the meeting. I didn't have time to check them first, since I was running late. I had no idea you'd have a surprise in there for me."

Audra snickered. "You presented that leather do-me teddy to the Chinese distributors?"

She tried to stifle her laugh as she imagined the faces of a bunch of guys ready for bridal wear and presented with wrist cuffs.

"Let's just say I don't think we'll be getting that particular account," Natasha said with a stiff laugh. "I guess it isn't that big a deal, since I didn't feel comfortable with them anyhow."

Audra winced, all laughter dying away.

She hadn't intended to embarrass her sister-in-law or do anything to jeopardize the account.

"Natasha—"

"Look, I know you didn't mean it. It's just, you know, one of those impulsive things you tend to do. And it's not a major loss. This was that impromptu presentation we snagged after I got over here. I hadn't even had a chance to check into the company," Natasha interrupted. Her words were obviously meant to reassure, but the underlying disappointment in her tone cut Audra deep. "I realize this design is probably a lot closer to your true style, Audra. But I thought you could balance that natural naughty bent with the kind of designs I need for Simply Sensual. Was I wrong?"

Audra started to deny it. But then she stopped.

After all, the naughtier designs *were* her preference. They were a natural expression of her bad girl side. They were who she was. But that didn't mean she could just shrug off Simply Sensual or what it offered her. Natasha had given her a shot, a career. Head designer, with her own lingerie line debuting in the fall.

Tension pounded a beat at Audra's temples. She had no idea what the right direction for her career was anymore. Hell, she didn't even know what the right direction for *her* was at this point. Ever-so-naughty Wicked Chick? Responsible businesswoman? Creative lingerie designer? None of them meshed; they were all in conflict.

No wonder her head felt as if it were going to explode.

"Natasha—"

"Just think things through," her sister-in-law suggested softly. "We'll talk when I get back, okay?"

"Yeah," Audra agreed. "But—"

"How's business been in the boutique?" Natasha asked in an obvious change of subject.

Audra considered refusing to follow her lead. But knowing Natasha, she wouldn't get anywhere pushing the confrontation. Even though it went against her personal preference, she sighed and let it go. Besides, she honestly didn't know what she'd have said.

"We've been really busy, actually," Audra replied finally. A lot busier than she would have preferred, given that Sharon was sick, leaving Audra to work the boutique alone while trying to get the last batch of designs done. "I'm guessing there will be just enough profit to cover your long-distance bill."

"Seriously, is it going okay?"

Depended on what the day's definition of okay was. Audra looked around the shop, unvacuumed, slightly disheveled and looking like a classy dame who'd partied a little too hard.

"Has it really been that busy?" Natasha persisted. "How's the inventory holding up? Do we need to reorder anything? You know Wednesdays are the deadline to order paper supplies."

Audra winced and averted her eyes from the empty hangers. She spied random threads strewn over the burgundy carpet and the empty boxes where the stock of gift bags were supposed to be.

Maybe she should do a little housekeeping before her date? She opened the storage cabinet and saw there were no more gift bags to stock. Maybe she should completely cancel her date?

If nothing else, this was a good distraction from the identity crisis throbbing in her head.

"Audra?"

"It's all good. Don't worry. The boutique will be exactly as you left it when you get back."

"I knew I could count on you."

Feeling sick to her stomach, Audra pressed her lips together. She spent a whole five seconds trying to tell herself to let it go and keep her mouth shut. Then she gave up.

"Look, Natasha, I'm sorry you were embarrassed by the design," Audra said. "I didn't send it to hurt you. I'm proud of that concept and wanted to share it, you know?"

"I know." There was a muffled conversation on the other end, then Audra heard her brother's raised voice. She rolled her eyes. She grabbed a piece of paper and pen, trying futilely to figure out which stock needed replenishing. She'd do better to list what she had on the racks, instead. It'd take less time.

"We'll talk when I get home, okay? But for now, your brother wants to talk to you."

"Drew? Why?" Audra asked, puzzled. She and Drew had a nice enough relationship going on. They weren't super tight, though, and she could count on one hand the number of phone conversations they'd had in her lifetime. Why waste money for a long-distance one now? Especially when he couldn't be pleased she'd embarrassed his wife.

Oh, man, he better not be planning to lecture her. Just what she needed, a kick in the butt to make life decisions via long distance. Audra's tension shot up another notch, this time slipping into anger.

"Why…" she trailed off as her brother's voice came over the line.

"Hey, Audra. How's it going?"

"Peachy. What's up, Drew?" Her tone was probably more defensive than he deserved, but she couldn't imagine this was going to be fun. She made her way to the stockroom and stared at the neatly labeled shelves of inventory. *Inventory?* Natasha was always boasting how easy stocking was thanks to her computer program. Maybe that'd help.

"I need your help," Drew said.

"You in the market for some sexy undies?"

Audra booted up the computer and glared at the inventory program Natasha was so proud of. She'd never tried to figure it out before. Then she remembered the carefully detailed instruction list, complete with color-coded bullet points. With a quick glance, she was actually able to punch a couple keys and get a list of what stock they'd sold that week and what they had in-house that she could restock on the sales floor. Neat trick.

Drew's laugh made some of Audra's irritation slip away. He sounded just like their late father when he did that. She heaved a sigh at the familial tug at her heart. She really needed to change her brand of water or something; she was getting all mushy lately.

"No thanks, I need a favor. Tash said it'd be a pain in your butt, but it's important to me."

"Sure, whatever you need." Even wallowing in her guilt over disappointing his wife, Drew was likely the only person on earth she'd give that open agreement to.

"Thanks. This is important. Remember old Joe? A regular at the Sports Bar? I think he used to buy you Shirley Temples and play Go Fish with you for pretzels?"

Audra grinned as the memory of the old guy flashed through her mind. "Looks like Popeye, right? Old sailor dude, tattoo of an anchor on his arm, always smelled like peppermints?"

"Yeah, that's him. Perfect, I'm glad you remember. He'll be glad, too."

"Will he? Why?" She took the computer printout into the stockroom and started gathering inventory to put out.

"Tonight's his birthday. It's been like a tradition since he started coming into the bar, back when Dad first bought it, that he comes in on his birthday for a drink. On the house."

"Okay? So what? You want me to call your manager and make sure she remembers his drink?"

"Nah, it's on the calendar. That's not the problem. The thing is, he always makes a fuss about how he's been served his birthday drink for the last twenty years by a Walker in the Home Run Sports Bar."

Audra paused in the act of restocking satin chemises on their padded hangers. "Twenty years? How old is the guy? He seemed ancient when I was a kid."

"I think he's in his eighties. So you see why this is so important to him?"

Audra squinted from the list in her hand to the phone. "I guess, sure. It sounds like this drink might be the highlight of the old guy's year."

"Exactly. So you'll do it?"

"Do what? I'm not following you, Drew."

"You'll go to the Home Run and serve him his drink?"

"Tonight?" No way. The only thing getting her through this hellish week was the fact that she had a date tonight to look forward to. She had to get the first of three dates with Jesse out of the way so she could get to the main event.

"Yeah, tonight. What? It's not like you can ask a guy in

his eighties to hold off a week or so, right? I mean, he might not last, you know?"

Her already tapped-out guilt meter flashing red, Audra's lower lip poked out and she dropped the silky midnight blue nightie she'd been hanging. Not last? Now that wasn't a pretty thought. Poor old Joe.

"Will you do it? You don't have to do much more than be at the bar around eight. The bartender will get his drink ready, you serve it with a rousing chorus of 'Happy Birthday,' maybe give him a kiss on the cheek if his heart's up to the excitement."

Shit. As if she could refuse that? Not only was Drew directly responsible for any successes she'd achieved, but he never asked anything of her. And old Joe? He'd taught her to bluff. She'd be a heartless bitch to say no to handing the old guy a drink and singing to him.

But what about her date?

"So? Will you do it?"

"Of course," she said with a sigh as she rehung the blue nightie.

Maybe Jesse was into sports bars?

JESSE STOOD outside the gilt-trimmed door of the boutique and ground his teeth. This was the last place he should be. On a date with a suspect he was in imminent danger of falling for.

A suspect, for that matter, whose worst crime to date had been flirting with a known criminal. Because other than the flirting, and Dave's conversation afterward, Jesse had nothing on Audra. At least, nothing illegal.

Especially now that they'd found out her sister-in-law had blown off the lingerie company in China that sidelined as a money-laundering front. Reports said the woman had barely kept the appointment. Whether it was because they were backing away from dealing with the triad, or because the women really weren't involved, Jesse couldn't tell.

Nowhere in the communiqués, the e-mails or the chats he'd hacked from Davey's computer was there any reference to Audra by name or by any description other than "hot babe." Without more, the only involvement he could pin on her on was whatever Dave had passed to her in the club. That, and the large sum of money conveniently deposited into the boutique's account.

Neither of which, so far, was enough to convict her. Which meant there was a remote chance she could be innocent.

Jesse should be focusing on the case. He'd finally made a breakthrough on Davey's computer system. The guy had accessed an off-site storage unit to transfer a large sum of cash. Jesse hadn't been able to break into the system yet. But the way his fingers tingled when he worked at it assured him it'd be the key he needed to blow this case out of the water. A little deep excavation and he'd have enough to nail Davey boy. And, if the strings he was pulling led where he thought they would, enough to take down the *Du Bing Li* triad too.

He should be working on that now instead of going through with this date. He was a lousy actor. There was no way he'd be able to pull off the smitten suitor bit.

But the captain had other ideas. Shale had as much as promised Jesse his coveted promotion if he nailed this case with no loose ends. A promotion that would prove, to Jesse at least, that he'd succeeded by doing things *his* way. Using his brains and those computer skills his father had so often disparaged. His family would finally accept that his brainiac tendencies were just as valuable as his father's flash.

So he squared his shoulders, reached for the door handle and prepared to reel in his last loose end.

Audra was bent at the waist talking on the phone. Her

back was to him so he had a mouthwateringly sweet rear view. Her short skirt hiked up to show the seams running up the back of her black stockings. Jesse swore he felt his heart stop. Other parts of his body, however, raced to full alert.

Damn, she had to be the sexiest thing he'd ever seen. When she straightened and turned, a glowing smile on her face as she saw him, he wanted to groan. She looked that good.

"So he's that good, huh?" she said into the phone as she blew Jesse a kiss. "You're definitely welcome."

With a quick goodbye, Audra clicked off the phone and leaned across the counter to set it in its cradle.

"That was my friend, Isabel, calling to thank me," she said with a wicked look on her face as she turned back to face him.

"For?"

"Bringing her over to the naughty side." She winked. "We have all the good sex over on this side."

Jesse's body stiffened in reaction. He wasn't going to give in to the naughty. He had a job to do, loose ends to tie up. And arrests to make.

"It sounds like she appreciates your bad influence."

"Definitely," she said, coming toward him. Those delicious, stocking-clad legs seemed to go on forever, from the edge of her short skirt to feet encased in gladiator-style spiked heels. Her hair was a solid black, giving her an oddly conservative look after her fuchsia-tipped ends of the previous week.

Audra reached him and, without hesitation, put both hands on his chest to lean up and press her lips to his. Against the soft pressure of her kiss, he opened his mouth without thought and met the sweet dance of her tongue.

Jesse's hands curved over her slender hips, and he pulled her flush against him. His body welcomed the feel of hers like a homecoming. It was all he could do to break away and end the kiss.

"I missed you," she said in her husky tone. That voice had haunted his dreams. In those dreams, he'd imagined her doing all sorts of decadent things to his body, describing each one as she did it. "I haven't been able to think of anything but you and our phone conversation since last night. How soon can we do it for real?"

"I missed you, too," he admitted. And he had. Not just because his body had been rock-hard every time her image popped into his brain. But he'd missed her sweetness, her fun outlook on life.

Then he shook his head and gave her a rueful look.

"I'm really not trying to be a tease or whatever you'd call it. But I do want to spend more time with you before we actually, you know…"

"You know? Last night, you told me how delicious I tasted, and today you can't say sex?" she teased with a laugh.

"Go figure." Jesse grimaced, then gave a laugh and a stiff shrug. Last night he hadn't been looking for evidence to arrest her. He'd do well to keep that fact front and center in his brain tonight. He had to get the goods to nail her, or cut her loose. "You ready to go? I thought we could get something to eat, spend some time talking."

"Sure. I just need to grab my jacket and shut down the computer first. Dinner sounds great. I need to make one stop first, if that's okay with you."

He followed her down the hall to the office and stopped in shock at the sight of the once immaculate room.

"Whoa. What happened here?" It looked as if someone had tossed the place. Maybe in search of missing or stolen information? "Did you call the cops?"

"Cops? Why on earth would I want to bring some busybody cop in here?" Audra followed his gaze around the room. As if seeing the mess for the first time, she winced.

"Ooooh, you mean the mess? If I claim a tornado set down in here, do you think Natasha will believe me?"

"You did this yourself?"

"It's been a hellish week. I guess I kind of let housekeeping duties slide." Audra's shoulders sagged and she ran her hand through her hair. "I don't suppose you'd care to have a seat and flip through some lingerie magazines while I tidy this up a bit?"

She eyed what was probably still a shell-shocked look on his face and wrinkled her nose. She looked around the mess of papers, piles of fabric and lacy things, and the half-buried computer. Then she grinned.

"I know, you're a computer geek, right? Want to play online or something? I won't be more than a quarter, maybe a half hour at the most. And I'll treat you to a drink afterward?"

Could it get any better? If she *was* crooked, she really needed to take lessons. The first rule of being a good criminal is not to trust anyone. Audra was practically inviting him to invade her privacy. Then again, she'd welcomed his fingers into much more private places than her computer keyboard.

Which didn't prove she was innocent, Jesse forced himself to remember. But, maybe a few quick strokes on that keyboard and he could at least figure out how guilty she was. Then he could find a way to make her a deal, get her to roll over on Larson. She'd be in minimal trouble, and he'd be there to set her on the straight and narrow.

"You can cruise the Net, play games or something. Whatever floats your boat."

Resolved and comfortable that it was for her own good, Jesse smiled back and flexed his fingers.

"What computer geek can say no to an offer like that?"

Audra laughed. "I wonder what would get you more

excited? A fully loaded, up-to-the-minute, technologically
advanced computer? Or me, naked?"

Jesse let the images flash through his mind and heaved a
delighted sigh. "How about both? You, naked, on my lap
while I use the computer?"

"Kinky. I like that." She cleared a couple bolts of silky-
looking fabrics in jewel tones off the rolling computer chair
and, after looking around, stacked them in a corner by the
door. "Here, get comfy. I'll run in and get you a soda. Then
it'll only take me a little bit to tidy things here and we can
go."

"Sounds great," Jesse said absently, his butt already in the
chair and fingers hovering over the keys. He waited until she
left the room before hitting her programs option to see what
bookkeeping software they used. He'd opened it, minimized
and was playing Tetris online when she came back.

"Cola, right?" She leaned over his shoulder to set in on the
desk, her breast brushing his forearm. Distracted, Jesse saw
the bars stack up on his screen through blurred eyes. A vision
of her, naked on his lap while he worked some complex
computer program, flashed through his mind.

Damn, he wanted her. And if he connected her to the crime,
she'd be so off-limits, he might as well lust after a cover
model as Audra. He'd have no chance with her. Who knew
regret could hurt so bad?

Unable to help himself, Jesse pulled her around so she sat
across his lap, her back cradled in the crook of his arm. Her
eyes sparkled as she smiled up at him and she curled both her
hands around the back of his neck and raised one brow in
tempting dare. She felt right in his arms. Sexy, but comfortable at the same time.

"I like this," she said.

"You'll like this better," he assured her before his mouth

descended. They went from tinder to flames in an instant. She met his tongue with hers, challenged him to keep up with her demand for more. Audra would accept no less than complete passion, breaking down all inhibitions and hesitations. For once, Jesse knew he held a woman who'd not only meet any and all of his sexual needs, but she'd encourage him to explore his limits.

As their mouths continued their sensual dance, Audra slid one hand down his chest, teasing his belly before those talented fingers moved to play with the snap of his jeans. Sensual anticipation grabbed hold of him. He wanted to feel those clever hands everywhere, to experience the intense pleasure he knew they'd bring.

Jesse wanted her to feel the same exquisite wanting, the same desperate need he felt. Oddly enough, he wasn't intimidated by Audra's experience or her grasp on the art of sexual pleasure. But he *was* determined to make one hell of an impression himself.

With that in mind, using the lightest of touches, he brushed his fingers over the tip of her breast. He felt the intake of her breath against his mouth and, taking it as a good sign, continued his barely-there teasing. After ten seconds, she gave the slightest squirm on his lap and Jesse wanted to groan himself. He palmed her nipple until it pebbled beneath his hand. She left off playing with his snap to scrape her fingernails down the zipper of his jeans, making his already straining flesh burgeon with need.

Unable to deny the rushing intensity of desire any longer, Jesse tweaked her nipple. Audra's fingers convulsed on his dick, making him groan aloud and pull away from her mouth.

Jesse buried his face in her throat and tried to gather some control. Damn, she was incredible. He was about ready to come in his jeans, from just the simple pressure of her fingers.

He hadn't seen the woman undressed yet, but he'd dedicated so many orgasms to her, he felt as if they were in a long-term relationship.

But they weren't. And they couldn't be. He needed to remember that. To remember why he was here, what his purpose in her life was. To save her, not to screw her. Maybe if he had it tattooed somewhere, he'd be able to remember that.

With a deep breath, Jesse pulled back and brushed a kiss over her forehead. He forced himself to meet her eyes as he tried to come up with an excuse to not go any further.

But when he looked into those wide, brown depths, there was no demand or expectation. All he saw was happy pleasure.

"Nice," she murmured.

"Same to you."

She grinned and patted his cheek before sliding off his lap.

"Play away, I'll just be a few minutes. Then we'll go, okay? I do have to be at this thing by eightish, so I'll hurry."

Jesse refrained from asking what kind of thing, since he'd be there to find out himself. Besides, the sooner she got to cleaning, the sooner he could peek at her books.

"Are you one of those people who can't concentrate if someone is talking to you?" she asked as she started gathering bolts of fabric from around the room to stack by the door with the others. "Or are you a social computer geek?"

"In between," he admitted, keeping one eye on her as he pulled up her bookkeeping program. He frowned. It wasn't even password protected? She was such an innocent. That'd go in her favor when he was trying to plea-bargain a good deal for her.

"If I'm doing anything intense, programming or something, I'm better without conversation. But for games, most computer work, talking doesn't bother me."

After that, Audra kept up a steady stream of chitchat. None of which required much response, but was fun to listen to all the same. She had a quirky way of relating a story, of describing clients and salespeople. It told him a lot about how much she liked the people she dealt with. This lingerie business was definitely a labor of love.

Jesse looked over to see her sorting beads and things into a plastic container and clicked on the recent list of deposits. And there it was. Ten thousand, cash. With the initials "S.S." and a notation of *China loan* next to it.

S.S.? Jesse flipped through the files in his brain, but couldn't connect any names—or even nicknames—to S.S. What was the deal? Loan? Not payoff? Could it be to cover their criminal activities? That didn't makes sense. Not when there was a payment schedule outlined, complete with terms.

"Hey, what d'ya know? Natasha really does have a desk. I just had to clear enough stuff to find it," Audra said with a laugh.

Jesse hit the Close button and laughed too, albeit a little stiffly. His mind was going in a dozen directions, and none of them made sense.

"You about ready to go?" she asked.

"Sure. You want me to shut this down?"

"Thanks, yeah. I'll just grab my jacket and I'm ready."

Jesse used the time she took to do that, turn off the lights and lock up the boutique to puzzle through what he'd found. By the time they'd reached their cars, he still hadn't figured it out. He'd have to do some further computer investigation after their date. Good thing he'd given her that good boy excuse; at least she wouldn't be expecting him to spend the night. Not that he wouldn't want to, but it was a hell of a lot easier to fight one person's wants than two.

"Do you mind if I drive?" she asked. She gave a little shrug and glanced at her watch. "You can follow me to my place and drop off your truck. It's on the way. We're running a little late and it'd be faster if I didn't have to give directions and all."

"Um, sure," he agreed. Jesse tried to hide his frown. It wasn't that he was uncomfortable with a woman driving. Just with a suspect driving him to a possible crime scene.

"Where are we going?" he asked after he'd followed her three blocks over to her apartment complex and dropped off his truck. He settled into the passenger seat, gripping the door as she zoomed out of the parking lot with barely a glance for traffic.

The woman drove like she did everything else. Wildly.

"There's this little place in Auburn I need to go to. I have to be there by eight, eight-fifteen."

"Sure, no problem. Are we meeting someone?" he asked as they sped toward the freeway. Was it some kind of handoff? He flipped through his mental files, but nothing in Auburn sounded familiar. The triad tended to meet in clubs, Larson in nudie bars. But always in Sacramento. At least, not so far.

She took the on-ramp at high speed, zooming in and out of slower traffic with an ease that had the tension in Jesse's neck unknotting just a little. For all her wildness, she seemed to be in complete control.

"It's a nice place, a little bar I know. We'll be in and out before you know it. Call it a quickie." Audra laughed and glanced over at him. Her scent, that sensual, musky rich perfume, filled the car's interior and Jesse's senses. His mouth watered, because he knew the scent was stronger right along her collarbone.

"Bar, huh? Not a club? That doesn't sound much like your speed."

"You'd be surprised how much time I've spent in this particular bar," she said.

She paused, and Jesse glanced over. Sadness tugged at the

corners of her eyes and she sighed. Then, catching his gaze, she pasted her sexy smile on and winked.

"But it is a nice place, and the people are great."

"Okay. But there are plenty of nice places with great people here in Sacramento," he teased.

"Sure there are, but not like this. Besides, I promised I'd be there. It's a matter of life or death, babe. I can't blow off a promise."

Jesse raised a brow. He wasn't sure why the Auburn location, but something big must be going down. After all, it was *life or death.*

Fifteen minutes later, brows drawn together, Jesse watched Audra park in the reserved parking spot in front of the Home Run Sports Bar. This was, just like she had said, a nice place.

This was her brother's place. Jesse recognized the name from her files. Did she use it often for illegal activities? He'd have to check into it.

A middle-income neighborhood in the suburbs, there was a restaurant on one side of the bar and a flower shop on the other. Both looked to be frequented by families. The cars parked along the street and in the shared lot all looked middle- to upper-class. It didn't look like he'd need to worry about calling for backup.

Not a strip joint in sight, so it was unlikely the person they met inside would be Dave Larson. Which left any of a dozen others, Jesse reminded himself as he came around the car.

"Nice neighborhood," he commented as he opened Audra's door for her.

"It's picked up the last five years. The neighborhood was a little rougher, a little seedier before. But, yeah," she gazed around with a fond, indulgent look on her face, "it is nice, isn't it?"

"It sounds like you're really familiar with the area," he commented as he grabbed the metal door handle to let her enter the bar before him.

She didn't have to respond. It was like something out of that Eighties TV sitcom, *Cheers*. Except, instead of everyone yelling out "Norm," they all yelled "Audra." Jesse blinked, taken aback at the warm welcome she received. Not that he didn't expect people to be excited to see her. But because they simply weren't the *kind* of people he expected to be excited to see her.

With most of the patrons in their mid-thirties, it was definitely not a party kind of place. Beer seemed to be the drink of choice, if the sea of frosty mugs was anything to go by. Instead of a guys' hangout, the bar appeared to cater to couples and groups. A dartboard, pool table and bank of television sets tuned to different sports completed the setting.

The green and blue interior showed a bit of age, as did the scarred hardwood floors. The tables and chairs all looked new, and the plants and flowers on each table were well cared for. Overall, it was friendly and welcoming.

And Audra fit right in. As she made her way to the bar, she greeted a few people by name, responded to questions here and there and fielded congratulations on her recent graduation. And, in typical Audra fashion, patted a few guys on the butt.

"Audra, sweetie, I'm so glad you came," the bartender cried out. The tall blonde looked as if she should be home baking cookies, not manning a bar. "I was worrying, what with Drew being off gallivanting like a wild man."

"So tell me, how often does Drew call in? Seeing as he's the owner and all into running the place himself?" Audra asked. She sounded a little persnickety, enough to make the bartender raise her carefully manicured brows.

"Let's see, he's been gone a little more than a week, right? He's called three, maybe four times."

"Total?" Audra leaned her elbows on the bar and shook her head. "I get more calls than that in a day from Natasha."

"Ahhh, being left in charge is fun, huh? Congratulations on the promotion, by the way. We're all proud of you."

If he hadn't been gawking at her, Jesse would have missed the faint blush that swept over Audra's high cheekbones.

"Thanks," she murmured. Then she turned to gesture to Jesse in an obvious change of subject, "This is my friend, Jesse. Treat him right, huh? He's a hell of a kisser."

Now it was Jesse who was probably blushing. He muttered a hello to the laughing woman behind the bar and slid onto the empty stool.

Why were they here? Old home week? Was this a kinky twist on Audra's bad-girl-style dating? Something illegal? If her sister-in-law was involved, it stood to reason that her brother was, too.

"So," Audra said, sliding onto a barstool and spinning so she faced the room. "Have you got it ready? Is he here yet?"

There must be a pickup or drop-off scheduled tonight. Jesse looked around at the middle-class clientele and frowned. It simply didn't compute.

The bartender tapped Audra's shoulder and nodded over to a gaggle of old guys huddled together around a small table with a cup of dice. Then the woman set a drink of what looked like scotch on the bar next to Audra's elbow.

"There ya go, tiger."

Audra grinned and slid off her stool. She leaned over and brushed a kiss over Jesse's cheek and gave him a wink.

"I'll just be a second, okay? Go ahead and order a drink. It's on the house."

With a kicky swing in her hips, Audra took the single drink, placed it on the serving tray and swayed across the room to a table where the trio of octogenarians held court.

The guy in the center had a smile as long as the Golden Gate. His wizened face showed delight beneath his sailor's cap.

"If it isn't sweet little Audra."

"Sure enough. Nothing but the best for your birthday, Joe."

And with that, she proceeded to sing the old guy "Happy Birthday" in perfect tune as the entire bar watched, then chimed in after the first line.

Jesse stared. This was her important task? Life or death? He absently thanked the bartender when she set a beer in front of him.

"Old Joe's been coming in here for years," she explained, her arms crossed over her chest and a wide grin on her face. "Back when Aaron was alive—back before he got so sick and let everything fall apart—he was the first to serve up Joe's drink and sing to him for his birthday. His son, or now his daughter, have carried on that tradition for over twenty years. He'd be proud."

From what little he'd gleaned from his investigation, Aaron Walker had been a hard-ass who'd died after a long, rough bout with cancer. Before he'd gotten sick, the man had single-handedly raised his children in this bar. Audra had gone to live with her estranged mother, but she'd obviously retained a strong affection for her onetime home and what it represented.

Ironic that they were both so strongly influenced by their fathers.

Jesse gulped down a swig of beer. He'd always looked down on his father for blurring the lines on a case. And now? Now he was falling in love with a suspect who was, if connected with the crimes he was investigating, guilty enough to be serve time in prison.

When had he turned into a conjugal visit kind of guy?

10

"THAT WAS sweet," Jesse said as he escorted Audra from the bar to her car.

Audra snorted, but didn't deny the observation. Not that there was much to deny. They'd stayed for a drink and shared a basket of nachos while the patrons had regaled him with stories of Audra's younger years.

Instead of being embarrassed, as he would have been, she'd just grinned. He'd never met anyone so comfortable with herself as she was. All aspects of her, not just the social mask she presented. Sure, occasionally she'd corrected someone's story. But only if they were making her sound too nice or goody-goody. Not that there had been too much of that. From the sound of the stories, Audra'd been a handful from infancy.

"They're a good bunch of people. I don't get over here too often, but it's always nice. I'm glad you had fun," she said. They reached her car and she gave him a considering look, then dangled the keys from her finger. "Wanna drive?"

"You don't mind other people driving your car?" Jesse frowned.

"Nah. Besides, we've already established we'd take turns leading. I led us here, you're in charge of the rest of our date."

His frown faded and he caught the keys she tossed to him. He unlocked her door and settled her into the passenger seat before going around to the driver's side. Her car was a lot sportier than his old truck. Eight horse-power, it'd be a pleasure to handle.

Much like its owner.

Jesse slid into the car. He started the ignition and glanced over at her.

"It sounds like you were a hellion growing up." Which was in keeping with the reputation he'd uncovered in his investigation. "And yet they all seem to love you."

Which wasn't in keeping with that rep. For a woman who'd grown up with juvenile delinquent tendencies, a neglectful father and a drunken mother, she had some amazingly well-developed people skills.

"Hey, I'm a lovable kind of gal. Hadn't you noticed?" she said with a laugh and a vampy look.

"So you grew up in the bar?" Jesse headed toward the freeway, determined to solve this puzzle, or at least a portion of it, before they got back to Sacramento.

"Over it, really. Dad's apartment was upstairs. My brother lived there off and on for a while, too. Mostly off. Then my dad got sick and my mom was forced to take custody."

Her tone was so matter-of-fact, Jesse almost misunderstood the words. A quick glanced showed no evidence of emotion on her face.

"Forced? You mean she won custody, right?"

"Nope. My parents weren't much for nurturing, if you know what I mean. My dad was a good guy, but he didn't know diddly about raising a kid, let alone a female kid. He'd had enough trouble with Drew, then I came along. He'd have preferred my mother raise me. You know, females belong together and all that jazz."

He slid her another glance. Like her words, her face showed no trace of bitterness. Her easy acceptance was a surprise. Especially since he was used to criminals who blamed their misdeeds on parents who'd denied them video games and candy.

"And your mom?"

"She's cool. We had some pretty wild parties. My place was the hangout, which gave me ready access to a lot of hot guys," she said in a teasing tone.

Parties. Jesse mentally reviewed Audra's file. She'd lived with her mom between the ages of fourteen and seventeen, including the time of her arrest at sixteen. Somehow he didn't think those parties included soda pop and spin the bottle.

"What about your brother?"

"My dad died when I was sixteen. Drew took it hard. He had the bar to run then, and was pretty busy. I hardly saw him again until I was an adult."

She shrugged as if it didn't mean much, but Jesse'd learned to look to her lips for a true reaction. Audra would be a hell of a poker player with that bland face and go-to-hell eyes. But when she talked about her father's death, the slight tremble in her lower lip gave her away.

Those years with her mother must have been hell. If he remembered right, it had been her brother who bailed her out of jail and had signed the court papers when she'd been arrested. Interesting.

"How about you?" she asked, turning the tables. "Tell me about your family.

Jesse gave a laugh. "My family? They're about as average a family as you can get, I guess."

"C'mon, that's a copout. You mentioned sisters before. How many? Are you older or younger? Where'd you grow up, what're your parents like?"

He shot her a shocked look. "All that?"

"Yes, all that. Now that you know just about everything

there is to know about me, it's only fair to share the knowledge. Besides, you are the one who wanted to do this dating thing to get to know each other. If you don't want to talk, I'm perfectly content to have sex."

His blood went south, instant reaction stirring at her words. Damned if his body wouldn't be perfectly content to have sex, too. But as long as she was a suspect, he'd keep his pants on.

"Fair's fair," he agreed. "I have four sisters. Bossy, interfering know-it-alls, every one of them. We grew up in Grass Valley, an ancient house with more leaks and problems than money to fix them. One bathroom, four primping girls. It's a wonder I managed to shower at all in my teens."

"You love them a lot, huh?"

He glanced over, expecting to see mild disdain at best, all-out derision at worst. Instead, her eyes were filled with warmth and interest, her lips tilted in an encouraging smile.

"They're good people," he finally said, borrowing her earlier words. "All four are married now, which makes my mother happy. She's on the warpath for grandkids, but nobody is in a hurry to accommodate the demand."

"Aren't you her main target? I'd think there would be that whole 'family name' thing to live up to."

Jesse bit back a sigh. She didn't know the half of it. Of course, in his family's mind, his being a cop meant he was living up to the family name. Thankfully, no one but him knew the truth behind his father's reputation as a cop. Or how hard Jesse worked to make sure he didn't follow suit.

"Nope, her ticking grandma clock seems focused on the females. She's had a hard time since my dad died two years ago," he heard himself admitting. "I mean, I know she'd like to see me settled down and all. But she's old-fashioned, I guess. It's okay to nag at her daughters, but once dad was gone, I became the man of the family. To her mind, that means I'm above questioning and nagging."

Like his father had been.

"A get-out-of-nagging free pass?" she joked. "It sounds like she's a cool mom. Tough but loving. Like those old-fashioned moms you see on TV Land."

He gave a little laugh. Then as he thought of just how old-fashioned she was, his laughter died and bitterness coated his tongue.

"As much as I love my mother, that old-fashioned system might work for bringing up a decent pack of kids. But sometimes I wish to hell she'd been less subservient to her husband. Maybe if she'd laid down the law with him as well as she had with her kids, he might have shown more loyalty."

Jesse glanced at Audra, curled in the seat next to him. Faint shadows of exhaustion rimmed her eyes, but she still managed to look hot, sexy and sweet, all at the same time. Her gaze was locked on his face, a look of compassion in those eyes.

"He strayed, huh?"

"Yeah. She never let on like she knew, though. So maybe he kept it from her." Jesse had only found out after joining the P.D. His father's exploits were stuff of legend at the cop shop.

"She knew," Audra said softly. "A woman intuitive enough to successfully raise five kids, not a screwup in the bunch? She'd know."

"She never let on," he repeated.

"Like you said, she's strong. And it sounds like her family was number one. Some women believe it's more important to keep the family intact than open those closet doors and clean out the skeletons."

He considered that, then nodded. "Would you?"

"Keep the door closed?" she clarified. At his nod, she grimaced and shook her head. "Nope. Then again, I'm selfish and greedy. If I ever end up married, he'll be loyal or I'll castrate his sorry ass."

Even though he felt the same way, Jesse couldn't keep from clenching his thighs in protest.

"After all," she continued, "if I ever loved someone enough to promise him forever, that means my body as well as my heart, right?"

Jesse tried to shove aside the sudden, overwhelming urge to pummel this imaginary guy who would be lucky enough to have Audra's heart.

"So," she said in a bright tone, "it sounds like your family is still close, though?"

"Yeah, I guess we are," he agreed. "How about you? Are you close with your brother now?"

"I guess we are, yeah. Once Drew and I hooked back up, I even lived with him for a while. Until he got married, actually." Audra leaned her head against the seat and laughed. It was a sweetly sentimental sound that made Jesse grin. "Drew even bailed my sorry butt out of jail once."

Feeling her gaze on him, Jesse feigned a surprised look as he shot her a glance. "Jail? What did you do to land there?"

"I broke a friend out of death row," she said quietly. This time, Jesse didn't have to fake the look of shock on his face. Not at her words, but at the pain in her tone.

"Death row? That's pretty serious."

"Definitely. Jack, my dad's dog, was scheduled to be put down. He was a mean, nasty thing. The only way to keep him from snarling and biting was to give him booze. But he didn't deserve an ugly death. He'd got out one day and the pound wouldn't release him to me. Drew was out of town. I didn't have a choice…"

Her words trailed off, then she sucked in a breath and gave him a big smile. "It was sexy as hell. Middle of the night, clandestine behavior. Too bad the cops were such jerks. Even after I explained why I was breaking Jack loose, they threw the book at me. I'm a suspicious character, apparently."

"You mean you were then?"

"Nah, it's never changed. Cops don't trust me. They take one look, see bad girl, file me under guilty." The frustration in her tone was so subtle he almost missed it. Jesse knew he shouldn't feel like a total jerk, but he did. Then she flashed her usual smile and shrugged. "It's too bad, 'cause one of them was really cute. I mean, usually I have no use for the police, but you gotta admire a man who carries his own handcuffs."

Jesse gave a surprised laugh. He wondered if his having handcuffs might outweigh his being a cop in her eyes? Probably not.

Which brought him full circle back to the sister-in-law and the trip to China funded by *S.S.*

"You've come a long way from then, huh?"

"To say the least," Audra replied with a roll of her eyes.

"So, you seemed a little frazzled when I picked you up. Is work always this crazy for you?" he asked, changing the subject. He needed to nail down those initials. It was better to focus on the case than on the fact that Audra was the sweetest woman he knew wrapped up in the sexiest packaging he'd ever seen. Damned if this wasn't a confusing night.

"This is way overboard on the crazy times. Things are definitely not business as usual for me," Audra told him. "With Natasha in China and all the complications we've run into, I've been stuck with a lot more responsibility for the boutique than normal. I'd like to say I'm handling it well, but that'd be a total lie."

Perfect opening to grill her on the China connection.

"I'm sure you're doing great," Jesse heard himself saying instead. She seemed so assured in most things, it was weird to hear her sound less than confident.

"No. Not great. Barely decent. If it was just the boutique, I'd be fine. Or just the fall deadline. But now there are custom designs, and my own special project."

Special project? As in the triad?

"What kind of project?"

She shot him a look and pursed her lips as if she were trying to decide if she was going to share or not. He tried to look trustworthy and encouraging.

"It's kind of, well, personal."

"Audra, I've had my hand down your panties. I think we can share personal information, don't you?"

She laughed, but he could tell she was surprised at the analogy. What? She didn't think sex was personal? Special?

Jesse vowed then, when they had sex—and once he helped her straighten out her life, they damned well would be having sex—he'd make sure it felt both personal *and* special.

"Well," she said, for the first time since he'd known her, her tone shy, "I've been sketching up some new designs. I call this line *Twisted Knickers,* mostly because that's what will happen when Natasha sees it, get her panties all twisted."

"I don't get it? You're the designer, right? So that's your job."

"Technically, my job is to design lingerie in keeping with Simply Sensual's target market," Audra said, her dry tone making him laugh. "In case you didn't notice, the boutique caters to the sweeter side of sex. These designs are anything but sweet."

"Is that a problem?"

He caught Audra's shrug from the corner of his eye.

"It could be. I mean, it's reaching a point that I have to make a choice. I love working with Natasha, and she gave me my start. But the more I work on these, the more I want…need to see them realized. If she won't go for them, I'm going to have to find another outlet."

From the sound of it, that was a bad thing.

Jesse tried to figure where this might fit in with the triad and his case. No matter how he replayed her words, they didn't seem to have any deeper meaning.

Her voice, normally so upbeat and sensual, drooped with exhaustion. Jesse looked over to see her leaning her head against the window with her eyes at half-mast.

"You must be worn out. Not just worrying about the designs, but all the rest of the boutique business. Tiring, huh?"

"Yeah. I wish Sharon could have come in to help more, but she hasn't been feeling good. Add keeping that from Natasha to my list of irritating duties."

"Why would you be hiding this person's illness from your boss?"

"Sharon is her aunt. She's a total sweetie, a great lady. She'd actually sold Natasha the boutique and Simply Sensual a couple years back when she was diagnosed with M.S. She usually clerks in the boutique a few days a week."

Audra went on to explain about the health issues Sharon was dealing with and how crazy the work week had been as a result, but Jesse barely heard her.

Sharon? Natasha's aunt, as in *Sharon Stover?* S.S.? Jesse reviewed all the information he'd amassed on Simply Sensual and Audra, and had a giant *aha* moment.

That money wasn't connected to the Larson/*Du Bing Li* case. Not at all. It was simple coincidence. There was absolutely nothing to connect Audra to this case, other than the fact that Dave Larson had supposedly given her something in the club and that large sum of money in her account. Now that he knew the money was clean, that meant Audra was, too. He felt like yelling his triumph out the window of the car. He felt like pulling off to the side of the road, getting out and dancing on the hood. More than anything else, he felt like grabbing Audra to hug her close and kiss her.

She was innocent. Oh, sure, there were still a few *i*'s to dot and *t*'s to cross, but this information, along with his gut instinct, was enough to assure him she was one hundred percent innocent.

Of any crimes, at least.

AUDRA relaxed in the passenger seat of her car and watched Jesse navigate the streets to her apartment.

This had been one interesting date. Not one thing they'd done had fit into her realm of experience. First, she'd taken him to her childhood home. He'd watched her give in to sentiment and sing to an old man. Then she'd spilled her guts, not just about her childhood, but her design dreams.

Then? If that all hadn't been weird enough, they'd gone to the movies. A romantic comedy, complete with an extra large buttered popcorn, soda and, of all things, M&M's.

"You know," she told him in a contemplative tone, "I don't think I've gone to the movies with a guy since I was ten years old."

"Your dad?"

"Nah, a date. But that's the last one that took me to the movies." She laughed at the mock glare he sent her.

"After your barside serenade, I couldn't think of a lot of options," he said defensively.

"Really? I can think of a bunch. Clubbing. Sex. A fast drive to the ocean. Sex. Music at one of the jazz clubs. Sex."

"I think I'm seeing a theme there."

"Oh, yeah?"

"Yeah. They're all things that would keep us up late."

Audra snorted. "Especially the sex."

"That's an all-nighter for sure," he agreed.

His husky tone sent shivers down her back. Audra could picture them, wrapped around each other's naked bodies as they tore up the sheets. From his clenched jaw, so could Jesse.

"So what's wrong with an all-nighter?" she asked.

"Besides the good boy thing?" he asked, reminding her of his stupid getting-to-know-her plan. "You're exhausted and we both have to work tomorrow."

Audra gaped.

"You'd put work before sex?" The concept simply boggled the mind.

Jesse started to say something, then shot her a glance. He shrugged and pulled into her apartment complex's parking lot.

"Yeah," he admitted quietly as he parked in the slot she'd pointed out. "I mean, in some cases, work has to come first."

Audra shook her head. Maybe it was the stress of the week, or the unfamiliar sexual frustration, but she had to force herself to hold back her snarky retort.

What the hell was she doing with a guy who put work before sex? A good boy who was more into having dialogue than getting horizontal? A guy who didn't think relationships were something to bullshit his way out of?

"Look," she began, about to let her remark fly.

Jesse shot her a surprisingly effective look, making her shift back in the seat and shut her mouth.

"Sometimes you have to do what's right," Jesse said. "Like your designs. Even though you have a sweet job, a nice title, you're willing to take a risk with something you value. You're ready to risk that to be true to yourself. To your vision and what you believe in."

All she could do was stare. Snarky retort forgotten, Audra tried to calm her suddenly racing pulse. Had anyone ever seen her so clearly, understood her so well? And still wanted to be with her? Not that she had some poor-misunderstood-me thing going. Quite the opposite. She was an open book. But people tended to only be interested in reading certain chapters. In connecting with certain aspects of her. Her friends were the perfect example, wanting her to fit their vision, rather than accepting that she was too much to fit in some easy definition. Natasha wanted her to fit her version, too.

But Jesse looked at her as if she were his every sexual fantasy just waiting to come true. And he listened. Not just to her, but he'd sat for hours this evening listening to stories *about* her. As if he couldn't get enough.

Audra had to swallow twice to get past the lump in her throat.

"You say that like it's a good thing," she joked, trying to distract herself from the unfamiliar feeling of vulnerability.

At his raised brow, she shrugged. "I suppose it is, although this is exactly the kind of thing my friend, Isabel, lectures me on. I mean, who is crazy enough to finally grab their dream, only to throw it away because it's not all that *and* fries on the side?"

"A woman who believes in herself enough to fight to make sure that dream is exactly what she wants it to be. A woman strong enough to hold out for what she's worth," he suggested.

Never one to doubt her self-worth on the surface, his suggestion still made her frown. Was that why she was hesitating? Did she really believe in herself? She believed in her sexuality. Her body. Her ability to bring a man to his knees and have him beg. And she believed in her talent as a designer.

Didn't she?

Jesse shut off the ignition and turned to face her. He traced the back of a finger down her chin and leaned closer. Close enough that she could feel his breath on her cheek. She could see the banked heat in his eyes.

Yum. An answering fire sparked in her belly. He presented the perfect distraction from her neurotic soul-searching.

Not willing to wait and see if he'd move on the desire so clear in his eyes, she did it herself. With a little growl, Audra leaned forward and took Jesse's mouth with hers.

She slid her tongue over his lower lip, then nibbled at the delicious pillow of flesh. She felt him relax, the surprised tension leaving his body as she massaged his shoulder.

Hmm, relaxation was never her goal in a kiss. As sweet as this was, Audra decided she was gonna have to kick it up a notch.

With that in mind, she turned up the heat. An all-out sexual assault of tongue, teeth and lips, she used every skill at her disposal as a self-professed kissing expert.

Damned if his body didn't tense right back up again. She grinned against his mouth in satisfaction, then gave herself over to the kiss.

His moan of appreciation was muffled by the sound of blood rushing through her head. Maybe it was the pent-up anticipation. Maybe it was the edgy attraction that'd been building for the last week, or the dreams. Or even the phone sex. Whatever it was, just the touch of Jesse's lips beneath hers had Audra primed, wet and ready to explode.

"We seem to be making a habit of getting naughty in my car," she said with a breathless laugh as he trailed his lips down her throat.

"It's that voyeurism factor combined with a safety net," he murmured, his lips tracing a delicious pattern down to her collarbone.

"Safety?"

"Yeah." He pulled back to grin at her. His hair was all finger-mussed so that a long black strand trailed down his forehead in a way that made her heart melt. "After all, this damned car is too small to really get carried away."

"Oh, I don't know. I'll bet you do pretty well in tight spaces," Audra purred. Then she laughed and leaned back. Detecting weakness, she scanned his face. He was turned on, for sure. But he still had that good boy glint in his eyes.

Could her bad girl self overcome his good boy reticence? She'd put money on it.

Audra leaned forward to brush that sexy strand of hair off his forehead and gave Jesse a long look from under her lashes.

"I suppose you're right. It's probably time for both of us to be getting into bed."

She watched his throat move as he swallowed and hid her grin. Excitement warred with relief. She wanted Jesse like crazy, but there was more to her excitement than simple wanting. She was grateful to know she hadn't lost her sexual mojo, but there was more to her relief than simple ego.

Bottom line? She wanted Jesse like she'd never wanted any man before. And since she didn't know what to do about it, she'd go with her fallback answer. Seduce him into a puddle of lust, and have her wicked way with him.

"I'll walk you to your door," he offered.

Smiling her agreement, Audra waited for him to come around and open the door before she slid from the car. As she stood, she made sure her breasts brushed his chest. Her breath caught at the delicious sensation. The dark desire in his eyes was gratifying thanks for her effort.

She led the way to her apartment, sexual energy zinging between them like an electrical arc. She had it all figured out.

She'd open the door, give him enough time to clear the threshold, then slam the door shut and pin him up against the wall.

Hot, wall-banging sex. What better way to see how high he rated on the orgasm scale?

11

JESSE TRIED TO FOCUS on something other than the hypnotic sway of Audra's hips as she led the way to her front door. Even though he knew, both instinctively and with the new evidence, she was innocent—at least of the involvement with the triad—she was still off-limits. Until he'd come clean, told her the truth, he couldn't give in to his raging desire.

Nope. Like he'd told Audra, he was a good boy. He had control. He wasn't ruled by lust.

Audra reached her door and pulled keys out of a tiny purse. The look she tossed over her shoulder, pure temptation combined with the promise that she could make his every dream come true, sent all the blood in his brain south. So much for control.

Clearly reading his struggle, Audra giggled. The sound was both sultry and sweet, filled with heat and delight. It summed her up perfectly.

Jesse realized, in that moment, he was lost. Body, heart and soul, he was hers.

Without a word, she pushed the door open and took his hand. Other than an impression of flash and color, he barely noticed the interior. His attention completely focused on Audra.

In a smooth move, she pulled him inside and shut the door behind him. One step, then two, and he was trapped against the door. She didn't touch, instead letting the promised heat of her body, the heady scent of her perfume, seduce.

"I decided to take your advice," she told him with a sultry smile as she tapped her finger against his lips.

"Huh?"

"I know what I want and know I'm worth having it."

She took a small step, just enough for him to feel the brush of her breasts against his chest. Jesse's head spun.

"I'm strong enough to take it, too," she informed him softly. "But I'd rather take turns."

The images flashed in fast-forward through his head. All hot, all naked, all intense. Each of them taking turns giving the other the ultimate pleasure.

Jesse tried to reel himself back. Tried to get control.

"Taking turns, huh? Maybe I'm not that kind of guy," he said.

"That's okay. I'm enough of that kind of woman for both of us."

His heart skipped a beat at the naughty promise in Audra's smile. Even the cocky arch of her brow excited him. She was a fantasy come true, with that slightly wicked, dark edge to her. The kind that came without guarantees or safety nets.

The kind of woman that forced a man to ask himself if he was sure he had what it took to handle her. To satisfy her. A warning voice screamed in his head to watch out. She was involved in his case, even if she was no longer a suspect. He stifled the voice with a reminder that he wasn't using her for information or to forward his investigation.

Jesse swallowed. She tilted her head to one side, obviously giving him a last shot at running. Instead, Jesse took that last emotional step and, throwing caution and good sense aside, slid his hands over her lush hips and pulled her against his straining body.

With that one move, he risked it all. His reputation, his self-image and his job ethics. And most of all, his shot at a real relationship with Audra after this was all over.

All hesitation took a fast dive down a sheer cliff when their lips met. One hand on the sweet curve of her waist, Jesse ran his fingers over the delicious length of her silk-encased thigh. His hand slid easily under her flirty skirt to cup her bare butt, realizing as he did that rather than panty hose, she wore stockings and a garter.

Their mouths battled for control. Neither of them tried to dominate the other; instead, they were both doing their damndest to drive the other crazy. Jesse traced the lace edge of the garter, running his fingers under the elastic to feel her warm skin. Skin he needed to see, ached to taste.

With a low growl, he pulled his lips from hers and stared down into her passion-clouded eyes. She stared back, challenge clear in the set of her chin.

"Not bad," she murmured in a teasing tone. "A kiss like that's a nice start toward at least a six on the orgasm scale."

"Six, my ass," he promised. "I'll have you seeing stars and crying my name before you can count that high."

"Big talk."

Jesse didn't bother answering. Instead, he dropped to his knees in front of her. Audra's grin was pure dare. She cocked her brow, then shifted so she leaned against the wall. In a deliberate move, she placed one foot on either side of his knees.

Her gaze holding his, she trailed the back of her hand over her cheek. He thought of their sexy phone call, heat intensified low in his belly. His gut clenched at the remembered intensity of their words, their shared fantasy.

Using the backs of her hands, Audra caressed her throat in a slow, sensuous slide until she reached her cleavage. Like a generous offering, she slid her hands down to cup her breasts, holding them in obvious pleasure.

Jesse swallowed hard as her thumbs flicked over the tips, just a couple swipes, and he could see the beaded nipples pressing against her silky blouse. He wanted to take those peaks between his teeth, suck them until she screamed.

But first, he had a six to beat.

His gaze still holding hers, he reached out to embrace her calves. His fingers smoothed over the fine seam of her stockings, climbing up the back of her knees, up her thighs until he reached the lacy top. Again, he smoothed over the elastic garter.

He groaned in protest when her hands left her breasts. Then she winked, reached down and lifted her skirt for him. She took the hem, tucked it into the waistband, baring herself to his hungry gaze.

"Just thought I'd make it a little easier for you," she said with a naughty laugh. Jesse didn't bother responding. He wasn't sure he could speak if he'd tried. He eyed the tiny magenta triangle between him and heaven. His hands left her garter and cupped the smooth, tight skin of her bare ass. One finger snagged the string of her thong and pulled. With a wiggle, she helped him release her femininity from its tiny bit of modesty.

"Should I start counting?" she challenged in a tone husky with desire.

Jesse cupped the feminine treasure she'd bared for his worship, the other still kneading her cheek. He slipped a finger into her folds, loving the wet heat that greeted him. The scent of her desire intensified the pressure against his zipper. Enough of the slow buildup; he was ready to hear her scream his name.

"Go for it," he instructed just before he took the slick folds into his mouth.

AUDRA'S BREATH shuddered out as Jesse worked his magical mouth over her. His tongue traced along her swollen lips while his finger slipped in and out, in and out. The tempo slowly increased, her breathing along with it.

Damn, he just might make a seven. She'd have bet that was impossible with clothes still on.

He sucked at her clitoris at the same time he shifted the tempo. All feeling, all of her focus, centered on those ever-so-sensitive nerve endings he was so expertly coaxing. Her slick heat coated his fingers as he moved faster. The pressure wound tighter, her breath came in gasps now as her body climbed.

Her eyes closed, and Audra grasped Jesse's head. Her fingers curled into the silky softness of his hair. She let her own head fall back against the wall, her hips undulating against his talented mouth. When his hand left her butt, she almost moaned in protest.

Then he reached up to cup her breast. He tweaked her stiff nipple at the same time he scraped his teeth over the swollen bud of her clitoris. That combination, with the swift pumping of his finger, sent her over the shuddering edge.

Audra panted, hanging on to the orgasm with all her might. Her body tense with the intensity of the sensations ripping through her, she finally gave in and rode the wave of pleasure to its crest.

Her head too heavy to lift from the wall, she couldn't even open her eyes when she felt Jesse move from between her legs. She heard a rustle, the metallic slide of a zipper, then the sound of ripping foil, telling her he was tearing open a condom package. Before it all registered, though, Jesse's hands tore the fragile fabric of her blouse from her with a loud rip.

Audra gasped and her eyes flew open just in time to see the almost feral look on his face as he stared down at her now naked chest. He met her eyes and gave her a tight grin before he cupped both breasts in his hands. He held her stiff nipples between his middle and index fingers, pinching them as he squeezed her breasts together with just enough pressure to make her catch her breath.

"It's going to feel so good you're going to scream," he promised just before he took one of those aching nipples into his mouth.

Desire swirled higher and higher, building and tightening until she was ready to scream for him to hurry. Audra felt as if she were running a race against her own body, rushing toward the promise of a pleasure so fine she'd never forget it.

She clutched at his shoulders, loving the feel of muscle rippling beneath her fingers.

With one large hand, he wrapped her leg around his waist and thrust into her. Audra whimpered at the delicious length of him as he embedded himself fully in her welcoming body.

When she grasped his shoulders, Jesse pulled away, his dick slick with her juices. She made a sound of protest and he grinned. Someone was getting a kick out of his power over her body. She'd have issue with it if it weren't for the fact that he was doing such a good job, he deserved all the jollies he wanted. In fact, she intended to make sure he got his jollies off like never before.

With that in mind, she trailed her hand down his chest, scraping her fingernail over his nipple. Jesse's eyes narrowed, and Audra could see the pulse at the base of his neck beat a little harder. Good. Time to show him a little of her power.

She wasn't sure why, was almost afraid to find out, but she'd never wanted to make a guy as crazy for her as she did with Jesse. Crazy for her body. For what she could do to his. For what they could do together. It was like a deep-seated need, more powerful than anything she'd ever felt before.

She smoothed her palm down his flat belly, her fingers tingling as they trailed over the crisp path of hair leading to his stiff dick. She curled her hand over his straining flesh, her fingers sliding easily over the wet, latex-covered silk.

Jesse growled and grabbed her hand. He raised it to his mouth, licking the damp evidence of her pleasure from her fingers. The desire, so tightly wound in her belly, speared out at the move, need spiking through her system.

Her hand still in his, he grabbed the other one, too. He raised her arms over her head, bracketing her wrists in one hand to hold her captive as he slowly, ever so incredibly slowly, slid back into her waiting flesh. His eyes holding hers captive, he pumped in and out. Audra pressed forward to meet each thrust.

It was the look in those eyes, that ever-narrowing look of hunger, that seduced her as much as the delicious things he was doing to her body.

The curling heat in her system climbed again. Her lower lip tight between her teeth, she watched his eyes for the signal of his own loss of control. Jesse's movements came faster, his breath harsher. Audra struggled to hold on, to keep control. She wanted his mouth against hers, but couldn't bear to release his gaze.

He thrust, held. His gaze flickered. Her entire body so tense she felt she was going to rip apart, she started to lose her grip. Audra's lids fluttered as the climax started deep in her belly, its power ripping through her in a vicious rush of pleasure so intense it bordered on pain.

Not willing to go over alone, she met his next thrust with a grinding motion, her leg wrapped around his waist so she used her foot to press him deeper. To hold him tight as she undulated against him.

Jesse's guttural cry of release was the last straw. Audra exploded with a panting cry of pleasure. The orgasm was like a wild storm, ripping through her with devastating ferociousness.

She'd finally met a guy good enough for her bad self. That

was her last thought before she lost all awareness of anything but the pleasure.

IT WAS at least five minutes before Jesse could even consider raising his head from Audra's shoulder and trying to breathe again.

"Damn," he muttered against Audra's hair. "I can't feel my legs."

Audra's foot did a long, slow slide down his ass and over the back of his thigh. Her spiked heel caught in the jeans pooled around his ankles. He winced at the reminder of his tacky haste. What kind of guy took a woman against the wall with his pants still halfway on?

Shame tap-danced its way over his conscience. What a jerk. He should be shot. Oh, sure, he'd made her scream as promised. But where was finesse? Gentleness?

Dread filled him as he forced himself to pull back.

An apology on his tongue, Jesse got a good look at Audra's face. Her head still against the wall, her features were slack with pleasure. A faint smile played around her lips like a naughty secret just waiting to be shared.

Sensing his stare, she opened her eyes to meet his gaze. After a couple seconds, she cocked a brow and tilted her head in a considering way.

"Well, well…"

Jesse's ego swelled at the considerable pleasure in her voice. He tried to keep the grin from taking over his face, but doubted his success.

"Look at you, all satisfied and smug," she teased.

"As long as you're satisfied and smug, too," he returned, sliding away from her with regret. "Never let it be said I'm the kind of guy to hog smug satisfaction all to myself."

Audra laughed with delight. Then, in a move that sealed

his heart's devotion to her forever, she stood on tiptoe to brush a sweet kiss over his lips. The act, pure affectionate joy, was even more emotionally intense than their lovemaking.

Jesse had to swallow his declaration of devotion. He was sure nothing could be more guaranteed to get his ass kicked out of her apartment and her life. And he planned to do everything in his power to stay in both.

Instead, he pulled away to dispose of the condom. He watched as she slipped off what was left of her ripped blouse. She eyed it, then him, and winked.

"I'm proud and humbled to say you, my amazing man, scored a sweet eight on the 'O' scale." She glanced at the shredded fabric again, then grinned. "Actually, I swear just the memory of that little session gives me a mini-orgasm. That has to kick you up to an eight and a half."

Pride and affection mingled as Jesse returned her smile. He brushed his finger over her bare breast, just above the nipple. Her body gave a satisfying response, the dark coral bud tightening.

"What do you say we try for a nine?" he suggested.

She rolled her eyes, but her smile told him she was pleased.

"I have to warn you, if you stay you won't get any sleep. I doubt I'll be able to keep my hands off you."

"I still don't want to leave," he admitted.

"I thought you were a good boy?"

"I'm good enough to score that nine," he promised.

"I like a man with a goal," she said with a laugh. Then she unsnapped her rumpled skirt and pushed it off her hips.

With a wink, she stood before him in a garter belt, black stockings, those wicked gladiator-style sandals and a glittery belly button ring. Jesse's body, so recently satisfied, stirred with interest.

"Let's try it horizontal this time," she suggested. Then she turned and led the way to her bedroom. She shot him a wicked glance over her shoulder. "Don't forget, it's my turn to take advantage."

His eyes glued to the hypnotic sway of her bare-except-for-the-garter-belt hips, he realized he couldn't wait.

A FAINT CHIME sounded from somewhere far away, tugging Audra from her deep sleep. She felt Jesse pull away from her, immediately missing the comfort of his warmth.

That thought pulled her the rest of the way out of sleep. With a frown, she watched Jesse's sweet butt as he bent over to tug the chiming cell phone from the pocket of his discarded jeans.

When had a man's body in her bed brought comfort? Pleasure? Often.

Satisfaction? Mandatory.

But this sweet sense of comfort and sappy emotions? Audra wrinkled her nose. What was up with this? Not that the sight of Jesse's naked body in the soft morning light wasn't a total turn-on. But to want to cuddle just as much as she wanted to make him arch his body in gasping pleasure beneath her mouth?

Panic overwhelmed the desire in her stomach, taking control and making her pulse skitter.

She understood sex. But emotions? What did she know about emotions? If she wasn't careful, she'd start thinking crazy. Start considering futures and having hopes and depending on someone other than herself.

Since the entire concept was impossible, and she knew it, she'd have to nip this in the bud. Send Jesse on his way with a thanks and a kiss, like she'd done so many guys before.

And if her heart spasmed at the concept, well, all the more reason to do it.

Audra caught sight of herself in the wall-to-ceiling mirrored closet doors. Her hair was spiked in bad girl wildness, and her chest was red with whisker burns. Swollen lips and heavy eyes greeted her inspection. She looked well-loved, satisfied and damned smug.

Exactly as she should after a night of incredible sex. Hell, Jesse had even scored the mythical nine. Maybe nine and a half, but she'd passed out, so it was hard to tell.

This wasn't gooey emotional crap, she assured herself. It was sexual satisfaction. No reason to kick the guy out of her bed for that.

Happy now that she'd settled that in her head, she raised her arms overhead, pointing her toes to the foot of the bed, and stretched the stiffness from her body. Thoroughly satisfied, she slid her hands over her breasts in pleasure. Maybe they had time for another go-round before work?

"I'm a little busy," Jesse said in a low whisper. "No, you handle it. I'll be in later. Right now I'm…" Jesse glanced over and winced when he caught Audra staring at him. "I'm busy," he finished.

With his sleepy eyes, tousled hair and guilty look, he was like a naughty little boy caught with his hand in the cookie jar.

It made a woman glad to be a cookie.

Audra gave him a wink.

He blushed.

She ignored the melting feeling in her heart and shifted to her side, letting the sheet fall away.

His gaze slid from her face to her bare breasts. The heat in his eyes was enough to make her wet.

Then the person on the phone said something, Jesse's eyes got huge and he ripped his gaze from her body as if he'd been slapped on the back of the head.

She giggled and opened her mouth to tease him, but he gave her a frantic hand motion to hush. One brow raised, she leaned across the bed to grab one of the pillows from the floor. Sliding back to a sitting position, she was glad to see Jesse's gaze back on her body. His glazed look promised she'd be starting the day quite nicely.

Audra grinned and plumped the pillow behind her back, then settled against it to listen to his conversation. And, of course, enjoy the view of his nude body and its gratifying reaction to her nakedness.

"Sorry," Jesse said as he pushed the Off button with look of relief. He tossed his cell phone back on his jeans and shrugged. "That was the office. There's a job they need me to take care of this morning."

"Isn't it awfully early in the morning to have to deal with business calls? That's what voice mail is for."

"I can't ignore the phone when I hear it. I guess it's a good boy thing," he said with a grin.

Then he curved his large, warm hand over her bare hip, and Audra shoved the curiosity aside and focused on the here and now. Tingles of awareness shivered through her. Desire, never far from the surface when she was around Jesse, flamed higher. Audra reached out and pressed her palm against his chest, combing her fingers through the smooth hair. She glanced at the clock. Six-thirty. Plenty of time for breakfast.

"You know," she said, leaning forward to run her tongue around his nipple, "I seem to have developed a serious yen for good boys."

"Oh, yeah?" Jesse's smile turned her on almost as much as the hand that was now caressing her butt.

"Yeah. So, seeing as I'm feeling generous, I think you should be rewarded."

"For being a good boy?"

"Well, that and the level nine orgasm you so awesomely

rocked my world with last night," she said with a delighted shiver of remembrance.

Jesse took her mouth with his. She leaned into his kiss with a purr. The taste of him filled her senses, his tongue dragging her deeper and deeper into passion. His scent enveloped her and Audra just wanted to grab his broad shoulders and never let go.

He slowly eased back, the kiss tapering from passion to soft, sweet nibbled kisses on her lower lip. When Jesse pulled completely away, Audra's lashes fluttered open. She met his rich brown gaze with a passion-glazed one of her own.

"That'd be a nine and a half, thank you very much," he corrected.

She blinked twice, then burst out laughing. "Can't forget that half, can we?"

"Would you want to?"

"Definitely not. And," she said, pulling away and giving him a pat on the cheek, "I'd say such a grand accomplishment definitely deserves a reward."

"What? A T-shirt proclaiming me the best sex you've ever had?"

"Your ego is no little thing there, is it?" she said with a roll of her eyes as she slid from the bed.

Jesse glanced down at his dick, then back at her with both brows raised. Audra got his point and couldn't keep from laughing.

"Okay, so you probably deserve a little stroking. Your ego, too. For now, though, will you settle for breakfast?"

Jesse's mouth dropped open. "Breakfast? As in you'd make me food? To eat?"

"You say that like it's such a crazy concept that I can cook." Audra tugged a T-shirt over her head, its hem brushing the top of her thighs. The bunny on the front proclaimed her Cute But Psycho.

Jesse swung his legs over the side of the bed and stared at her in puzzlement as he pulled his jeans on. "I can imagine you doing just about anything. Hell, I *have* imagined you doing any number of things. It's just that cooking isn't anywhere on the list."

"Ye of little faith."

With a heavy dose of body English in her hips, she led the way to the kitchen. She gestured for him to have a seat at the tiny bistro table.

He watched avidly as she sauntered to the pantry. Audra shot him a naughty look over her shoulder, then reached in and pulled out an octagonal-shaped jar with a gold foil label.

Jesse's eyes lit up like fireworks at the sight of the chocolate fudge topping.

"You went out and bought that?" he asked in delight.

"Nope. I've had it a while. It's actually my favorite ice cream topping. Among other things."

"Breakfast?" he asked.

"Breakfast in bed," she corrected as she dipped her finger in chocolate, then rubbed it over his bottom lip.

12

HE WASN'T REALLY a spiritual man, but Jesse had to admit if there was a heaven, this was his idea of it. An incredible night, out-of-this-world sex and the perfect woman. He vowed to make damned sure not to lose any of them.

He lay back on the cool sheets of Audra's bed, the scent of their lovemaking mingling with the exotic vanilla aroma of the candles she had all over the place. Morning light filtered through the filmy curtains, giving the room a soft glow.

Of course, the woman standing at the foot of the bed, her nude body a work of art in the golden light, could never be termed an angel.

Thank God.

"How hot do you like it?" she asked with a teasing grin. She used her index finger to stir the chocolate sauce still in its glass jar. The rich scent of chocolate overlaid the other scents in the air.

Jesse's body stirred, realizing this woman was about to make one of his wildest fantasies come true. Could life get any better?

"I'll take it as hot as you can get it," he assured her, folding his hands behind his head as he leaned back against the headboard.

Audra peered at him, then shook her head and tut-tutted.

"What?"

"You look much too comfortable there. Like you're a despotic king about to enjoy being serviced."

Jesse burst out laughing. Had he ever had so much fun with a woman? Sure, the sex was the best in his life. But just the fun? Even more than sexy, Audra was quirky and sweet. The woman, he realized with sudden, absolute conviction, he wanted to spend the rest of his life with.

The realization didn't even bother him. It just felt good. Felt right. He probably best keep it to himself, though. Or she'd kick him out of bed without chocolate.

"Despotic?" he asked instead.

"Yeah. Like you're so sure you know what's coming next and it's all about you."

"All about *us*," he corrected with a grin. Because no matter who did what, he'd be getting pleasure beyond belief. *That* he knew. And there was no way he'd be stopping until her pleasure was ripped from her while she screamed with ecstasy.

With a roll of her eyes, Audra slowly shook her head.

"Never get too comfortable," she warned. "The last thing I'll ever be is predictable."

With that, she pulled her fingers out of the chocolate and lifted them to her mouth. Holding his gaze, she sucked first one, then both fingers into her mouth. Her tongue slid down the length of her hand, sipping up the chocolate that had dripped down to her wrist.

Jesse swallowed, trying to wet his suddenly parched throat. More than anything, he wanted to taste that chocolate. But only if it was off her body.

Eyes narrowed, he watched her dip her fingers back in the jar, coming up with a scoop of the rich brown liquid. He held his breath and waited to see where she'd put it. And wished with all his might it was somewhere he could lick it off.

"We're gonna play a little game," she informed him.

Her words seemed to be coming from a distance through the blood roaring in his ears. She lifted her chocolate-drenched fingers to her breast, the deep brown confection a vivid contrast to her pearly white skin and coral nipples. All his concentration was focused on the sight of those fingers swirling the sweet syrup over her nipple.

Jesse leaned forward and grabbed her by the waist. Audra knelt on the mattress between his spread legs, but that was as close as she came. He sat forward, trying to get a taste, but she leaned back, limbo style.

"Nope," she said. "It's my game."

"Are you going to tell me the rules?" he asked.

"Of course not," she said with a light laugh.

He'd have objected, but she was now spreading chocolate over *his* nipples.

"I'll give you a hint, though. The first round—"

"Round?" he interrupted. His dick was already so hard it could drive nails and she planned to go *rounds?* The woman was crazy.

"The first round," she said again with a raised brow, "is follow the leader. You have to do what I do, match for match."

Jesse grinned. Given the directions were already painted in chocolate, this would be a definite pleasure. Anticipation making him cocky, Jesse reached out and flicked his finger over her chocolate-covered nipple.

"But," she said as he stuck his finger in his mouth and sucked at the bittersweet flavor, "I'm the leader. Which means you can *only* do what I do. No improvising."

"No…"

"None." She tilted her head to the side and, watching him through hooded eyes, cupped her hand under her breast as if offering it up for his pleasure. "Can you follow the rules?"

"As long as I get to set them for round two."

"Deal," she agreed.

Then she leaned forward and used that amazing tongue of hers to drive him insane.

His head spinning with sensations, Jesse gave in to the game. He followed her lead, reveling in the sensations as she tormented his body with her mouth, her hands and her own sweet body.

On his turn, he gave equal measure. Jesse wasn't sure which was more exciting—the satisfaction of Audra's body writhing with pleasure beneath his mouth, or how incredible she felt and tasted. Jesse's mind was a fog of sharp, edgy need. All he could think of was the woman in bed with him, even as his body screamed for release.

With slitted eyes, he watched Audra lean back and scoop in another fingerful of chocolate. Sitting forward, she took his mouth in deep, biting kisses. He was so into it that it wasn't until he felt her grip his dick in her slick fingers that he realized they'd moved on to the pinnacle of round one.

She scooted down to kneel between his legs, and Jesse knew this was heaven. Barely holding on to control, he watched as she licked away the chocolate and knew he wasn't going to last much longer.

With a groan, he pulled her up to meet his mouth.

"My turn," he said against her lips. "This time, we'll see who can make the other scream first."

AUDRA'S BREATH shuddered at the look in Jesse's eyes. His face tight with desire, he slipped around so they both lay on their sides facing one another with his feet toward the foot of the bed, hers toward the top, their mouths within easy kissing distance of each others.

"More follow the leader?" she asked after he brushed a soft, sweet kiss over her mouth.

"Follow my lead," he said, trailing his lips over her jaw, then down her throat. Since he was essentially upside down, his chest was now in front of her face.

Nice.

Audra took advantage of the delicious expanse of well-muscled flesh. Gliding her hands over the smooth plane of his chest, she used her teeth and tongue to tease his nipples.

She wanted to focus on making him scream. Proving her own sexual prowess by driving him wilder than he'd ever been before. But he had his mouth on one breast, nibbling little kisses in an ever-tightening circle. And all she could think was *Please hurry.* She had to feel his mouth on her nipple, his teeth. Something.

As if he'd heard her silent plea, Jesse took one stiff bud in his mouth at the same time he tweaked the other with his fingers. Already dripping with desire, Audra squirmed.

Gentleman that he was, Jesse released her breast and slid his open palm down her body until he reached her aching core. Audra gasped when his fingers flicked her throbbing center. She was ready to explode. And damned if she'd go alone.

She pulled away and slid down so his hard length was in front of her face. Jesse shifted so he was on his back, she on her knees over him.

Audra took him into her mouth at the same time he licked his tongue along her swollen lips. She pressed herself to him and used every bit of talent she had with her mouth and hands to send him higher and higher.

Her breath coming in gasps, Audra lost her focus. Forgotten was her intent to drive Jesse crazy. She couldn't find the energy to care about proving her prowess. She sucked his delicious flesh into her mouth, her hands cupping his jewels and giving him a gentle squeeze.

She felt the tension in his body, the involuntary pumping of his hips and knew Jesse was right there…so close.

And with a swirl of her tongue and the lightest scrape of her teeth along his head, she sent him moaning over the edge. She swallowed deep, taking in his essence.

With barely enough energy to grin at her triumph, Audra focused on the feelings surging through her body. The sensations reached that painful edge between pleasure and pain, winding tighter and tighter. Then, like an overwound spring, the desire suddenly snapped.

The orgasm ripped through her in a wild torrent. Like free-falling over a cliff, Audra could only feel. She lost herself in the incredible power of her climax, vaguely aware of Jesse's hand smoothing the small of her back. Grounding her body to reality while the rest of her floated somewhere in a wild never-never land of pleasure.

Audra wasn't aware of whether Jesse moved or if she did. But when she finally became conscious of anything other than the aftershocks of pleasure surging through her, she realized Jesse was holding her against him, her head tucked against his shoulder.

Audra sighed and cuddled in the warmth of his arms. This was good. The best sex of her life, and the greatest guy she'd ever met. Love didn't suck as bad as she'd thought it would.

With a start, Audra's eyes flew open and she replayed the discovery. Her body was too worn out from a long night of deliciously decadent sex, but her mind was suddenly wide-awake.

And totally freaked-out.

This couldn't be love. Could it?

Unlike the guy she'd thought she loved when she was seventeen, Jesse appreciated her. He'd never ask her to drop out of school to join him on a cross-country trip, only to leave her stranded in Nebraska.

Instead, Jesse seemed to accept every aspect of Audra's personality, including her odd little quirks and weird habits. He had more faith in her designs that even she did. And that was saying a lot. He made her feel good inside. A kind of good she'd never experienced before. The kind that lasted through fights, sexual dry spells, old age.

The scary kind.

She wasn't ready for love. Hell, she didn't know who she was anymore. How could she share her heart with another person when she was in the middle of an identity crisis? The last thing she needed was a guy—even a guy as hot, sexy and sweet as Jesse—confusing the issues even more.

Besides, it was too soon. They'd only just had sex. There was no way to know if a physical relationship this intense had any shot at lasting more than a few orgasms.

Audra ignored the little voice in the back of her head mocking her fancy steps around the issue. She had enough to deal with already. She'd worry about finding an acceptable definition for what she felt for Jesse later.

After a few more of those orgasms.

She groaned as he moved against her. He had to be kidding. She'd just had a mind-blowing orgasm, followed by several very sweet smaller trips over pleasure hill. He couldn't want to do it again?

"Shower?" he murmured against her hair.

"That way," she said, half-heartedly pointing toward the bathroom.

"Join me?"

Audra pulled back to see his face.

A night's growth covered his cheeks, giving him a tousled pirate look. His eyes gleamed with satisfaction and something else she was afraid to try to identify. She was too tired and worn out to even worry, though. The man had just experienced the best sex of his life. He had a right to look a little smug.

"As many times as you rose to the occasion, so to speak," Audra teased, "I doubt you'd be able to do justice to a dual shower."

"Wanna bet?" he challenged.

She wasn't sure if she had enough energy to actually walk to the bathroom, let alone go another round of sexual gymnastics.

But she'd be damned if she'd back down.

So Audra winked and reached around to pat his ass.

"Babe, I'm all yours. Let's see what you've got."

There was nothing like good chocolate to top off a night of excellent sex. Audra popped an M&M into her mouth and savored the delicious taste. She hummed a little as she slid her leg into the silky welcome of her stocking. With a practiced move, she hooked the garter and stood, shaking out her skirt.

Music pounded through the living room speakers, giving a nice downbeat for her impromptu dance of joy. She felt great. Sexy, satisfied and unstoppable.

With a shudder of remembered delight, Audra glanced at the bed. Nine and a half. Jesse was definitely a keeper.

One last look in the mirror assured her she was ready for her date, even though Jesse wasn't due for another fifteen minutes.

Which was a testament to her feelings for him, since Audra's policy was never to hurry date preparation. But she couldn't wait to see him. And not just for the sex, although the thought of that had kept her juices stirred all day long.

Just as her thoughts were heating up, her cell phone rang. "When You Wish Upon a Star" chimed out.

"Speaking of good sex," Audra said with a grin as she answered her phone. "Hey, Isabel."

The only thing more satisfying than a night of the best sex of your life was knowing your friends were getting their own. It made gloating so much easier. Audra bit her lip, hoping Isabel hurried with her greeting so she could share the awesomeness of her nine-and-a-half night.

"Don't mention sex to me," her friend growled.

"What?"

"Live a little, you said. Go ahead and let loose, enjoy. Great advice, Audra."

With a frown for the hurt beneath the snippy words, Audra sank to her bed. "What happened?"

Isabel hiccuped, then sniffed. Audra's heart dropped. *Damn. It was bad.*

Her mind raced. Kinky sex? That'd freak Isabel out for sure. Even years of Audra's influence hadn't prepared the woman for fur-lined handcuffs. Bad grooming? That wasn't so bad, but Isabel wouldn't have gone for the guy if he were a slob. How bad could it be?

"Randy's married."

Shit. That *was* bad.

"You're sure?" Audra asked quietly.

A rare sense of guilt felt like a lead weight in her belly as Audra listened to Isabel.

"He says he's separated. That's why he has his own apartment. He claims they're getting divorced, but have to work out the details first."

Audra grimaced. Those excuses wouldn't matter to Isabel. Hell, they wouldn't matter to Audra, either. Separated meant still married. While that might be a fine distinction, it was an important one. It put him off-limits until he'd dealt with his issues. The only thing worse than a man who cheated on his wife was a man who was still tied up in a marriage he claimed was over. Those strings were usually ugly and painful.

"Isabel, I'm sorry. I shouldn't have encouraged you to let go and get wild. At least, not without warning you to do a status check first."

"It's not your fault," Isabel said with a sigh and another hiccup. "I've listened to you advising those status checks often enough, I should know better. I just never thought it'd happen to me, you know?"

"I know." Audra glanced at the clock. Jesse was due any second. "Look, do you want me to come over? I can pick up some ice cream, grab a couple DVDs. We'll eat junk food and dish dirt."

"Nah. I'd rather be alone."

After a few more minutes of bad-mouthing the worthless Randy and assuring herself that Isabel would be okay, Audra finally hung up. Just as she did, the doorbell rang.

Even as she moved to open the door for Jesse and their hot date, she couldn't help but wonder if her bad girl ways were to blame for her friend's heartbreak. How ironic that she was turning into such a goody-goody over Jesse, and yet she still managed to be a bad influence.

DAVE LARSON shielded the apartment door with his shoulders as he worked a long piece of metal in the lock. Piece of cake. He'd go in, look around for his tie, be back out in fifteen minutes flat. And since this Audra chick was such a good friend of his Bea, he wouldn't even lift anything. Well, unless it was cash. Cash always came in handy. Once he'd snipped this nagging little thread, he'd be on his way to easy street. With the second half of his payment, he'd be *on* easy street. The perfect life. Riches, high-powered connections and the woman of his dreams.

Watch out, world, Dave Larson was about to make his mark. And for once, he was making it in style, with a hot chickie by his side. The luscious Bea, woman enough to inspire him to even give up his porn. He'd shower her with jewels, buy her way onto the cover of any magazine she wanted.

All he had to do was retrieve that chip and make sure his ass was covered with the triad.

He could barely keep from patting himself on the back. Tracking down the Walker chick had been easy. A few questions to Bea while she'd serviced him, a few clicks of the computer mouse. That's all it had taken to get the name, home and work address of the only person who might block his road to success.

With a quiet snick of the lock, he swung her front door open and sneered. He was as good at breaking into buildings as he was hacking computers.

Wiping a bead of sweat from his chin, Davey scanned the sparsely furnished apartment. It was like pictures he'd seen of Mardi Gras. Bright colors, a lot of shimmer and shine. Dave eyed the wide purple couch. He'd bet it saw a lot of action. Other than the couch and a pile of oversized throw pillows, some big, fancy dresser with doors holding a TV and stereo and a few plants, it was empty.

He took a quick look around and then headed for the bedroom. Fifteen minutes later, Davey was sweating up a storm. Nothing. No tie. No evidence of any triad connections on her computer, either. He had found sex toys, plenty of leather and enough lingerie to dress the entire cast of his favorite weekly porn series. But that was it. Could she have thrown it away? Probably. This was a waste of his time.

He checked out the other bedroom. It was small, almost claustrophobic. The sketch-covered walls didn't help the suffocating effect. Ignoring the deficiency of air, he took a minute to appreciate those, given they were of women in lingerie. Fabric was stacked on the corners, piled on the floor.

A rope hung from one wall to the next, fancy strings, beads and trim stuff draped over it. He rifled through them. No tie there. A quick glance over the large drafting table didn't reveal any fabric. No tie there. Just as he was turning to leave, though, something caught his eye.

Dave grabbed the paper with a frown. The words, written in a loopy scrawl, made his gut churn.

A list of names and addresses. All in China. He recognized one as a money-laundering front for the *Wo Shing Wo* triad.

Son of a bitch. Sweat slid down the back of his neck as Dave tried to catch a breath. This Walker chick had obviously duped him. She had connections in China. Crime connections that were going to end his life. Dave didn't recognize the address on the paper, but it was all the proof he needed that he'd been double-crossed.

Rage surged through him, a black film coating his vision as his ears rang. Nobody, especially not some damned woman, screwed over Dave Larson.

Giving in to the fury, he shoved the table across the room. He grabbed the rope, yanking it from the wall. Beads clattered against the window, their loud pings sounding out like shots. He kicked a few piles of fabric, then started to punch his fist into the wall. Just inches from it, though, he remembered how much he didn't like pain, and how valuable his hands were. Instead, he kicked it a couple times, then stormed out of the room.

He glanced at the clock. Ten on a Friday night. God knew when she'd be home. With a breath, he shoved the address in his pocket to look into later and rocked back on his heels. Did he wait for her in here or not?

He could hang out, but she might not be alone. Given the state of her apartment, she'd probably be whining to the cops before he could get back in here and deal with her.

He'd deal with her later.

On his way out of the apartment, Dave glared at the mess. He had planned to keep his visit secret as a favor to Bea. He knew she wouldn't want her friend upset. Just break in, grab the tie and maybe a souvenir or two, then leave.

But he wasn't the kind of man to let a little thing like lust stand between him and someone who screwed him over. Rage, still simmering, stirred an idea in Dave's head.

He stormed back into the trashed office and grabbed one of the sketches he'd ripped from the wall. He snatched up a pen and with strokes so deep they ripped the paper, he left a message. One he was sure would get the two-timing bitch's attention.

Nobody ruined Dave Larson's dreams and got away with it. She'd get him that tie, or she'd pay. Dave Larson wasn't going down alone.

IT'D TAKEN Audra a few hours and two phone calls to get over her worry about Isabel. One more point in Jesse's favor was how understanding he'd been of her need to check up on her friend.

"Thanks for the fun night," she said, leaning into Jesse's side as he walked with her to her apartment door. "I had no idea miniature golf could be such a turn-on."

"It's all in how you use your putter," he assured her with a straight face. "If you nail those balls just right, it can be the hottest game in town."

Audra rolled her eyes at the lame joke, but couldn't hold back her smile. Even though he'd acted as if he had something serious to discuss with her when he'd picked her up, as soon as he found out how stressed she was over Isabel, Jesse had been pure entertainment.

Between the jokes, a delicious dinner and the sexual sparks Jesse kept stoked to a low flame, Audra was finally relaxed. Now for the best part of the evening. Jesse, naked, in her bed.

Anticipating an eight, maybe an eight-point-five, given that they were both tired after last night's lack of sleep, she slid her key into the lock and swung open the door.

It stuck.

Audra shoved. "What the…"

She slapped at the switch on the wall next to her. As light filled the room, her stomach pitched.

Jesse's broad shoulders crowded behind her. She felt their warmth as she gaped at the mess strewn over her apartment.

"I take it this wasn't a visit by your cleaning service?" he teased. But under his light words was a cold, clinical tone she'd never heard. It both comforted and made the tiny hairs on the back of her neck stand up.

"Someone trashed my place?" She felt tears well in her eyes, but blinked fast. Wicked Chicks didn't cry. With a deep breath, she shoved aside the pain and lifted her chin.

"Well, we might want to delay our hot sex," she joked stiffly. "I think I'd better tidy up first."

Not meeting his eyes, she stepped over the bolt of cloth that'd been blocking the door and made her way into the room. At second look, it wasn't as bad as she'd originally thought. It was a mess, and someone had obviously invaded her space. But nothing looked broken. Her TV was still in the armoire, as was the stereo. So why were her hands trembling?

Audra took a shaky breath and tried to calm the pained emotions swirling through her system. It was just stuff. Just an apartment. Maybe if she told herself that often enough, the devastating pain would subside.

She bent down to pick up a few paperback romances that looked as if they'd been kicked around. Jesse grabbed her arm.

Startled, she looked up at him. He was shaking his head,

even as he pulled his cell phone from his pocket. He punched a couple of keys and held it to his ear.

"I'd like to report a break-in," he said into it. His eyes held hers as he gently pulled her to him. He wrapped an arm around her shoulders and, despite her stiffness, rubbed his hand over her back. She should pull away. She didn't need soothing. But she couldn't bring herself to leave the haven of Jesse's arms.

The tension slowly left her body and she let herself lean into him. His strength enfolded her as Audra tuned out his words and closed her eyes to the devastation of her home.

And, for the first time in her life, she lowered her guard, and her heart, enough to let herself be comforted.

13

JESSE WAVERED between amusement and irritation as he watched Audra lead the investigating officer around by the…nose.

"She's not much into cops, is she?" Rob Dutton asked, a scowl creasing his freckled forehead. Jesse's partner leaned against a doorframe, tapping his pen against his blank notebook.

Jesse just shrugged, trying to ignore the sick knot in his belly. He'd had no idea Audra's warm, sexy charm could take on such a sharp edge. Her mood didn't bode well for him. How would she take his eventual confession?

"You think it was Larson?" he murmured, indicating the trashed office.

"Pretty sure," Rob agreed. He glanced at the nasty missive he'd pulled from Audra's wall, the angry words glaring through the clear plastic of the evidence bag. "Even though the guy's a notorious wimp, I'll put an APB out on him. Walk me out, huh?"

Jesse frowned.

Ignoring Audra's questioning glance, he followed Rob out of the apartment. A soft evening breeze stirred the dark night. The two men were silent until they reached Rob's car, lit by the streetlights.

Jesse frowned again at the note, sealed in an evidence bag. *You're not getting away with it. Give it back, bitch. Or you'll pay, and pay big.* Apparently Davey was getting desperate.

"We picked up a bimbette tonight," Rob said without preamble. "While she was shoveling dirt to get her ass out of trouble, she tossed a few clumps at the triad. She also said she was stiffed on a deal. She was supposed to pick up a handoff of goods a week or so ago at The Wild Thing from ole Davey boy."

Ahh. Last piece of the puzzle. Jesse nodded his satisfaction. Audra was clear. A few knots he hadn't even realized he had loosened in his shoulders.

"You don't seem surprised." Rob took the evidence bag and tossed it into the backseat before leaning against the car and crossing his arms.

"I'm not. You weren't in the office this morning, but last night I'd discovered where the cash came from. As far as I'm concerned, Audra's clean. Nothing ties her to the triad or Larson except an accidental meeting."

"And the goods he passed off in the bar," Rob reminded him as he got in his car and started the ignition. "You might want to keep that in mind. Especially since whoever tossed the place obviously has a hard-on for your girlfriend."

Jesse winced at the reference to Audra. But there was no condemnation in Rob's eyes, just sympathy and a hint of worry.

"Don't wait to break the case against the triad," Jesse ordered. "Larson's a threat to Audra. Pick him up, maybe we can get him to roll on the them."

"You're kissing your promotion goodbye if you don't pull down the big boys. You know that, right?"

With a nod, Jesse shrugged. He wordlessly watched Rob drive away. The promotion had been important. Proof that he was as good a cop as his father. But it wasn't worth Audra's safety. Nothing was.

Between the bimbette's confession and the break-in, Audra was pretty much cleared. But, unfortunately for Jesse, it moved her cleanly from suspect to target.

And shoved her right back to the off-limits list. If he thought sleeping with a suspect was dirty, sleeping with someone under his protection was simply taking advantage.

Five minutes later, Jesse confirmed the drive-by schedule with the uniformed officers before closing the door behind them. Then he eyed the sexy woman across the room from him.

"Well, that wasn't quite how I planned to start off our wild night of hot loving," Audra said. Her tone was joking. But the stiffness of her smile and the stress bracketing her eyes gave away her turmoil. Even so, she stood in her usual, hip-cocked sexy stance and gave him a wink.

Was it any wonder he was crazy about her?

"Crime has a way of ruining the mood," Jesse shot back, figuring she'd appreciate the joke more than his observation of her emotional state. "I'll help you clean this up, huh?"

She looked around silently and then gave a sigh and a shrug. From where they stood, they could see the barely touched living room and bedroom, and the very trashed room that served as her office. Other than Davey's mess, her place was sexy as hell. Much like Audra herself.

"Did you want to come home with me?" he asked as they gathered CDs and books to put back on the teak shelving unit between the bedrooms. "Is there someplace else you'd rather stay tonight?"

"Stay? What are you talking about? I'm staying here."

"Here? You heard what the cop said. You should find someplace to stay until they catch that dirtbag who did this."

"Cops say lots of things. Most of them irritate me, so I rarely listen." At his frown, she shoved the last handful of books on the shelf, the red paperback spines willy-nilly and teetering precariously, then stood.

"Look, I'm sure he had good intentions. Serve and protect, and all that jazz. But this is my home. No lowlife is going to drive me out of it. Like I told the cop, I have no idea why someone would threaten me and definitely have no clue what that note was blathering about. Besides, that one guy in the jeans, the one you were so chummy with?" She shot him a look that made Jesse's shoulders twitch. It was a combination suspicion, curiosity and underlying trust. "He said they'd be doing drive-bys and keeping watch on my place."

Jesse rose and stood over her. Trying to throw off his guilt over ignoring the question in her eyes, he offered his fiercest frown. "Drive-bys are all well and good, but they are no guarantee of safety. Are you willing to take that chance? Willing to go climb into your bed and hope he won't be back?"

Rather than turning pale, stuttering or even looking thoughtful, Audra lifted her chin and gave a chilly smile.

"Let him try."

"Fine. Then I'm staying with you."

Her cold smile turned to steam and she gave him a look hot enough to melt his shorts. Beneath it, though, was a vulnerability he'd never imagined in Audra.

If he'd had any illusions of keeping his hands off her until after the case was closed, that look shot them straight to hell. But not tonight. That'd just be wrong. His body was putting up a fierce argument, but Jesse tried to convince himself he wasn't led by his dick.

"Look, you've had a rough night. The break-in, the threat. You're probably emotionally overwhelmed right now." He ignored her wide-eyed stare and gestured to the now tidy hallway. "I'll stay the night, but on the couch. I'm not going to take advantage of you in a vulnerable state."

Audra's jaw dropped, a look of blank shock on her face. After five excruciatingly long seconds, she burst into laughter. He wasn't sure if he was relieved to see she wasn't overwrought, or offended.

At the sight of her delighted grin, he settled for relief.

"I can't remember the last time anyone took advantage of me. It sounds fun, though. Wanna take turns?"

She took a step toward him and her foot hit a string of beads, sending them flying across the room with a reverberating rattle. They watched as the string hit the wall, bright red orbs flying every which way on impact.

Jesse grimaced at the mess and glanced back at Audra to ask her where she kept her vacuum. His heart clenched at the sight of her face, silent tears swimming in her huge eyes.

With a barely audible groan, Jesse stepped forward and pulled her into his arms. Her scent, the heady richness of it, wrapped around his senses. Jesse rubbed her shoulders and murmured comforting nothings as she pulled in a shaky breath.

"You okay, babe?" he asked.

"Yeah," she said against his shoulder. "I'm just pissed. And a little freaked that someone would hate me enough to break into my home and mess it up so bad. It's hard to fight someone when you have no idea who they are or how you pissed them off, you know?"

Jesse winced. He had to tell her. As much as he'd like to put it off, to protect her—and, if he was honest with himself, protect his place in her life—he had to clue her in.

Somewhere in the back of his mind, Jesse realized once he'd arrested Dave Larson and kicked his ass for breaking into Audra's apartment, he'd likely thank the guy for bringing her into his life.

That was, if there was a chance she'd still have anything to do with him after she learned the truth.

With a heartsick sigh, Jesse knew he didn't have a choice. It was time to confess. Both for her own good, and to find out if she had any idea what Dave had been trying to hand off that night.

But damned if he wasn't positive his admission was going to screw him but good with her. And not in the way he'd enjoyed last night.

FEELING LIKE a wimpy idiot, Audra sucked in a deep breath and tried to tamp down the fear whispering in her head. That note had been so angry.

Audra shuddered. Then she frowned. How dare someone come into her home and threaten her. As she'd told Jesse, she'd be damned if some dirtbag was going to mess with her or scare her out of her own place.

Or worse, screw with her sex life.

With that in mind, she took a deep breath and cleared her face. To push back the fear, she pictured Jesse naked, his hard body poised over hers just before he took that wild plunge of pleasure.

She pulled back and gave him her *let's-get-dirty* look.

"Since you're staying the night, why don't we go in the bedroom and get comfortable? I can deal with this mess tomorrow. I had other plans tonight, and I'll be damned if some loser is going to keep us from having fun."

Audra watched the expressions chase across Jesse's face. Maybe it was stress overload, but she was definitely getting a weird vibe off him. It had started when he'd been all chummy with that cop. And now he had a guarded look in his eyes. It was as if all emotion had been wiped away, giving him a blank, official kind of look. The kind Child Protective Services had always worn when they'd come to check on her mother.

She tried to brush off the sick feeling in her stomach. But the tiny hairs on the back of her neck wouldn't lie down, and she suddenly felt like hurling.

Audra had never fallen apart in front of a guy before. Never let her rarely admitted vulnerability show. She'd never felt an emotional connection with a guy that made her feel safe enough to even consider it. Until tonight. Until Jesse.

And now? Now he was pulling away, distanced and cold. With that closed look on his face.

All bad signs.

"What's up?" she asked.

"I have a confession to make. Something I need to tell you." His casual tone sounded forced, as if he didn't want to scare her off.

Audra bit her lip. From his tone and the look on his face, she didn't think she was gonna be giddy with delight over whatever it was he wanted to share.

Since it didn't look like she could put off the conversation until she'd regained a solid emotional footing, Audra gestured that he go ahead. Jesse swallowed uncomfortably and winced. Then he gave a shrug and took her hands.

"Okay. Here goes… I'm not just a computer geek. I'm a cop. With the Cyber Crimes division of the Sacramento P.D."

She blinked.

Huh? A cop?

Son of a bitch. The longtime bad girl in Audra pulled back a few inches. Her entire body tensed up, her defenses going to automatic full alert. That would explain his ease with the cops who'd tramped through her house. His private powwow with the one in charge.

"Okay," she said slowly, trying to figure out if the anger building inside her was because he was a cop, or because he'd lied to her. "Why didn't you tell me this before? I thought you worked with computers."

"I do. Work with computers, that is. Cyber crimes are just that, computer crimes. I spend most of my time working with a keyboard."

"Oh." Should she be relieved? Had he actually lied? Maybe

not, but it sure as hell felt like it. Audra forced herself to unclench her teeth and smooth out the furrows digging into her brow. "That would explain why you were so chummy with that dude tonight. The cop in jeans."

"He's my partner," he confessed with a grimace.

"Partner? Why…? What's going on, Jesse."

Needing to be away from him, Audra stepped back. Still able to breathe in the spicy scent of his cologne, she took another step back. She needed all the distance she could get to clear her head and get a freaking clue as to what was going on.

"I was in the club the night we met because I was on a case," he confessed.

"I thought you just said you worked behind a computer?"

"Usually, I do. But I went undercover. It was a dare, of sorts."

Of sorts. Audra winced at the memory of that night and her own dare. Of how and why she'd hooked up with Jesse.

"I was there tailing the dork. That guy you'd had the 'sort of' dare date with. Remember him?"

Audra nodded slowly.

"Dave Larson, that's his name. He was there to make a connection. To pass off a chip of stolen IDs. He's involved on the fringes of a Chinatown-based crime ring and was selling the information to them. My plan was to identify his connection, trail her back to the crime ring."

"Her?" It was finally all clicking together. Audra's stomach had stopped swirling, now it was clenched like an angry fist. "If I remember right, the only woman that geek hooked up with at the club was me."

"Well…yeah."

It didn't take her long to connect the dots. Betrayal slapped her with a stinging blow.

"You think I'm a criminal?" Shock made her tone sharp enough to cut glass. She'd thought he was different. Someone who looked at her and, yeah, recognized she was a bad girl, but realized that didn't mean she was a bad person. But no. Jesse was just like all the other jerks in her life. He'd not only had low expectations of her, he'd pegged her for a criminal.

"Look, that's not the point right now. What matters is that I'm sure it was Larson who broke in here and threatened you. You have something he wants, Audra. I need to find out what it is and get it so I can protect you."

Audra swore she felt her heart actually crack. Pain like she'd never felt, even during her father's prolonged illness and death, poured through her. Her breath caught at the intensity of Jesse's betrayal. At the misery of realizing he not only didn't return her feelings of love, he'd used her.

This was one hell of a time to find out that whole stupid cliché was rooted in reality. A red film of betrayed anger glazed her eyes, and Audra glared to clear her vision. She grabbed on to the fury, glad to have it there to shield her from the misery tearing at her heart.

"Not the point?" she hissed over the pain. "You think I'm dirty of some crime and that's not the point? You used me. You slept with me, all the while thinking I was a…what? A criminal? An accessory to something?"

"Don't make this into more than it is. There was a lot of evidence against you."

"Why? Because I talked to some geek? How the hell does that make me look guilty of anything except bad taste?"

"It was the money in your company's account. The trip to China. A lot of little things," he said in a stiff tone, misery clear in his eyes.

Audra didn't care how bad he felt. He deserved it. After all, he'd done the unforgivable. He'd made her open her heart. And for what? A police investigation? She pressed her hand against her stomach.

"You checked me out? You poked into Simply Sensual's finances and investigated our business?" Outrage made her words shrill. She thought back to that night, the club. Then the parking lot. How could she have been so stupid? She'd been worrying about forgetting a damned condom and the whole time she should have been worried about her blind trust. What Wicked Chick worth her stilettos didn't sense a setup?

To hide her heartache, Audra sneered. "I suppose that invasion of privacy was a piece of cake, though. After all, you had your hand in my panties first, didn't you. Your job sounds like so much fun."

Jesse stiffened. "Look, I cleared you. You might be a little grateful instead of nasty."

"Grateful? For what? I wasn't guilty of anything. Except believing your bullshit."

He wasn't in love with her. Hell, he probably wasn't even in like with her. He'd slept with her in the name of the job. She, her heart, they didn't count. Only her connections to his nasty little crime. And she'd thought he was a good boy?

Audra gulped back the tears clogging her throat and stiffened her lower lip before it could quiver. No way in hell she'd give him the satisfaction of knowing what he'd meant to her. To know she'd fallen in love with him.

"Look, Audra, it's not like that. I mean, yes, I didn't tell you everything, but I couldn't."

"Nope, can't tell the criminals you're on to them, right? Or should that be *on* them? Under them? In them?" Jesse made a sharp gesture for her to stop, but Audra just glared and raised one sardonic brow. Anger was the only thing keeping her from falling to pieces. "Behind them? That was nice, huh?"

"Stop it," he snapped. The way he cringed assured her

she'd hit a tender spot. Good. Now that she knew where to strike, she could get him the hell out of her face.

"You're good at giving orders, Jesse. What rank are you? Bet you're high up there, a man like you, willing to do anything to get the job done. Or is that do anyone?"

"Audra, quit. Stop demeaning what we have."

"Had." Forcing herself into action, she sauntered over to the front door, making sure she put enough body English into her hips to make a blind man drool. "What we had. We have nothing now. We're through."

"You can't do that. Don't end it like this." Jesse followed her. He put a beseeching hand on her shoulder. She gave his hand a look, then met his eyes. He let go.

"This, whatever it is, is over." She wanted him out before she started crying.

"Audra—" he started.

"No," she interrupted. "I want you to go. We're nothing. We never were. All I was to you was a suspect, then a means to an end. And all you ever were to me was a dare," she lied.

"A what?"

She took grim satisfaction in the look of confusion on his face. Good, let him feel betrayed, too.

"A dare," she said with relish. "I told you that night in the club about dares, remember? Well, you were mine. All I had to do to keep my Wicked Chick status was sleep with you. I guess I should thank you for the extra credit points. You were pretty good, too."

"I thought that was a blind date."

"Hardly," Audra said with a sneer. "That was a dare. That's why I went up to your creepy criminal that night in the club. The girls dared me to do the first guy to come through the door. You were close, but he was first."

"Do?"

"Do. Screw. Down and dirty. Sex, Jesse. You remember sex, don't you? You were pretty good at it in there." Audra made a sharp gesture toward the bedroom. "I'd never have pegged you for a cop, being as you came off as such a good boy. But then, you were undercover, weren't you."

"You went after Larson for sex?"

"You got it." She gave him an evil smirk, then raised a brow. "Or got me, if you prefer. He was my dare, but his little chicken ass ran out. You, by default, were my backup dare."

Brows furrowed, Jesse tilted his head as if he didn't understand. "Are you trying to claim you only had sex with me for a dare?"

"Exactly."

The anger suffusing his face didn't even come close to the level burning in her gut, but Audra blinked anyway. For the first time, she felt intimidated by Jesse.

All the more reason for him to leave.

"I don't believe you." Fists clenched at his hips, Jesse glared at her. "There's too much between us to be some stupid game."

"What? Your crime? Get real. There's nothing between us. After all, I just remembered there's a good reason I don't do good boys. And I especially don't do cops."

Audra had to swallow to get past the lump in her throat. Knowing she couldn't keep herself together much longer, she gestured to the door.

"Go. I don't want to do this anymore."

"We need to settle this between us, Audra. And I need to find out about that night, ask you some questions about what Larson said to you, if he gave you anything." At Audra's vicious look, he frowned, then shrugged. "If you can't do this now, fine. We'll wait until tomorrow. But we have to talk, Audra. Soon."

Fear pounded in her head as she shook it in denial.

She couldn't talk to him again. Couldn't stand to see him and know there was nothing there but a case. It already hurt too much. Not knowing any other way to get him to leave before she completely lost it, she did the only thing she knew how. She pulled her hard-ass attitude around her like a shield and lashed out.

"You try to say another word to me, and I'll turn you in for sexual harassment. I'm sure there are some rules in your good boy book against lying to and sleeping with a suspect."

Jesse gave her a long look, then shook his head. "We need to discuss this. But if I've learned anything from my sisters, it's that it's pointless to push when a woman is so pissed she looks like she's ready to rip my head off. I'll call you later, we'll get together and talk."

"Don't bother. I only had to do you once, and since we're already well over that quota, I don't have any further use for you."

He shot her an indecipherable look. One that scared Audra to her very soul. Then with a shake of his head, he opened the door. Once through, his hand still on the knob, he looked back.

"You don't reach a nine and a half on just a physical level, Audra. That's about emotions. That's a connection that goes beyond two bodies and sex. It's about love."

He shut the door behind him with a quiet snick. She stood and stared at the white expanse of wood until it blurred.

It wasn't until she moved to slide the dead bolt into place that she realized everything was blurry because of the tears streaming down her face.

It looked as if she'd finally found the answer to the identity crisis that had been plaguing her the last couple of weeks. Dare achieved or not, she'd lost her bad girl status. Because Wicked Chicks didn't cry. Especially over men.

14

"HE's A COP and he slept with you while you were under investigation?" Bea asked, her breathy voice tinged with shock. "That's terrible."

"Men suck," Isabel claimed in a rigid tone. Her pale face, hair pulled back in a punishing ponytail and baggy sweats were all clear signs of man trouble. Given her discovery that her first-time fling was a lying cheat, Audra figured the fact that she wasn't burning a well-endowed male effigy and spitting on the flames was a miracle.

"Be fair," Suzi said with her usual logic, "Audra did a number on him, same as he did her."

"There's a difference," Bea insisted.

Suzi just laughed. A cynical, mocking sound that played on Audra's already raw nerves.

After she'd kicked Jesse out, she'd thrown a nice little temper tantrum. Two hours at the gym trying to exhaust her body and a carton of Heath Bar Crunch had only made her angrier. She'd come home and ripped the sheets from the bed to remove all traces of her night with Jesse. Then, when that hadn't made her feel any better, she'd waited until dawn, and called for reinforcements.

She hadn't really felt up to company, but she'd known being around her friends would force her to put on her game face and suck up the hurt. And true friends that they were,

Isabel, Bea and Suzi had jumped right out of bed—in Suzi's case, someone else's—and come right over.

She sat with the other women on the floor of her office, sorting through the mess of designs, trim and beading. With a sigh, she scooped up the shredded pieces of her fall design boards. Like her love life, her career was sucking hard.

"I know," Bea offered, "Let's spend the day pampering ourselves, then tonight we'll get dressed up, hit a few clubs and see how many hot dudes we can reel in."

"I thought you were seeing that photographer guy?"

"That wasn't going anywhere," Bea said. She jingled her wrist, the pale morning sunlight glinting off the diamonds in her bracelet. "I mean, he was just too clingy and weird. I guess I should let him know it's over, huh?"

Audra groaned. "Jeez, Bea. You haven't told the guy it's over yet?"

"Nah. I hate hurt feelings. I keep hoping he'll clue in when I don't call him back."

"That's not fair. If you're going to end it, do it clean."

"He's a man," Isabel said with a roll of her eyes. "It probably serves him right."

"You're a little on the bitter side, don't ya think?" Suzi asked with a surprised stare.

"I just don't think this guy had any right to let the relationship go as far as the bed," Isabel insisted, ignoring Suzi's question. "Men are pigs. Lying left and right just to get a woman into bed."

"Sure guys lie. So do women, it's not like truth is exclusive to one sex or the other," Suzi said dismissively. "The bottom line is, Audra did her dare. It wasn't like she fell for the guy or anything. Right?"

She peered at Audra, her face looking oddly young and almost sweet without its usual polished makeup. Blue eyes

Audra knew as well as her own were filled with questions. It wasn't the curiosity that worried Audra, though. It was the sympathy.

"It was good sex," Audra retorted with a shrug. As long as she forced herself to treat it like any other encounter, she could keep away the pain. "A little practice and he'd have hit the fabled ten on the orgasm scale."

"That good, huh?"

"Yup."

"It'd be a shame to let go of someone who could toast your buns so perfectly."

"Let him go? I never had him." Maybe if she said it enough she'd believe it, too.

"Maybe you should report him," Isabel mused.

"Why? Do they give medals for sexual prowess? He deserves one, sure, but I don't usually go in for ego strokes, you know?"

"Stop it. You're as bad as Suzi." Isabel quit straightening and stacking a pile of designs to glare. "Don't blow this off. Not only did he take advantage of you, you were—are—in danger."

Done sifting beads, Audra closed the lid of the plastic case. She stared down at the rainbow of glass shapes until they blurred into a kaleidoscope of running colors. She tried to shove the pain back down, but it was like the lid she'd kept on her emotions for so long, once peeled open, refused to shut.

Finally, she looked up and met Isabel's outraged gaze, her own eyes sheened with tears.

"He didn't take advantage. You know that. Sure, I was a suspect, but he was a dare. Which of us took advantage of the other?"

Isabel pressed her lips together as she considered, then she shook her head.

"But he hurt you," she said softly. Her own eyes were liquid with sympathy.

"Yeah." Audra drew in a shuddering breath and tried to shrug. But as hard as she wanted to ignore the pain, it wouldn't go away. "But it wasn't like he owed me anything. We didn't make any promises, you know?"

"Oh, my God, will you stop being so damned fair," Suzi snapped in an abrupt about-face. "Quit it. I don't give a rat's ass how he was a nice guy, how he was doing his job or how good in bed he is. Isabel's right. None of that excuses him hurting you."

Walls crumbling, Audra's lip trembled for a brief second before the dam burst and tears poured free. Damn Jesse, he'd totally ruined her Wicked Chick vow to never cry over a man.

When her friends' faces crumbled too, Audra knew she was done. The tears poured free. The other women sniffed, rubbed her back and gave each other helpless looks. Audra still couldn't stop.

Finally, Isabel got up and went to the kitchen. She came back with a grocery bag. She pulled out sour cream and onion potato chips, pretzels and Doritos, along with a four-pack of wine coolers and a big bag of jelly beans.

"Breakfast of champions," Bea pointed out.

Even through her misery, Audra had to giggle.

"What? No chocolate?" Suzi asked with a watery laugh of her own.

"No," Isabel said quietly with a sympathetic look at Audra. "I'm pretty sure Audra's had enough chocolate."

Audra eyed the fattening feast spread over the tattered remnants of her designs. "So much for my Wicked Chick status, huh?"

"What are you talking about?" Bea asked, tearing into the chips.

"This heartbreak over some guy," Audra specified. "It's so totally against all the rules. Next thing you know, I'll be whining in an Internet self-help group while eating a pint of Chunky Monkey in my flannel jammies."

Suzi snorted, but Isabel just stared.

"Since when do Wicked Chicks follow rules?"

Audra frowned, but couldn't think of an answer so she shrugged instead.

"You of all people should know being a bad girl is all about attitude," Suzi pointed out as she handed Audra the bag of Doritos. "This crappy one of yours sucks right now. But that's not a permanent thing. More like a temporary breakdown. We're all entitled to those."

"Even you?" Isabel teased.

"Sure. But if it were me, I'd lose the flannel. Hell, all I own in the sleepwear department is Audra's stuff anyway. Even if most of it is sweet and fluffy."

They all laughed, but Audra had to blink a few times to keep the tears from starting again. For a badass friend, Suzi was pretty damned wonderful.

"So what are you going to do?" Bea asked around a mouthful of jelly beans.

"Yeah, are you going to go after this guy? Or are you going to trade him in for three guys and a bag of Doritos?"

"I don't want three guys," Audra said as she shoved a nacho chip into her mouth.

"Then what *do* you want?"

Good question. Audra licked the orange powder from her thumb and considered. She remembered how good it'd been with Jesse. The laughter and the jokes, the simple enjoyment of his company. Who knew it'd be those things, instead of the wild sex, that would send her head over heels for a guy?

He was a cop. A cop who'd used her. Lied to her and suspected the worst of her.

And he was a dare. One she'd used to prove herself.

Which made them even, in her mind.

She knew what she wanted. The real question was, could she handle it? The Wicked Chick and the cop? It was so far-fetched, what were the odds?

Then again…she was a Wicked Chick. Damned if she couldn't play those odds and win.

"I want Jesse," Audra admitted.

Bea took the bag of chips from Audra's hands and pointed to the door. "Then fix your crappy attitude, take your bad girl self and go get him."

LATER THAT MORNING, after a cold compress and a change into her sexiest lingerie and a leather skirt, Audra sauntered into the Good Times Sports Bar. Attitude at full throttle, she was ready to deal with the first of her tiny problems.

Once she'd confronted Natasha, she'd either be out of a job, or have the creative freedom she needed to do her current one.

Then she'd go tackle her other problem.

Jesse Martinez, good boy cop.

The bar was empty, as she'd figured it would be at eleven in the morning. She waved to the daytime bartender, then made her way to the back stairs that led to the second-floor apartment where her brother lived.

Since they were expecting her and because she was in the mood to seize the upper hand, Audra knocked once, then walked right in.

"Hey, Audra," Drew said from the couch. He aimed the remote at the TV, hit Off and tossed the wand on the coffee table. With a grin, he rose and gave her a hug.

Audra let herself lean into him for a whole five seconds. There was something comforting about Drew. Maybe his resemblance to their father, maybe his easygoing manner.

Either way, she figured she might as well snag her hug

while she could. Who knew how he'd feel about her once she'd had her say.

"Hey, you look like China agreed with you," she said when she pulled away. And it was true. With his red hair mussed and his face the most relaxed she'd seen in a while, he looked like a guy who'd had a great vacation.

Natasha walked in, her face a study of cool, composed breeding. Audra wondered, not for the first time, how the hell such an uptown lady had ever hooked up with Drew.

"It was a good trip," he was saying. "We've got pictures. I'll put you to sleep with them later, huh?"

"Vacation pics?" Audra asked in mock horror. "Ack, no."

"There are a few you'll really like," Natasha assured her as she offered a hesitant smile.

Audra's stomach clenched at the reserved look. It didn't bode well for her long-term job prospects.

She lifted her chin. So what? She wasn't sidelining her beliefs anymore. Like Jesse had said, she believed in herself enough to fight, to hold out for what she felt she was worth.

"You don't mind me stopping in, do you?" she asked them. "I figured this was a better place to talk than the boutique with all its distractions."

"No, this is perfect. I wanted to talk to you before we settled into the work week anyhow, and weekends are always so crazy." Natasha gestured to a chair. "Have a seat, I have to get something. I'll be right back."

Audra raised an inquiring brow at her brother, but he'd slapped on his poker face. He pointed to the chair, then sat himself back on the couch.

"So," Natasha said as she joined Drew on the couch, a large folder on her lap, "let's talk design."

"Let's," Audra agreed. Natasha opened the file, and there on top was the naughty little design with the wrist ties. Audra looked at it and felt a surge of mingled pride and excitement. It was one of her best pieces. Innovative, sexy and unique.

She lifted her chin and met her sister-in-law's gaze with her own level stare.

"I didn't intend for that to be shown in China, but I did intend for you to see it," she admitted. "I realize you want to wait until later, if at all, to introduce any changes to Simply Sensual product focus. But as much as I enjoy designing for you, I need to be able to expand my portfolio. Creatively, I can't keep stifling the naughtier, wild designs that come to me."

In a totally bullshit show of calm, Audra leaned back in the chair and gave a little shrug. She was sure the nerves jangling through her system didn't show on her face.

Unfortunately, she couldn't read anything from Natasha or Drew's expressions, either. They glanced at one another, then Drew got up and headed for the kitchen.

Chickenshit. He probably didn't want to have to watch his wife fire his sister.

"I'd hate to be responsible for stifling creative expression," Natasha said slowly. She lifted the design and gave a little laugh. "And leave it to you to find inspiration in that butt-ugly tie. Keeping your designs from the world would be an absolute shame. You're talented and deserve to make the most of your gifts."

Audra pursed her lips. Nothing like a few pats on the ass before you got booted.

"So, I'd like to offer you full creative control of Simply Sensual's new line. Since it's your designs, and you'd come up with such a clever name, I thought we'd call it Twisted Knickers. And, if you'll take it, partnership in the company."

Stunned, Audra stared. She gave a little shake of her head, the only sound in the room the tinkle of her dangling earrings.

"You're kidding, right? This is a joke to get me back for embarrassing you in front of the distributors?"

"Why would I do that?"

"You were pissed."

Natasha grimaced, then shrugged. "Yes, I suppose I was. I'm used to being in control of my business. And, I guess, feeling that I know what's best."

"What changed, then?"

"Drew."

"Huh?" Audra squinted at her, totally lost.

"While I was having a meltdown over how much more interested the distributors were in your naughtier design than what I'd brought to present, Drew looked at it." With a glance, she passed the board to Audra. "He pointed out that this was likely your best work yet, and after I got over the urge to throw something at him, I had to admit he was right."

Her brother had stood up for her? Audra's heart did a little happy dance.

"What about Simply Sensual? What about the money constraints and marketing and all that other stuff?"

Natasha lifted one shoulder. "The spicier line will be marketed under the Twisted Knickers label and distributed separately. I've worked up the specs, and it's all doable. As for money," she glanced over as Drew returned with a bottle of champagne and three glasses, "the Chinese distributors are placing much higher than expected orders, based on your naughty design. And if we need more financial backing, Drew's offered to bankroll Twisted Knickers."

Her brother had that much faith in her succeeding? Tears sprang to Audra's eyes. Oh, God. She was turning into a total wimp. She tried to take it all in. Not just what was being said, but what was going unsaid.

Her brother's faith in her. Natasha's willingness to take a chance on her. The fact that they were offering her the world.

Excitement dueled with joy in her belly, doing a happy little cancan. Jesse had been right. Her dreams were worth standing up for.

And now that one was being handed to her, wrapped up in a black leather bow?

She didn't want to take it.

"Don't be pissed," she said slowly, "but I'm going to say no."

"What?" Drew yelped, the champagne slopping as he poured.

"Why?" Natasha asked, her tone a lot calmer.

"I'd suck as a partner, Natasha. I mean, the design aspect, well, that's a dream come true. I'd love it. But running the boutique, well… I blew it. Things got messy, the store isn't as well stocked as it should be."

Audra sucked in a deep breath and kissed the best business offer of her life goodbye. Then she grabbed the half-full glass of champagne from her brother and downed it.

"It's just not my gig," she admitted. "If I've learned anything the last couple weeks, it's that I've got to be true to what works for me. And that boss thing, well, that isn't it."

Feeling sick and a little miserable, Audra held out her glass for a refill. Drew, though, was staring at Natasha. The two of them were doing that whole silent communication thing.

Then Natasha nodded. With a smile, she rose and came around the coffee table to pull Audra out of the chair and give her a big hug.

"How about the design offer, then? They aren't a package deal."

Like the sun had come out on a bitterly rainy day, hope shone again. Audra grinned. Then for the first time ever, she grabbed her brother and sister-in-law both in a huge hug.

JESSE WATCHED Shale peruse the case file. He wished he felt even half the level of triumph the gloating grin on the captain's face indicated.

"You're sure of this?" Shale asked.

Jesse nodded.

"You did it, Martinez. You nailed them. Not only Larson, but the whole *Du Bing Li* triad as well. You've tied them to China and gave us the connection's name."

Jesse tried to smile, but he was sure it looked more like a pained grimace.

"Once Larson accessed his off-site computer storage unit, I was able to trace his connection. Hacking into it was easy at that point. He's a tidy thief. Everything was neatly labeled, ready to download. I'd bet the triad warned him to ditch the IDs once he'd handed them over, but a guy like Davey likes to have backup."

"Have you physically located his off-site unit?"

"No, not yet. He's smooth. Without the chip he was reputed to hand off, this won't be as easily admissible in court, but we can make it stick. Especially since I was able to access the list of IDs. The triad's moving human cargo from China and already assigned at least a dozen of those IDs to their people. It's not all tied up with a bow, but it's a solid case."

"Too bad we didn't have that chip, or we'd blow it wide open. Even so, this is more than the chief had hoped for. Good work, Martinez. It'll go far toward that promotion. I gotta say, you have a lot of your father in you."

"Yes, sir," Jesse agreed with a grimace.

Yup, he was one righteous bastard, just like his father. Here he was, justifying sleeping with a woman involved in his case. Good ole dad couldn't have done any better.

"Although, if you don't mind me being honest with you, as much as I admired Diego, he didn't have your knack for tying up loose ends. Or your care to make sure the bystand-ers and victims in your cases are taken care of. To be honest, his methods were sometimes a cause for concern."

"Sir?" Jesse stared across the desk and wondered if he'd heard right. Didn't everyone universally adore his father's methods?

"Don't get me wrong, Diego had a sterling rep and a solid arrest record. You take that extra care, though. People are more than just names and means to ends for you, Martinez. I appreciate that, and I'm proud to have you on my team."

Jesse wasn't sure what to say to that. Shale didn't think he was like his father? Not in the ways Jesse was worried about. Sure, he'd let his emotions get the better of his common sense with Audra, but maybe that wasn't the same. He'd been with Audra despite the case, not because of it. Which meant maybe, unlike his father, he wasn't destined to lousy relation-ships. He thought back to Audra's parting shot, her anger and swaggering attitude. And now that he was remembering it without the cloud of guilt, he felt the faint stirring of hope.

All he had to do was convince her to give them a chance.

For the first time in fourteen hours, Jesse smiled. Hell, yeah, he'd convince her. Audra was meant to be his, and he'd show her exactly why. Jesse knew her—appreciated her—like nobody else in the world. And he'd use that knowledge to court her, to lure her back. Then he'd marry her and tie her to him for the rest of their lives.

AUDRA SLID into her car, the grin still plastered to her face. Rock on. She'd shown up ready to be fired and ended up with her own line of lingerie. Better yet, she'd realized that she really did know what was right for her and what wasn't.

Now to do something about the man who was right for her.

Audra would be damned if she'd give up a guy who not only got her, but got what made her *her*. What made her special.

She fingered the design Natasha had returned to her, eyeing the scrap of that ugly tie. She remembered Jesse's words about being true to herself. How clearly did he see her? More clearly than she saw herself, apparently.

So what was she going to do about it? Did Jesse really care, or was his interest in her based on his good boy genes trying to justify his naughty foray into down and dirty sex? Could he handle the real her?

Audra thought back over her time with him the last two weeks. He'd never shown any hesitation in accepting her, even when she hadn't been able to do the same.

Maybe she'd underestimated herself. As crazy a concept as it was for a woman who'd always been sure of her own strengths, Audra thought back over her brother's words.

Drew gave her credit when she didn't herself. He was willing to stand up and fight for her when she'd settled for being shuffled aside. Nobody had ever done that before, she realized.

Like Jesse, Drew believed in Audra's talent. In her vision and her ability to make her dreams a reality.

Audra stroked the ugly material she'd hacked off the end of the tie. The cheap, poorly constructed polyester felt slick beneath her fingers. Then she came to the tip, and winced. It really did feel as if someone had left a needle or something in the fabric.

With a frown, she tugged the tie free of its staple and tore at the material. A small chip, about the size of her thumb and encased in plastic, fell into her lap.

Well, well. It looked as if Jesse had been right. She was guilty, if unknowingly.

Audra pressed the tiny chip between her fingers and considered her options.

She'd always been proud to be unique, to march to her own drumbeat. All of this worry about who she was and soul-searching were a waste of energy. She was who she was. A bad girl with a soft spot for good boys. One hell of a designer with a knack for the naughty. A wild woman who was strong enough to make her dreams come true.

And a woman in love.

Which brought her to the real question.

Was Jesse man enough to accept her? The whole her, totally?

She rubbed the chip again.

Maybe it was time to find out.

15

JESSE LEFT Shale's office and tried to keep his triumphant grin from splitting his face. He'd nailed it. The case, and his internal struggle over his choices and work methods. And damned if he didn't feel good.

Now to get Audra to talk to him again, find a way to work things out with her, and he'd be great.

"You look like a happy man," Rob said as Jesse approached. Feet up on his desk, the redhead looked like he was about to fall asleep. Jesse raised a brow.

"The case is pretty much nailed," Jesse said with a frown. "What's up?"

"You had a phone call."

"Informant?" Jesse dropped into his chair and booted up his files. He wanted to make sure his case against the triad was as solid as possible. No loose ends, no easy walks.

"Nah. Girlfriend."

Jesse's fingers froze on the keyboard. "Audra called?"

"Yup. Said she had something you might be interested in."

He was interested in everything she had. That didn't narrow things down much. He squinted at his partner.

"She didn't leave details. Just said she had something you might want to check out."

Jesse was already out of his chair and halfway to the door when he thought to ask, "Did she say where she'd be?"

"Nope. But she mentioned a leather couch."

AUDRA TURNED the sign on the boutique door to Closed, but didn't lock up. Just in case Jesse decided to drop in. Would he? She was pretty sure he would, despite her nasty slams the other night. After all, his parting comment had made it clear he was either emotionally invested or the best damned actor this side of George Clooney.

Of course, he had a major investment in retrieving the tiny computer chip she had tucked away in the pocket of her mini-skirt, too.

But she'd ignore that possibility until she saw him face-to-face.

Audra checked her appearance in the gilt-framed mirror on one wall. A tweak here, a shimmy there, and her leather skirt and chiffon blouse were just right. The glint of her rhine-stone belly-button ring showed through the sheer top. She fluffed her hair, liking the redone magenta tips, and grabbed her purse to find her gloss and add more shine to her lips.

Shoulders squared, Audra took a long, hard look. Damned if she didn't like what she saw. A Wicked Chick with an attitude, but a solid grasp on her future. Not bad.

Not bad at all.

The front door rang a gentle chime as it opened. Anticipation swirled a whirlwind through her belly and she lifted her chin. Showtime.

She gave her reflection a wink, a seductive grin curving her lips as she turned.

"Hey, big boy."

Oops. It wasn't Jesse.

Instead of her sexy hunk, some geeky guy sauntered into the shop. Short, dark and unimpressive.

Audra squinted. He looked familiar, but in the designer sunglasses, it was hard to tell.

"Can I help you?"

"Since you owe me, I'd say you're definitely going to help me now."

"I beg your…"

The guy whipped off his sunglasses at the same time he pulled out a nasty-looking knife.

"What the…"

"Game's over, hot stuff" he snarled, his tone pure anger. "You've screwed me over and now it's time to pay."

"Screwed you over? I have no freaking clue who *you* are," Audra explained, taking an automatic step backward. This was a joke, right?

Except the knife in the geek's hand was anything but funny.

Geek.

Oh, my God.

"Dave Larson?" she whispered, her mouth suddenly as dry as the Mojave. His laugh sent chills down her spine.

"I'm glad you're not playing dumb," he said with a friendly smile. That smile worried Audra more a lot more than the shiny knife in his hand. It was pure ice, with an edgy anger that made it clear he was a man with nothing to lose. "I'd hate to think I'd have to educate you. This way, we're on the same page and can help each other out, hmm?"

"Just because I know your name doesn't mean we're on the same page," Audra told him.

His icy smile melted. Apparently, she should have kept her mouth shut.

"Thanks to you, I'm screwed. Not only did you sell me out to the triad, you ruined my love life. Because of you, I've lost everything."

Audra tried to make sense of his words. Sell him out? He must mean something to do with the chip she had in her pocket. That part she got. But his love life?

"Dude, you can't pin a lousy love life on me. I gave you a

chance for a wild time once already. You're the one who ran away."

Like the mercury in a thermometer on a hot day, she watched the color climb Dave's cheeks in slow heat.

"Bea was mine," he claimed in a low, empty tone. "She was totally into me. Then I find out you're dirty, that you double-crossed me to the triad. And suddenly she's not returning my calls. She's too busy to see me. I know a kiss-off when I get one. It's your fault. It has to be. You ruined things. Every-thing."

This guy was Bea's photographer? God, that girl had rotten taste. Audra tried to swallow, but her throat felt as if it had closed up. She drew in long breaths, trying to push back the black haze from her vision. She'd never passed out before and she'd be damned if she'd do it now. Not over some geek with a grudge.

"Look, let's talk about this," she said, gesturing to the high-backed velvet chairs. "I'm sure we can figure some-thing out."

"I've already figured it out. You screwed me over, you'll pay." The knife held low at his side, he took a measured step toward her.

Audra sucked in a shaky breath, and the geek's gaze dropped to her breasts. The heat that flared in his beady eyes turned her stomach. Then it sparked an idea.

Jesse would come. She had to believe in him, believe that he'd really meant it when he'd said what they had was all about love. She'd never believed in love before. Not enough to trust it. Not enough to trust anyone to believe enough in the emotion to actually be there when she needed them.

But she believed in Jesse. He'd be here. And she'd be damned if he'd find her cowering from some geeky loser. Still scared, but determined, Audra racked her brain to figure a way out of this mess.

She gave Dave a long look up and down. The guy had a good sixty pounds on her. While he didn't look very muscular, she'd bet anger gave him more strength behind that knife than she wanted aimed at her.

At her look, he preened a little. Shoulders pulled back and he visibly sucked in his belly. Audra narrowed her eyes, assessing the signs. She knew men. More importantly, she knew how to read the male species. Dave wasn't immune to her charms. He'd run from her once. Could she do it again? It was worth a shot.

"Look, we can work this out," she said in a smooth, husky tone. Audra pulled out all the stops, giving him her sultriest look and running the tip of her tongue over her bottom lip. With a little extra swing in her hips, she slowly stepped toward him.

His eyes glazed over.

Audra pulled her shaky courage around her like a paper-thin chemise and sauntered closer to Dave. She fluttered her lashes and gave him her best *do me* look.

Dave swallowed audibly.

"We don't have to have all this tension between us, you know. I'd be happy to work things out so you're completely...satisfied."

A bead of sweat trailed down Dave's face.

"You get me back that chip," he demanded, trying to sound tough. "You do that, I'll make a deal with the competition. I can even cut you in," he offered with a leer.

"Cut me in, hmm? Sounds like you'd take good care of me. But what about Bea?"

"She was just a passing thing, you know? To get to you, track down my chip."

Audra was so glad Bea had dumped the jerk.

Triumph surged as he closed the blade of the knife and

dropped it into his pocket. Now they were on a more even footing.

"I'm confused," she admitted. "When you came in here, you accused me of sending that chip to China. What makes you think I can get it back? Or even if I could, that we'd get away with it? I'd think whoever has it would have already used the information, wouldn't you?"

"This chip is password protected. Your contacts in China won't be able to open it. They'll either be contacting you soon for instructions, or sending it back. A smart man always has a backup plan. And I'm one helluva smart man. That chip is worth a fortune, and only I know how to use it," he said, his hands shaking as they ran over her shoulders.

Audra had to force herself not to throw up at his touch. Thinking fast, she eyed the filmy pink robe on the hanger by the dressing room.

"Why don't we make ourselves a little more comfortable and discuss this, hmm?" Taking his hand in hers, she had to hold tight to his fingers to keep the sweaty appendages from slipping away. She led him to the public dressing room and gestured to the open door with her chin.

"So tell me," she asked as he eyed the narrow room and its plush red velvet chair, "do you like it better on top? Or on bottom?"

His hand shook so hard at that point, she gladly let it go. Audra reached over and pulled the sash from the robe, holding it taut as she pressed it against Dave's chest to push him backward. His legs hit the chair, and he fell into the seat with a clumsy thump.

Audra mentally rolled her eyes and pasted what she hoped was a simpering look on her face.

"All this intrigue talk has me all turned on." Audra licked her lips and, with a slight wince, straddled the geek in the chair. "When I'm this turned on, I just want to be kinky. Wild." She leaned close, as if to give him a wet, openmouthed kiss. She pulled back before she made contact, though. "A smart guy like you, one who takes such huge risks, I'll bet you're good at the kinky stuff."

Sweat flew from his forehead as Dave nodded so hard, he should have had whiplash.

Audra reached down to take his hand and, holding it inches from her breast, she wrapped one end of the rosebud-pink sash around it. He frowned. She grabbed his other hand and wrapped the sash around it, too.

"I'm not into pain, but I'm huge on dominance," she said, reading his arousal clearly. She swallowed as nausea rose at the image, but kept bluffing. "I want to tie you to this chair. While you watch, I'll strip off all my clothes, then all yours. Then I'll run feathers, so soft and light, over your body."

She swore there was drool on the guy's chin.

With a tight square knot, Audra secured each end of the sash to the arms of the chair. Then, sucking in a shaky breath, she rose. Crossing her arms in front of her, she gave Dave a seductive look and grasped the hem of her blouse. Hopefully seeing her bra would be enough to keep him giddy until she could run out on the pretext of finding those feathers.

"Audra? You here?"

"What the…" Dave started, pulling at the scarf.

Panic and relief surged in equal doses at the sound of Jesse's voice. She hadn't even let herself consider what she'd do if he hadn't shown up. And now that he had? Were the knots tight enough? Had she put him in danger?

Her vision blurred with anxiety, Audra had to swallow twice to find her voice.

"In the front dressing room," she called out. "I've got company, though. You might want to be careful."

"Hey," Dave protested with a yelp. He started to get up. Worried he might escape, Audra moved fast to plant herself on his lap. She knew she couldn't hold him down, but between her body weight and his tied hands, she could keep him at a disadvantage.

Jesse stepped into view, and she drank in the sight of him. His hair brushed the collar of his black T-shirt and worn jeans curved over hard thighs. His face was blank, although his eyes flashed what was either irritation or surprise at the sight of Audra on Dave's lap.

She winced. Maybe not a smart move, but if it kept Jesse safe, it didn't matter.

"This is a private party," Dave said, his tone pure male posturing. "Get lost, dude."

"I got your message," Jesse told her. "I'm going to hazard a guess this," he indicated Dave, "isn't what you had for me?"

"Hardly. This was an unfortunate surprise," she replied.

With a relieved sigh, Audra slid from the geek's lap. His hands still tied in front of him, Dave glared at them. So glad to have Jesse there, and safe, Audra just winked back. Dave's glare turned to acid, then he got a rat-like look on his face.

"I don't know where you get off, buddy, but we're busy here. We don't need an audience, so you can get lost."

"Pink's a good color on you, dude. You always let yourself be tied up for public sex?" Jesse asked snidely.

"Hey, she likes it kinky, if you know what I mean."

"Right," Jesse said with a roll of his eyes. He reached behind him and pulled a set of handcuffs from a tiny leather pouch on his belt. "You'll have plenty of time to imagine kinky sex in jail, I'm thinking. Although they might restrict your access to porn, Davey boy. Bet that'll be rough."

The geek stiffened. His eyes narrowed, first on the handcuffs, then on Jesse's face.

"Jail? You can't lock me up for dirty sex, dude. This one," he pointed to Audra with his chin, "will vouch for me. We're doing the sex thing. She seduced me, tied me up and now we're going to play with feathers. It's a two-person game, so you're not welcome."

"Actually," Audra said, gesturing toward Jesse with a sigh of relief, "I'd much rather do sex things with him. I've had him already and he's—" she gave Dave a wicked look and a slight shudder of delight "—incredible."

Dave narrowed his eyes, then his face tightened in fury.

"You wanted me. You were so hot, you couldn't stop yourself from climbing all over my body. Hell, you even came up with the kinky idea to tie me up..." As his words trailed off as he caught a clue. As he realized just how well she'd played him, his anger was a visible thing.

Now that Jesse was here, though, it didn't scare Audra in the least. She wiggled her brows and flicked the pink bow at Dave's wrists.

"To be honest," she told him, "you're really not my type. I'm not much into criminal lowlifes with teensy little... knives."

Dave lunged for her, ripping one of his hands free of the scarf. Audra skipped back a few steps.

"You go ahead and say that for your boyfriend, here," Dave said with a sneer. "But you're the one that came on to me, remember? You are the one who wanted me so bad in the club that you were practically in my lap begging."

Audra rolled her eyes. What an idiot. "All three of us were in the club that night, *dude.* And two of us watched you run like a scared little virgin when I flirted with you."

"Regardless," Jesse said, obviously fighting a laugh, "your sexual prowess—or lack thereof—isn't the issue here, Larson. You're under arrest for identity theft, conspiring with known criminals and breaking and entering. And that's just the appetizer."

Obviously realizing this was bigger than he'd thought, Larson turned pale. He shook his head, then got a crafty look in his eye.

"You won't make it stick," he claimed. "Besides, what kind of guy arrests his own girlfriend?"

Audra gasped.

"What are you talking about?" Jesse asked.

"You take me down for this, you're gonna have to take this little bitch, too. She's in as deep as I am. As a matter of fact, she was my handoff that night. She's a smart one, though. She bypassed the local triad and hooked herself up with the big boys in China."

Audra growled low in her throat at the blatant lies. She'd been plenty bad in her time and had no problem owning up to her naughty ways. But she'd be damned if she'd have some geek wrapped in a pink ribbon spout lies about her.

Before she could call him on it, though, Jesse made a low humming sound.

"She's dirty, is she? Want to give me a few details?"

Eyes huge, she stared. Jesse didn't meet her eyes, focusing solely on Dave as the guy babbled details that meant nothing to Audra.

Her breath hitched, her stomach was tied in knots. What was Jesse thinking? Did he actually believe the jerk? She couldn't tell from the bland look on his face. Was her trust misplaced? Was all that stuff he'd said about level nine needing an emotional connection just fluffy emotional crap?

Or did he actually care, but he'd arrest her anyway?

Because, as any bad girl knew, the naughtier she looked, the naughtier she was. And Audra was one of the naughtiest.

"So you're telling me Audra was your handoff to the *Du Bing Li* triad? And that tie you gave her had a chip, right? But she didn't give it to the locals, she sent it direct to the Chinese contingent?"

"Yup," Dave said, leaning back against the velvet cushion with a look of smug satisfaction. He obviously didn't mind going down as long as he took someone else with him. "She's the handoff. She's got ties with both triads."

Jesse gave a slow nod. He didn't even glance at her. The room was silent. Audra wondered if her brother would be willing to shift his funding from her new lingerie line to her criminal defense. Obviously, there was enough circumstantial evidence here to make Dave's claims believable.

Most people would accept them as true. The question was…what did Jesse think? She tucked her hand into her pocket, fingering the tiny chip. She could hand it over now, prove Dave wrong. But she needed to see what Jesse did. What he said.

After years of people believing the worst about her, she had to know what he believed.

He pursed his lips, then smiled.

"Dude, you just admitted to your crimes. Thanks, you made my job a little easier."

"I didn't… I mean, I… Sure, I was involved, but just on the very outermost circle. This bitch is guiltier than I am. Hell, she's probably cheating on you, going down on the leaders. Look, you want dirt, I'll give it to you. You give me a deal, I'll give you enough evidence to nail this double-crossing bitch to the wall, along with the triad."

Anger flamed on Jesse's face. He reached down, grabbed Dave by the pink sash still tying one hand to the chair, and yanked. The cloth ripped free as Dave flew to his feet. "I think you might want to apologize to the lady, Larson. On top of everything else, you probably don't want her to press charges, do you?"

"Screw her. She's guilty and she knows it."

Jesse's face darkened with a rage like Audra had never seen. She hurried to his side and placed a hand on his shoulder.

"He's not worth the trouble," she murmured. "Besides, I have something for you."

Jesse held Dave's frightened gaze for another solid ten seconds before slowly sliding a look toward Audra. She held the chip between her fingers, the metal catching the gleam of the overhead lights.

Jesse reached out and took the chip without comment. Then, for the first time since he'd busted in, his gaze met Audra's. There in those chocolate-brown depths, she saw love. And complete acceptance.

Audra couldn't hold back her relieved grin. "You're not buying his claim?"

"That you're involved? Nah. I told you already, I knew you were innocent." At her raised brow, he laughed and corrected, "Innocent of any crime."

Like a warm blanket on a chilly day, his love settled around her. Unlike their sexual games, this wasn't edgy and wild. Rather, it was both empowering and comforting at the same time.

Audra realized then Jesse knew her to the depths of her soul. And he not only accepted all of her, he appreciated her.

It was enough to turn a girl to mush.

"MARTINEZ?" called out a voice from the boutique.

"Back here," Jesse called out, glad to have reinforcements here. He'd had enough of Larson's bullshit. All he wanted was to get the guy out of his sight so he could hold Audra. Leaving the frilly bow in place, he slapped the cuffs on Larson's wrists and pushed him through the door at a waiting uniformed officer.

Audra's eyes widened as she looked into the shop. He followed her gaze. It probably looked as if cops had overrun the entire boutique.

"I see you brought the cavalry?" she said softly.

"I called it in when I saw his car out front," Jesse said. He shot her a glance, then winced. She was as pale as the white walls behind her. As if her usual tough shell had been peeled away, she looked vulnerable and unsure. He wanted to think it was because of his emotional declaration. But being threatened by a desperate criminal at knifepoint probably had a little something to do with it.

Jesse gave a few orders to the gathered cops. Within thirty seconds, they'd cleared the boutique. Audra visibly relaxed when they heard the front door close.

"I found the chip this afternoon. I'd totally forgot about the tie the geek had tossed at me that night in the club. I didn't mean to ruin your case, but I had no idea that chip was in the tie when I cut the tip off and sent it to my sister-in-law," Audra explained. She obviously realized she was babbling, because she abruptly stopped talking and pressed her lips together. He watched the adrenaline fade and her hands start to shake.

"You didn't ruin the case. We nailed Larson and the triad. That chip will help us make sure the case is rock-solid, though. Thanks to you."

At his words, she threw herself into his arms. Jesse buried his face in her hair and inhaled the musky rich scent with a groan of pleasure. She fit perfectly against him. He wanted to make sure she stayed there.

"I'm sorry," she murmured against his chest.

"No," he said. Jesse pulled back to see her face and lifted her chin. "I'm sorry. I'm sorry I kept things from you. I wasn't using you, I swear. I can see why you thought so, but honest to God, Audra, I wouldn't have slept with you if I wasn't sure you were innocent."

She gave a watery laugh. "I've been a bad girl so long, I'm almost used to being guilty. Or at least naughty. But to have a cop declare my innocence like that is strangely gratifying."

"Despite the previous evidence to the contrary, I hope you finally believe I'm totally on your side. I've wanted you from the first moment I saw you," he vowed. Then he gave her a teasing wink. "Even if it took a do-me dare to get you interested in me."

"You gonna do me now?" she asked with that smile he loved. The one that promised sex, but hinted at the humor and fun that went with it.

"I'll do you anytime," he vowed. "I hope you keep all those do-me dares just for me from now on, though."

Vulnerability like he'd never seen was clear in her eyes as Audra stared up at him.

"You're looking for an exclusive?" she asked hesitantly.

Jesse took a deep breath, the adrenaline quieting in his system, just leaving pure nerves. What if he'd misread her? What if they were just about sex to her?

Damned if he'd let a *what-if* get in his way, Jesse kissed her. When they finally came up for air, he looked into Audra's eyes.

"I love you," he said simply. "I guess you'd say I'm definitely angling for an exclusive. How about you?"

Her eyes went huge and her mouth moved, but no sound came out. Then she gave him that slow, sexy smile that sent his heart reeling and his body into overdrive.

"Yes," she said.

"Yes?"

"I want you," she admitted. With a deep sigh, she curved her hands over his biceps and pressed against him. "I'd blame it on all that leftover adrenaline, but that'd be a lie. I want you, Jesse. Always."

He frowned, looked around the dressing room, then out the door to where cops were probably waiting.

"Here? Now? Um, can it wait a bit?"

"I'll wait as long as you want," she admitted. Then, with a deep breath and in typical bad girl fashion, she laid it all on the line. "I want you for more than just sex, even though you've achieved immortal status with that nine and a half."

Jesse knew his smile was pure smug male satisfaction. But he didn't care. Obviously, she didn't, either, since Audra grinned back and shrugged.

"I want you for your humor and your sweetness. For all those good boy traits that make you so strong, so special. I want you for the way you make me feel. Sexually and emotionally." She took a deep breath. "I love you, Jesse. I want you for good."

Jesse's heart did a flip. He'd followed his conscience and stuck to his beliefs in this case. And look what it got him. Every possible dream he'd ever had, right here in his arms.

Life didn't get much better than this. He'd bet his father would be proud of him.

"For good, huh?" He leaned down to brush a kiss over Audra's mouth. He'd intended it to be a sweet gesture but, as did most things with Audra, it quickly turned hot and wild. Their tongues dueled, her hands gripping his shoulders. Desire, always close to the surface when he was with her, surged. A sound in the boutique reminded him they weren't alone.

Jesse pulled back just a little and caught his breath. "For good sounds perfect," he said. "Especially since I'd planned to tell you the same."

"You're sure you can handle me? All of me?"

Could she doubt it? He tugged her hips tighter to his, letting her know just how much he wanted her.

Her roll of the eyes made him laugh.

"Always," he answered. "In every way."

Her smile lit up the small dressing room.

"Shall we commemorate it?"

"Let me take that loser down and book him, tie up a few loose ends, then we'll celebrate."

"Celebrate?"

"I'm thinking something with whipped cream, chocolate syrup and jar of cherries."

A burst of happy laughter escaped Audra, and she hugged him again. She winked. "Bring those handcuffs, huh?"

"I'll bring them," he agreed, "but you don't need them to keep me with you for the rest of our lives."

Who knew? A Wicked Chick and a cop…forever.

His own personal fantasy.

* * * * *

Mediterranean Nights

Join the guests and crew of Alexandra's Dream,
*the newest luxury ship to set sail on the
romantic Mediterranean, as they experience
the glamorous world of cruising.*

*A new Harlequin continuity series
begins in June 2007 with*
FROM RUSSIA, WITH LOVE
by Ingrid Weaver

*Marina Artamova books a cabin on the luxurious
cruise ship* Alexandra's Dream, *when she finds out
that her orphaned nephew and his adoptive father
are aboard. She's determined to be reunited with
the boy…but the romantic ambience of the ship and
her undeniable attraction to a man she considers
her enemy are about to interfere with her quest!*

Turn the page for a sneak preview!

Piraeus, Greece

"THERE SHE IS, Stefan. *Alexandra's Dream*." David Anderson squatted beside his new son and pointed at the dark blue hull that towered above the pier. The cruise ship was a majestic sight, twelve decks high and as long as a city block. A circle of silver and gold stars, the logo of the Liberty Cruise Line, gleamed from the swept-back smokestack. Like some legendary sea creature born for the water, the ship emanated power from every sleek curve—even at rest it held the promise of motion. "That's going to be our home for the next ten days."

The child beside him remained silent, his cheeks working in and out as he sucked furiously on his thumb. Hair so blond it appeared white ruffled against his forehead in the harbor breeze. The baby-sweet scent unique to the very young mingled with the tang of the sea.

"Ship," David said. "Uh, *parakhod*."

From beneath his bangs, Stefan looked at the *Alexandra's Dream*. Although he didn't release his thumb, the corners of his mouth tightened with the beginning of a smile.

David grinned. That was Stefan's first smile this afternoon, one of only two since they had left the orphanage yesterday. It was probably because of the boat—according to the orphanage staff, the boy loved boats, which was the main reason David had decided to book this cruise. Then again, there was a strong possibility the smile could have been a reaction to David's attempt at pocket-dictionary Russian. Whatever the cause, it was a good start.

The liaison from the adoption agency had claimed that Stefan had been taught some English, but David had yet to see evidence of it. David continued to speak, positive his son would understand his tone even if he couldn't grasp the words. "This is her maiden voyage. Her first trip, just like this is our first trip, and that makes it special." He motioned toward the stage that had been set up on the pier beneath the ship's bow. "That's why everyone's celebrating."

The ship's official christening ceremony had been held the day before and had been a closed affair, with only the cruise-line executives and VIP guests invited, but the stage hadn't yet been disassembled. Banners bearing the blue and white of the Greek flag of the ship's owner, as well as the Liberty circle of stars logo, draped the edges of the platform. In the center, a group of musicians and a dance troupe dressed in traditional white folk costumes performed for the benefit of the *Alexandra's Dream*'s first passengers. Their audience was in a festive mood, snapping their fingers in time to the music while the dancers twirled and wove through their steps.

David bobbed his head to the rhythm of the mandolins. They were playing a folk tune that seemed vaguely familiar, possibly from a movie he'd seen. He hummed a few notes. "Catchy melody, isn't it?"

Stefan turned his gaze on David. His eyes were a striking shade of blue, as cool and pale as a winter horizon and far too solemn for a child not yet five. Still, the smile that hovered at the corners of his mouth persisted. He moved his head with the music, mirroring David's motion.

David gave a silent cheer at the interaction. Hopefully,

this cruise would provide countless opportunities for more. "Hey, good for you," he said. "Do you like the music?"

The child's eyes sparked. He withdrew his thumb with a pop. *"Moozika!"*

"Music. Right!" David held out his hand. "Come on, let's go closer so we can watch the dancers."

Stefan grasped David's hand quickly, as if he feared it would be withdrawn. In an instant his budding smile was replaced by a look close to panic.

Did he remember the car accident that had killed his parents? It would be a mercy if he didn't. As far as David knew, Stefan had never spoken of it to anyone. Whatever he had seen had made him run so far from the crash that the police hadn't found him until the next day. The event had traumatized him to the extent that he hadn't uttered a word until his fifth week at the orphanage. Even now he seldom talked.

David sat back on his heels and brushed the hair from Stefan's forehead. That solemn, too-old gaze locked with his, and for an instant, David felt as if he looked back in time at an image of himself thirty years ago.

He didn't need to speak the same language to understand exactly how this boy felt. He knew what it meant to be alone and powerless among strangers, trying to be brave and tough but wishing with every fiber of his being for a place to belong, to be safe, and most of all for someone to love him....

He knew in his heart he would be a good parent to Stefan. It was why he had never considered halting the adoption process after Ellie had left him. He hadn't balked when he'd learned of the recent claim by Stefan's spinster aunt, either; the absentee relative had shown up too late for her case to be considered. The adoption was meant to be. He and this child already shared a bond that went deeper than paperwork or legalities.

A seagull screeched overhead, making Stefan start and press closer to David.

"That's my boy," David murmured. He swallowed hard, struck by the simple truth of what he had just said.

That's my *boy.*

"I CAN'T BE PATIENT, Rudolph. I'm not going to stand by and watch my nephew get ripped from his country and his roots to live on the other side of the world."

Rudolph hissed out a slow breath. "Marina, I don't like the sound of that. What are you planning?"

"I'm going to talk some sense into this American kidnapper."

"No. Absolutely not. No offense, but diplomacy is not your strong suit."

"Diplomacy be damned. Their ship's due to sail at five o'clock."

"Then you wouldn't have an opportunity to speak with him even if his lawyer agreed to a meeting."

"I'll have ten days of opportunities, Rudolph, since I plan to be on board that ship."

* * * * *

Follow Marina and David as they join forces to uncover the reason behind little Stefan's unusual silence, and the secret behind the death of his parents....

Look for From Russia, With Love
*by Ingrid Weaver
in stores June 2007.*

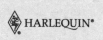

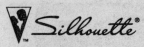

Silhouette®

Romantic
SUSPENSE

**Sparked by Danger,
Fueled by Passion.**

*This month and every month look for
four new heart-racing romances
set against a backdrop of suspense!*

Available in June 2007

Shelter from the Storm
by RaeAnne Thayne

A Little Bit Guilty
(Midnight Secrets miniseries)
by Jenna Mills

Mob Mistress
by Sheri WhiteFeather

A Serial Affair
by Natalie Dunbar

Available wherever you buy books!

REQUEST YOUR FREE BOOKS!

2 FREE NOVELS PLUS 2 FREE GIFTS!

HARLEQUIN®

Blaze®

Red-hot reads!

HARLEQUIN®

Super Romance®

Acclaimed author
Brenda Novak
returns to Dundee, Idaho, with

COULDA BEEN A COWBOY

After gaining custody of his infant son,
professional athlete Tyson Garnier hopes to escape
the media and find some privacy in Dundee, Idaho.
He also finds Dakota Brown. But is she ready for the
potential drama that comes with him?

Also watch for:

BLAME IT ON THE DOG by Amy Frazier
(Singles...with Kids)

HIS PERFECT WOMAN by Kay Stockham

DAD FOR LIFE by Helen Brenna
(A Little Secret)

MR. IRRESISTIBLE by Karina Bliss

WANTED MAN by Ellen K. Hartman

Available June 2007 wherever Harlequin books are sold!

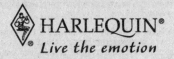

HARLEQUIN®
Live the emotion

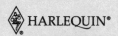

HARLEQUIN®

American ROMANCE®

**is proud to present a special treat this
Fourth of July with three stories
to kick off your summer!**

SUMMER LOVIN'
by
Marin Thomas,
Laura Marie Altom
Ann Roth

This year, celebrating the Fourth of July in Silver Cliff,
Colorado, is going to be special. There's an all-year
high school reunion taking place before the old
school building gets torn down. As old flames find
each other and new romances begin, this small
town is looking like the perfect place
for some summer lovin'!

Available June 2007
wherever Harlequin books are sold.

HARLEQUIN®

Blaze™

COMING NEXT MONTH